WA
1717 AUSTIN AVE
WACO TX 76701

MW01531199

THE ROYAL ROGUE

KARINA HALLE

Metal Blonde Books

Copyright © 2019 by Karina Halle

2nd edition published 2022

All rights reserved.

No part of this book may be reproduced in any form or by any electronic or mechanical means, including information storage and retrieval systems, without written permission from the author, except for the use of brief quotations in a book review.

Cover by: Rachel Skye

Edited by: Laura Helseth

Thank you to my husband, to my prince

CONTENTS

PREFACE

A note to the reader:

While Monaco has a royal family, I have taken extreme liberties with the Grimaldis' and made them a work of complete fiction. Though the Franco-Monégasque Treaty of 1918 did exist, I have bent this to suit the story of The Royal Rogue.

Also, people who live in Monaco but aren't native to the country, are called Monacoians. People who are native to Monaco are called Monégasques. For simplicity, I have referred to the people of Monaco as Monégasques in this book.

The same goes for the royal family of Denmark with regard to fictional liberties. However, both families have very interesting histories, with the truth a little stranger than fiction at times, and are worth a look.

I hope you enjoy The Royal Rogue.

CHAPTER 1
STELLA

E very family needs a black sheep—even the royal ones.

And in the Danish royal house, that black sheep is me.

I might have the title of princess, but that doesn't seem to mean much these days. I'm forgotten about by the world at large, and yet somehow still hounded by tabloids that like to rip apart my parenting skills and what I'm wearing that day (and who I'm *not* seeing). At any given time you can pick up *Hello Magazine* and see a picture of me on the cover, usually in the corner, usually me bending over in see-through leggings that I swore were opaque when I left the house, with an arrow pointing at my cellulite and poor choice of underwear. The accompanying article for this *riveting* piece of journalism will then discuss whether "letting myself go" has contributed to my lack of love life and nun-like status, and also open up the age-old debate if leggings should be considered pants.

At least I know my opinion on the latter.

Needless to say, I don't give those magazines a second glance. In fact, I rarely find myself leaving the house because

I know I'm just setting myself up for that shit. I'm quite content with being a hermit at our estate in Southern England, making my life only about my little girl Anya (who seems to get terrifyingly older—and smarter—with each single day that passes). It's just the two of us, hiding out from the world.

Except for those few situations that I'm roped back into my royal duties, such is the case every time my brother, the King of Denmark, decides to leave the palace and go on vacation.

In the past, he never went anywhere. That's because poor Aksel was depressed over the death of his awful, unfaithful ex-wife Helena (er, I guess rest in peace and all that?) and being thrown into the role of king far earlier than he would have liked. As a single father to two little girls, Aksel was one hundred percent committed to his role as a royal and as a parent.

Since then, however, he's shed that relentlessly grumpy and bitter persona as he fell head over heels in love with his nanny. Yes, the Australian nanny to his girls, Aurora, got under his skin and now they're married, have one-year-old twin boys who are more than a handful, and she's the new Queen of Denmark.

I'm happy for them. Truly, I am. Aksel deserves it and Aurora is lovely and has enough spunk to keep him on his toes. They're terribly happy with their growing family. As for her having the title of queen, while I'm forever a princess? Honestly, it's not a big deal. I had never been groomed for the throne and it was never on my agenda.

What is a big deal is, now that they're married and still in their honeymoon phase (twins aren't slowing them down), they're jetting off all over the world at any given time: Morocco, Greece, Argentina. You name it, they're there, this time with all their kids in tow.

Which means that I have to step in as Royal Regent, taking over any of Aksel's duties. It's like I'm a substitute teacher for the King and, like a substitute teacher, the pay sucks and I get zero respect.

"What time is the royal family supposed to be here?" I ask my aunt Maja, as if I haven't already asked her that a million times already.

"They said four," she says, eying the grandfather clock in the corner of the room. "But who knows with that bunch."

That bunch in question is the royal family of Monaco. For whatever reason, they've decided to pay Denmark a visit and then embark on some royalty tour of northern Europe. That's the way it is with royals. When they're not at home, they go around visiting other royals. I'm not really sure why. I mean, is it because we all have something in common? Is it just about crashing at other palaces and inspecting how they run the show? Surely all these families can't possibly get along, especially with all the money, and politics, and big fucking egos at stake.

Nonetheless, the royal family of Monaco are coming to pay us a visit. They know Aksel isn't here—I told Princess Consort Penelope that *many* times—and yet they decided to come anyway. I've never met them before (I haven't been in the company of that many royals lately), but I've heard rumors about them.

Mainly that they're a bunch of eccentrics.

Mind you, this isn't much of a secret since the tabloids are always reporting on Princess Consort Penelope's face-lifts and affairs with boy toys, and on Prince Pierre's obsession with big-game hunting, and then there are the kids, the twenty-something twins, Prince Francis and Princess Matilde, who are rather quiet and charitable, unlike their older brother Prince Orlando. I only know about him because he's been dubbed as the "Royal Rogue" by the media ever since he was a teenager, and he's been featured in the tabloids for his hard-partying as much as I have been for being a single mom and divorcee.

"I wish they'd waited until Aksel was here," I tell Maja, wringing my hands together. "I don't know what their insistence was. What am I to them? Nobody."

My aunt raises her thin brow and gives me a dry look. "You're somebody, Stella."

She then sighs and taps her thin fingers along her knee. Both of us are fidgeting, sitting side by side on uncomfortable chairs in the receiving room. It has an actual proper name, but I don't remember what it is, all I know is that, while growing up, this is where the guests would come to meet my parents. There are a ton of old paintings of important monarchs on the wall, as well as some fine pottery on various side tables. The walls have pale blue-and-white striped wallpaper and there's this smell, like centuries of potpourri have seeped into the walls, that's giving me a major headache.

"Besides," she adds, "they're nuts. All of them. And that Princess Penelope is so damn pushy. She said they had been planning on this trip forever but when I called Aksel, he said they'd never contacted him before. So there's that. Bunch of liars, too." She sniffs, her chin raised.

Great. So I'll be entertaining a bunch of pushy liars for the next while. In the past, I haven't had to do much when acting as royal regent because most people know to wait until Aksel gets back. But this bunch apparently isn't "most people." Thank god it's only a dinner. With any luck, they'll do all the talking and then drink enough to get tired and go home. Or wherever they're staying.

Oh wait.

"Are they staying here?" I ask Maja.

She gives me another tepid look. "Of course they are. The

rooms are all set up. Where else would they go? A Best Western?"

Well, no, I figured that maybe they'd opt for one of the fancier hotels in Copenhagen, as is sometimes the case. Oh, who knows, I obviously don't do this enough.

Suddenly a head pokes into the room, Erik, one of the younger staff members. Butler apprentice, or whatever.

"They're here," he says, his voice frantic, his eyes wide.

That's not a good sign.

I look at my aunt for comfort, but her mouth is set in a firm line, her de facto expression, as we both get to our feet.

Before I can say anything, the door to the room opens wide, with the head servant Henrik announcing the guests.

"May I present to you His Serene Highness, Prince Pierre of Monaco," Henrik says, bowing just as Prince Pierre comes in the room.

He's a short, rotund little man with grey hair and a big bushy mustache. You know the father of Prince Charming in *Cinderella*? Yeah, he looks like that. A cartoon of a king.

Henrik is about to announce us to him, as per the protocol, but Prince Pierre just barrels on over to us and thrusts his hand out to mine, grasping it hard and shaking it vigorously.

"Such a pleasure to meet you, Your Highness," he says in heavily accented English, his mustache moving as he talks, showing big, rabbit-like teeth beneath. "You're so beautiful, too. It's a pity no man has seen himself worthy to be your king." He takes my hand and kisses the back of it.

It's happening so fast that I can barely squeak out a word, though I want to remind him that I'm just the princess, not a queen, and also his mustache is tickling me and I'm pretty sure this is inappropriate.

Meanwhile Henrik is clearing his throat, seeming aghast at the way the prince busted on through. "May I present to you Her Serene Highness, the Princess Consort of—"

"Oh, they all know who I am, everyone does," the Princess Consort, Penelope, says to Henrik, waving at him dismissively as she enters the room and hurries on over in her black ball gown that looks straight from the Victorian era, long sleeves, high neck and all. I suppose it's better than what I've usually seen her wear in the tabloids, low-cut, high slits, etc.

"Pierre, you can let go of her now," Penelope chides him, and nearly hip checks him out of the way. "So sorry about my husband," she says to me, taking my hand in hers and giving it a limp shake with long, pointy nails that almost stab the vein in my wrist. "He doesn't know his manners." She then looks at Maja. "You must be the aunt. Such a shame what happened to your sister."

I stiffen at that, though Maja lets it slide with a polite smile. Any mention of my mother, who is under the permanent care of the hospital thanks to her Alzheimer's, usually gets my hackles up. People don't seem to understand the situation and make plenty of assumptions.

Luckily, Penelope glosses over it and turns around abruptly to wave at the door where Henrik is standing uneasily, unsure of how to proceed with these royals. To be fair, I'm not sure how to proceed either.

"Bring the rest in, I'll do the introducing," Penelope says.

What I do know about Penelope is that she wasn't raised royal, or even upper class. She's a Spaniard, raised by a single mother in Barcelona. She won a lot of beauty competitions, which later led to her being an on-air personality and host who captured Prince Pierre's eye after his first wife, Princess Selene, died from breast cancer when Orlando was just nine years old. I guess even though Penelope has been a princess consort for at least twenty-five years, the protocols and etiquette haven't rubbed off on her yet.

And so, with Henrik stepping back and out of the way,

shooting me a quick *I don't know what to do* look, the rest of the Monégasque house steps in.

"This is my son Francis," Penelope says to me proudly, as a young man in his late twenties with spiked brown hair, black-framed glasses, and full lips steps in. He's dressed in a black suit, powder-blue shirt underneath with matching pocket square in his suit jacket.

"Pleasure to meet you, Princess Stella" he says to me, giving me a curtsey, which I can't help but smile at, followed by a wink. "I've heard a lot about you."

"All good things, I hope," I tell him.

"It all depends on how you want to look at it," he says smoothly.

Before I can question what that means, his mother introduces his sister, Princess Matilde.

Matilde is the spitting image of Francis—tall, brown hair, warm brown, almost seductive eyes framed by heavy, dark lashes that work as natural eyeliner. They're definitely twins.

As if she can hear what I'm thinking, Matilde gives me a smirk and says, "Don't worry, I'm the good twin." Then she gives me a quick curtsey, holding out the side of her gown which is all nude tulle and layers, a little bit princess, a little bit boho. "Enchanté," she says, before doing a quick little dance as she joins her mother, her dress floating behind her.

I'm thinking about how charming and unusual she is when all of the attention suddenly goes to the door.

There's more?

But of course there is.

"Finally, my husband's oldest, Prince Orlando," Penelope says, as he walks in the door. And when I say walk, what I really mean is that Orlando struts, like the man is powered by just his own confidence, as if he owns every room in every building he steps into.

Okay, so if we're going by looks alone, I guess you could

say they were saving the best for last because Prince Orlando's real name should be Prince Sex-on-a-Stick. A six-foot-two, broad-shouldered, wide-chested hunk of royal man-meat dressed in a finely tailored navy suit. He's got that tawny Mediterranean glow, and he's built like a tank with dark-blond hair that's cropped close at the sides and longer at the top, with a smattering of rugged facial hair. Normally, I don't go for blonds (my brother is blond, so that doesn't help) but Prince Orlando is in a whole other league.

Don't get me wrong, I'm not usually the type of woman who goes around objectifying men like this. Or at least, I wasn't until my ex-husband put me through the ringer, so I think I'm owed a little fun. I can't remember the last time I was with someone, let alone the last time I saw someone I thought was attractive. Plus, Prince Orlando seems like the type to do the same to women, so I don't feel so bad about all the lewd thoughts and ogling.

Naturally, though, I keep it all under the radar. Prince Orlando is looking around the room like I should be honored to be in his presence, not the other way around, and that instantly puts my guard up. Playboys, fuckboys, whatever they're called these days, the last thing they need know is that they're as sexy as they think they are.

His eyes come to mine and for a moment I've forgotten all about keeping it cool because there's something in his eyes that pulls the rug out from under me. Their color reminds me of being in Capri, looking at the sea close to shore, where the light bounces off the shingled beach. Crisp, clear water, impossibly blue. Refreshing and rich.

But it's not just the clarity, it's the warmth behind them. A warmth I didn't exactly expect to see from him. For a split second it was almost like looking at someone who *knew* me.

Then a smirk comes across his lips, touching his eyes with

a wave of arrogance and I manage to keep my wits and composure.

I raise my chin, lips pressed together tightly in a way that would make my aunt proud and wait, channeling every haughty princess part of me as I stare him down.

Prince Orlando stops right in front of me and chews on his lip for a moment before he finally bows. "Princess," he says, and I swear he says it like a nickname. "Lovely home you have here."

"It's my brother's," I blurt out, and I hear my aunt clear her throat from the back of the room. I guess the correct thing to say is "thank you." After all, this is my home as much as Aksel's.

"Right, I forgot," Orlando says, looking me over before he shrugs with one shoulder. "You don't seem like you'd belong here anyway."

My brows come together. What does that mean? Is that the correct thing to say to the royal regent?

But before I can ask him to clarify, Penelope comes over to him and grabs the crook of his arm. "Now that the boring introductions are over," she says, grinning at me. "How about you show us to the bar before dinner begins. I'm sure you have some Scandinavian liquor that we'd be more than happy to try."

I glance at my aunt, trying not to look confused and frantic, but she's nodding politely to Prince Pierre who is going on about something excitedly and holding his hands apart like he's telling her about the fish that got away.

I give Penelope my most complacent smile. "Well then, follow me."

I know earlier I had said that being royal regent was a lot like being a substitute teacher, but it's also a lot like being a house sitter. In this case, I feel like Aksel is going to return

---

and learn about all the forbidden rooms the guests were in and the liquor cabinets that were raided.

I walk past Henrik, exchanging a bewildered look with him, and head out of the room and down the hall toward the living room. This isn't usually where guests are entertained but I know it's where Aksel and Aurora spend a lot of time in the evening when the kids have gone to bed and where they keep the good stuff.

I'm not used to playing host, not even at home. It's just me and Anya most of the time, with the occasional help from Margaret, my nanny. That's who Anya is with right now since I didn't want to pull her away from her riding camp while I came down to Copenhagen. Our typical Friday nights might involve a board game and a glass of wine (for me, not Anya). Maybe a reality TV show, if I'm feeling loose.

And yet here I am, wearing a glittering gown that's a smidge too tight, leading a group of royals to find the King's secret alcohol cabinet. I feel painfully out of place, even if I grew up in this palace. What Prince Orlando assumed, happens to be true.

Once we're all gathered in the room and I start pulling out the Aquavit and Cloudberry liquor from Aksel's bar, Maja grabs me by the arm and takes me just outside the door.

"What are you doing?" she says in a hush. "This isn't part of the plan."

I roll my eyes. "If it's not obvious by now, there is no plan. And by the way, you could step in more and lead the way. I don't know what I'm doing."

"You're the royal here, Stella, not me," she says. "And you're the princess even when you aren't being the royal regent. This is your job."

"And as I just said, I don't know what I'm doing," I remind her. "You tell me. What am I supposed to do? They wanted a Scandinavian drink and so now they're all going to get smashed on it. We're supposed to cater to the guests, aren't we?"

She shakes her head, pressing her lips together. "I'm not sure Aksel will like this."

"Aksel doesn't have a choice. He's the one galivanting wherever he is. I mean, really, where is he this time anyway? Greece?"

"Cyprus," she says.

"Do we have a private compound there too now?"

She nods. "No one bugs him down there."

"How lucky for him," I say dryly, as I cross my arms. "Meanwhile I have to entertain the royal family of Monaco who seem to operate on some weird wavelength and with a strange agenda. Please tell me they're just staying the night."

She shrugs. "That I know of." Then she sighs and looks down the hall at Henrik who is approaching us uneasily. She waves him closer. "What's the status on the dinner? Any way the cooks can hurry it up?" she asks him.

"At least another hour," Henrik says apologetically. "Anything I can do to help?"

"Do you know any magic tricks?" I ask him. He frowns and I add, "They could use some entertainment."

Even though I was totally joking, Henrik nods. "If you have a guitar, I think I could play them some music."

"You play guitar?" I ask.

"I spent a lot of my youth busking on street corners."

This is news to me. Though Henrik is in his mid-forties, I feel like he's been a part of this palace since the dawn of time, first as the driver and now as the head butler. "Do you know anything, I don't know, Danish or Scandinavian? Folk songs?"

"I know 'Wonderwall.'"

Of course he does.

I hold up my hand to stop him. "You know what, it's okay. I'll handle it."

I square my shoulders and walk back into the room, head held high, a polite smile on my lips.

Prince Pierre and Princess Penelope are squeezed together on a loveseat, her elaborate ebony gown covering most of him. Come to think of it, I think Penelope is always in black for some reason. The bottle of Aquavit is in her hands and she's pouring her husband a glass as he's talking excitedly in French to Francis about something.

Matilde is sitting in a big armchair by herself, scrolling on her phone, not drinking, while Orlando is on the big couch, his legs splayed. In his hands is a glass of what is probably Scotch, considering the Scotch bottle on the coffee table across from him. The very rare, very expensive bottle of Scotch that I know Aksel favors.

Hmmm. Maybe this wasn't the best idea. What if the bottle is priceless?

"Sit down, relax," Orlando says to me, his full lips curled up in a slick smile. He pats the place beside him on the couch.

Relax? My brows shoot up. I don't want to sit down next to him. It feels, I don't know . . . risky. In ways I can't even explain, like he's being way too comfortable around me.

I'm about to decline, make up some excuse, but then Maja promptly takes the other armchair, leaving me no choice.

I give Orlando another quick smile and then gather my gown, sitting down beside him, but putting as much distance between us as possible. Any closer and I feel I'll be sucked into his orbit, like he's a black hole of sex. Or something.

"Drink?" he asks, leaning forward to grab the bottle while dipping his finger in an extra glass and bringing them over to me in one smooth motion.

"I'm quite all right," I tell him.

I mean, *lies.*

I look off at the rest of the room, but I feel his eyes boring into me, studying me. Finally he says, "Ah. I figured."

Don't fall for it, I tell myself. *He's baiting you.*

"What?" I ask him anyway.

"Nothing. You just seem the type who doesn't like to lose control."

"You seem to make a lot of assumptions about me," I counter.

That smirk appears, and for a moment, I'm dizzy. Those eyes again are pulling me in, propped up by deep dimples. He's making me stupid just by sitting beside him. That's why I thought sitting here was risky.

He gives a light shrug with one shoulder as his finger traces around the rim of the empty glass in slow, deliberate circles. There's something overtly sexual about the movement, or it could be I haven't been this close to a man like this since . . . well, probably ever. I think he's the most sexually magnetic creature I've been around.

For a split-second my brain fills with the image of him placing those long, capable fingers between my legs and making the same motion, over and over again. A quick glance at his eyes, slightly hooded and sparkling in their intensity, tells me he's doing it all on purpose. Jackass.

I swallow hard and look away, squeezing my legs together subtly to make the ache go away. It's like all the hair on my arms and back of my neck are standing at attention, my skin prickling, my body coming alive for the first time in years, in a very inappropriate place.

This man, this royal rogue, is going to be some bad, bad news for me.

I can already feel it.

CHAPTER 2
STELLA

S omehow, I manage to make it through cocktail hour and most of dinner without doing anything embarrassing. Not that I'm sure what I'd do. Just because being in Prince Orlando's proximity is making me think tawdry thoughts doesn't mean I'm going to climb across the dinner table and act on them. Even so, I barely have anything to drink, just to keep in control (he was right about that, too), and instead I keep my eyes on the rest of his family, even when all I feel are his eyes on me.

His family is a bit of a shitshow. I'm not one to judge, since my own family history is complicated at best, but it's like they revel in their scandal and eccentricity. They own it, no apologies, which is actually pretty admirable in a way.

Still, I'm out of my element. Penelope drinks nearly a whole bottle of Cloudberry liquor, which is something you should either mix or have in small doses, and that's when she starts telling everyone about all the famous people she's met, alluding more than a few times that she's had affairs with them. Once she starts going off on how sexy Prince Viktor of Sweden is and what she wants to do to him (in somewhat graphic detail, mind you, completely ignoring the fact that he's married), Francis pulls her to her unsteady feet and has a talk with her out of earshot. And by talk, I'm pretty sure it's a lecture.

Then there's Prince Pierre. He doesn't even seem to hear Penelope at all. Instead he won't stop talking about hunting giraffes in Botswana, even after his daughter Matilde tells him to stop. When that doesn't work, she literally gets to her feet and starts yelling at him about how he only hunts because he knows it hurts her and that he's a monster and a horrible father.

It's . . . a lot. I keep looking over at Maja, both our brows raised until they can't possibly go any higher. Thankfully, when dinner is announced it gives everyone breathing room and a chance to calm down.

Everyone except Orlando—he was already calm. Throughout the whole ordeal he didn't even react. Just sat back and watched. If anything, his head was in an entirely other place—except for when he was looking at me.

He managed to sit across from me during dinner, which again was highly distracting. On one hand, it made me take small bites and eat daintily, on the other hand, who gave a fuck what he thought of me eating?

"Oh fantastico, dessert!" Penelope exclaims, clapping her hands together as the servants bring around the rice pudding, placing the dishes in front of us. Though she was mainlining champagne with dinner, she seems to be more under control than earlier. Maybe the food did her some good.

Meanwhile, I'm heading in the opposite direction. Feeling more at ease that the dinner is almost over, I start drinking the champagne, feeling it relax me as the bubbles go straight to my brain.

Maybe I've got this. I mean, everyone more or less seems

to be having a good time. I may not have Aksel's role as a royal, but perhaps I'm good at faking it?

I'm just about to dig into the rice pudding when suddenly an awful scream fills the whole palace. Penelope drops her spoon with a clatter while Pierre is pushing back his chair and standing on top of it, his arms out like he's holding an imaginary rifle.

"Where's the warthog? I know that squeal anywhere," he says, eyes scanning the dining the room as if he's on safari.

Warthog?

As another scream sounds, followed by thumps and the pattering of quickly moving hooves, I realize what's happening. It's not a scream but a squeal, and it's not a warthog but Snarf Snarf.

The royal pig.

Oh for fuck's sake.

I look at Maja but she's shaking her head, her way of telling me to deal with it.

That's the hidden fine print of being the royal regent for Aksel—having to deal with his pet pig. Or should I say, Clara and Freja's pet pig. Once upon a time, Snarf Snarf was easier to manage. He was a tiny little thing. They'd said he was a mini pig.

But mini pigs are a big fat lie. They never stay mini. Instead, they grow up to be the three-hundred-pound porkers that everyone knows, and that's what Snarf Snarf is now. A sweet boy for sure, but big as hell and with a rebellious streak.

Normally he's kept in the backyard in his own pen, so I have no idea why the pig is now in the house, but as I look to the hallway and see Snarf Snarf burning it past the dining room in a flash of fleshy pink, followed by a frantic-looking Henrik, I know that he escaped.

I sigh and throw my napkin down on the bowl. I can't sit here and eat dessert and pretend that this will get handled because if Aksel comes back and discovers his house was destroyed by that pig, I'm the one who is going to get the blame.

I get out of my chair and give everyone my most serene smile.

"You may have heard about the royal pig, Snarf Snarf," I tell them, clasping my hands together. "He gets loose from time to time. Allow me to go deal with it and you just finish your rice pudding. It's a Danish tradition."

"The pig being loose or the rice pudding?" Francis jokes.

"You're going to need my assistance," Pierre says, climbing down off his chair. He reaches over and grabs a knife off the table.

Quickly, Matilde reaches out and grabs her father's wrist. "You're not going anywhere. He's a pet, not food, not a trophy."

"It's quite all right," I tell them both. "I deal with this all the time." Which is a lie. "Now, if you'll excuse me."

I head out of the room and down the hallway where muddy cloven hoofprints lead the way, standing out against the cream and gold carpet. To tell the truth, I think I'd rather be out here on a Snarf Snarf mission than back in there where I never quite felt comfortable.

"Hey," Orlando says in a low voice and I jump in surprise, turning around to see him standing behind me. "What are you doing?"

Seriously? He couldn't just stay put?

"I'm going to go capture that pig," I tell him, and then nod back to the room. "Don't you have dessert to finish?"

"You shouldn't have to do this by yourself," he says. "Pigs are dangerous." Then his eyes coast up and down over my body in such a way that I can almost feel the heat on my skin.

"And I'm rather picky about dessert. I only put the sweetest things in my mouth."

Wow.

I open my mouth to speak but the words don't come out right away. I clear my throat. "I'm not doing it by myself. I just saw Henrik run after him."

"But you don't trust him to do his job?" He takes a step toward me until there's barely any distance between us. I should take a step back until I'm up against the wall. Give him a dirty look. He's invading my space.

But I don't step back. I stand where I am. I do give him a dirty look, though.

"I like to make sure things are done properly," I say, glaring at him.

"Uh huh." Another slick smile. "I was right about you, you know," he says, voice dropping a register and getting all gravelly, the kind of tenor that you feel vibrate between your legs. "Not much of a princess."

I raise my brows. "Excuse me? I'm plenty enough of a princess. I just don't sit back and let other people do my job. My brother will have my head if he comes back and finds the palace destroyed by that pig. If doing dirty work means I'm not much of a royal, if it means I have to be in control, so be it."

He grins and bites his lip and my eyes are drawn to that bottom lip, full and pink, and those perfect white teeth. "I knew we had a lot in common."

"What?"

His gaze drops to my mouth now. "That both of us like to get dirty. The dirtier, the nastier, the harder, the better."

I narrow my eyes at him to deflect the way he's making me feel all hot and wet and wanton. "If I didn't know any better, I'd say you're just another pig running around this palace."

He blinks at me and then lets out a sharp laugh. "Did you just call me a pig? Whatever for?"

"All your inappropriate innuendo," I say haughtily.

"Innuendo, huh?" he says, stroking his scruffy chin with his fingers, that shit-eating grin still on his face. "I'm sorry, Princess Stella, but I have no idea what you're talking about. I've just been talking to you, royal to royal, though I must say it's not unusual for a single woman to get the wrong idea about me, especially if she hasn't been with a man in a while."

Oh my fucking god.

I don't even know what to say to that. My cheeks flush with anger and embarrassment and I quickly turn away from him and hurry down the hall.

What the fuck is wrong with him? I try to listen to the sounds of squealing and Henrik's shouts and head in their direction, but I'm absolutely livid over Orlando. What an asshole! Like hell none of that was innuendo.

I shouldn't have played into his game. Should have just ignored him. The moment he stepped into this place he made it more than obvious that he was into me, that he's been sending me a steady number of signals.

Or was he? Maybe he was right. Maybe I did get the wrong idea. Maybe he was just teasing me to see if I'd bite. As much as I hate it, he was right about me not being with a man in a while.

Wait a minute.

How dare he!

Anger flares on my cheeks and I stop mid-stride in the middle of the hall, turning around to see him still standing where he was before, watching me curiously. I march all the way back to him, wishing I wasn't in this stupid, form-fitting gown and heels, and thrust my finger in his face.

"What do you mean, I haven't been with a man in a while? You don't know shit about me. Do you know how damn rude it is to surmise that about anyone, let alone a woman, let alone the Royal Regent of Denmark?"

The tip of his tongue shows briefly through his lips as they curve into another arrogant smile. "I'm just going by what the tabloids write about you."

"And if I go by what the tabloids write about you, you're supposed to be a reformed player, currently coupled with a long-term girlfriend, some famous tennis star, and yet here you are being inappropriate with me. Seems you're not so reformed anymore."

His gaze hardens for a moment, the first time I've seen him be serious, even if for just a second. "I don't belong to anyone," he says steadily. "I have no commitments. And once again you call me inappropriate. Sounds like you might be projecting."

As unladylike as it is, I swear I'm this close to driving the pointy tip of my heel into his shin, that is until I hear Henrik yell, "Your Highness!" followed by the sound of thundering hooves.

The floor shakes underneath me as I turn in time to see Snarf Snarf barrelling toward us, Henrik running after him and yelling.

I don't have time to react. I'm about to be run over by a pig.

Then Orlando reaches over and grabs me by the waist. I cry out as he somehow manages to hoist me up in the air, my knees drawn up, as Snarf Snarf passes beneath me and gallops back toward the dining room.

"You can thank me later," he says, practically throwing me back on the ground before he runs a few strides and then leaps into the air, tackling Snarf Snarf before he's about to run into the dining room.

Chaos ensues.

Orlando and Snarf Snarf roll over on the floor, bumping

into the wall, and it's just a mess of prince and pig, the squeals filling the air, the shouts and cries from the dinner party join in as they realize what's happening.

"Don't hurt him!" I yell at Orlando, not wanting an injured pig on my hands, just in time for Snarf Snarf to open his mouth and chomp into Orlando's forearm in defense.

"Ah!" Orlando yells, but he doesn't loosen his arm which is wrapped around Snarf Snarf's chest. "This porky fucker bit me!"

All of the Monaco royal family appears at the dining room doorway, looking down in shock as Orlando and Snarf Snarf battle for dominance. Henrik rushes past me holding a rope and leans down over the pig, slipping the rope around his head.

"Come on Snarf Snarf!" Henrik yells, followed by a string of Danish expletives. Probably not the right decorum for the head butler, but considering he just roped the pig, he's allowed. Besides, so far this evening it seems like anything goes and anything is currently going.

Finally Henrik is able to pull Snarf Snarf up securely and Orlando lets go, rolling over on the ground and moaning. I'm more concerned about the pig than the prince, but so far Snarf Snarf seems fine. If anything, he looks a little proud and defiant, even as Henrik leads him away.

Orlando is another deal. He's sitting up on the floor, holding onto his forearm and wincing, his suit torn and covered in Snarf Snarf's dirt.

"Oh dear," Maja says, looking through the gathering crowd. "Stella, you better sort him out."

Me again? I give her a contemptuous look but she's already turning around and trying to convince the royals to go back to their dessert.

"That was fucking wild, man," Francis says, wide-eyed, before turning back to the room.

Matilde looks at me. "Do you need any help?"

I sigh and glance down at Orlando who is getting to his feet. "I'm fine," he says.

But he's not fine. He looks wrecked and we need to make sure that Snarf Snarf didn't do any real damage. I've never seen him bite before—I guess I never even thought that was a hazard—but since mobsters have a history of feeding people to pigs, I'm guessing they can do a lot of harm. I really hope that Aksel and Aurora don't return here to find that Snarf Snarf has discovered an appetite for human flesh.

"Come on," I tell Orlando. "Let's go get you cleaned up."

"I'm fine," he says again, shaking out his arm but his expression is pained.

"You don't know where that pig's been, and he's at least torn through your suit jacket." I gesture for him to follow me and he does so begrudgingly.

We walk down the hall to a bathroom where I know Aurora keeps a spare first-aid kit under the sink. I had to use it once when Anya got her face cut up during a snowball fight gone wrong.

Once inside I get the kit out and place it on the countertop and gesture for Orlando to take off his jacket.

"I'm telling you, I'm fine," he says as he takes it off, and for a moment I'm distracted by the fit of his white shirt and the hint of tanned skin beneath the collar, before seeing the blood on his forearm.

"Oh shit," Orlando says, staring at his arm. "This is how I'm going to die, isn't it?"

I reach over and gently roll up the sleeve of his torn shirt.

He sucks in his breath.

"Sorry," I tell him, before lifting it back to see the wound.

It's a bloody mess. It's a good thing I can handle the sight of blood. I like to chalk it up to one of the superpowers of being a mother.

"Just a flesh wound," he says, though there's a strain in his voice.

"Let's hope."

I bring him over to the sink and turn on the warm water, gently sticking his arm under it. I'm pressed up against his shoulder, one hand gripping him by his elbow. His muscles are taut and tense, and he smells good. Like mint and something woodsy. I close my eyes for a second and tell myself to keep it together.

The water washes away the blood and we can see the wound more clearly. It doesn't look that bad, just a puncture wound from one of Snarf Snarf's tusks. I think he could have done some major damage had he meant to.

"Told you. Just a flesh wound," he says, glancing at me over his shoulder. He gives me a wry smile. "I've had worse."

"You've been bitten by a pig before?" I ask him, dabbing a cloth onto the wound to stop the bleeding.

"No, this is my first time for that," he says.

"Well, I'll put some antibacterial lotion on it and bandage it up, but you're going to want a new shirt, and if it gets worse, you're going to need to go to the doctor tomorrow for antibiotics."

I reach for the antibiotic cream.

"You're welcome, by the way," he says.

My fist clenches and I nearly squeeze all the cream out of the tube. "Excuse me?"

"Don't know if you remember, but I saved you from a similar fate back there."

"Snarf Snarf only bit you because you tackled him." I give him a steady look.

"And I tackled him because that was the only way to stop him. Your staff is incompetent."

"First of all, they aren't my staff," I tell him, dabbing the cream on his wound, maybe a little too hard.

"Ow."

"Sorry."

"What's the second 'of all?' I'm curious to see where your argument is going. After all, had I not saved you, you would have been trampled. Had I not stopped that damn pig, he probably would have had a ball tearing up the dining room. I'm practically virtuous."

I snort. "You want a medal?"

There's a pause and I look up from dabbing the cream on him to see his eyes burning into mine. "I want a thank you."

I fight the urge to roll my eyes. "Thank you, then."

"You owe me one."

Now I'm rolling my eyes. "Oh, of course I do. Dare I ask what I owe you?"

"Let your hair down a little," he says, and with his other hand he reaches over and takes the diamond clip out of my updo. My blonde hair spills down around my shoulders.

I'm so taken aback by the gesture, the fact that his hand is now at the back of my neck, his palm warm against my skin, that I drop the tube. It tumbles into the sink.

I turn to get it and his hand falls away.

"That's better," he says. "This is probably the real you, isn't it?"

I clear my throat, feeling heat on my chest and cheeks. "I'm not sure you'd want to meet the real me."

"Why not?"

I look away, busying myself by putting the tube of cream away and taking out the gauze and bandages. "There's nothing interesting about her."

"You're a princess, aren't you?"

I shoot him a dry look. "And you think that automatically makes someone interesting? You should know better than that. Though maybe you don't, since your family has to be the oddest royal family I've ever met. Actually, oddest family, period. No offence."

"None taken. They are what they are. And you are what you are."

His blue eyes flit over my body and up to my face. This time it doesn't make me uncomfortable. This time, I rather like the way he's looking at me, like he's trying to understand me. I can't recall ever feeling that way before. It's like no one bothers anymore.

"You have an odd approach," I say after a moment.

"I've been told," he says, watching me as I start to wrap the bandage around him. I twist around to get a better position, my ass pressing against the counter, and as a strand of hair falls in front of my face, he reaches over and pushes it back, his fingers trailing along my cheek as he tucks it behind my ear.

What on earth is happening? Just finish bandaging him up and get out of here.

But the words are slow in my mind. Everything else seems to expand, my senses heightened. I'm so very aware of the feel of his fingers on me, like shooting sparks, aware of his scent that makes the heat grow in my core, aware of the warmth of his body in this small space.

I'm aware of his roaming eyes, which never waver in their intensity, only in their tone. Curious, compelled, humorous, cocky, lustful, and wanting, they're constantly conveying something to me as they never leave my face and body.

I secure the end of the bandage and try to find my voice. "All done," I tell him quietly, afraid to meet his eyes.

He takes his bandaged arm and puts it on one side of me, so that I'm bracketed against the sink, trapped between him. "But we're not done," he murmurs, and I glance up at him. He licks his lips as he tilts his head and gives me a slow smile. "I think you know that, princess."

I gulp.

What do you want with me?

"I wouldn't want to get the wrong impression," I say carefully, bringing up his denial in the hallway, pre-pig collision.

"Maybe I just like to play games," he says. "Until I don't. And I don't want to play games anymore."

I blink at him, my breath hitching in my throat. "So what do you want?"

"I think it's quite obvious what I want," he says, raising his hand to hold the tip of my chin, looking deep into my eyes. I feel completely captive, my heart pounding against my ribs, the counter pressing against my ass, the strength in his shoulders and arms as he keeps me locked in. "But the real question here is, what do *you* want?" He leans in, his lips just inches away from mine, pressing his thumb harder into my chin. "Not in life. Not in your future. What do you want right now?"

Is this really happening?

Am I going to tell him the truth?

There's a chance that I won't even be able to put the truth into words.

But it might be a chance worth taking.

CHAPTER 3
STELLA

W hat *do* I want?

My throat feels thick as my eyes focus on Orlando's lips. Wondering what it's like to kiss them, to have them on my body. Knowing that I have the power to wonder no longer. I can make it happen or I can walk away and go back to the dinner party and the role I've been pretending to do.

"I don't know you," I whisper.

His lips curve into a soft smile. "What do you want, Your Highness?" he repeats.

"I'm not sure I can explain with words," I admit slowly, meeting his eyes. "I'm not even sure it's a want. I think . . . I think it might be a need."

"I can work with that," he says. "Do you need me to kiss you?" He lowers his mouth until his lips brush ever so briefly, ever so softly against mine. "Here? On your lips?"

He then moves his head and buries it in my neck. His hot breath is causing my body to erupt in flames. "Or here."

His mouth very gently presses against my skin, not quite a

kiss but enough to leave me yearning with no doubt in my mind what I really want and need.

Him.

I need him.

This man who showed up into my life today and awoke something inside me. Not a want but a need. A need to feel special, to be desired. A need to be free of my roles and my life and everything that's expected of me.

A need to have a little fucking fun for once.

"How about here?" he asks in a murmur, as his hand releases my chin and slowly trails down over my chest, to the edge of my dress. I hold my breath as he pulls the neckline of my gown away, exposing my breast. My nipple immediately hardens, and I grip the corner of the counter until my knuckles turn white.

He lowers his head and gently blows on my chest, the feeling causing a cascade of shivers to roll down my spine and for my legs to clench together in an aching want. I can practically feel my panties growing wet. I'm this close to begging him to kiss me, lick me, devour me.

"Do you have a better idea now?" he asks, voice like silk, as he brings his face up to mine. I'm quite aware that I have one tit hanging out of my dress and I'm nearly panting with desire. "Or should I keep guessing?" He brings his hand to my breast and slowly brushes his thumb over my nipple. "Is it these fingers?"

The circles he was making on the glass earlier are now swirling around my nipple, sending waves of pleasure throughout my body, both intoxicating and coupled with urgency.

His touch is incredible.

"Or is it my cock?" he says, taking my hand and placing it on his crotch. His dick is hot even through his fly, the shape of him thick and hard as concrete. It literally takes my breath away. "Because I could give this to you so hard and so thor-ough, it will be like you've never been fucked before. Is that what you're wanting? What you're needing? My big, hard cock deep inside your tight little cunt?"

My eyes go wide. There's dirty talk, and then there's Prince Orlando's dirty talk, and I don't think you can even compare the two.

I end up gripping him through his pants, my body now taking on a mind of its own and I decide to let it do what it wants, dictate the show.

"Yes," I say, the word coming out breathless and hoarse.

He bites his lip and grins at me. "That's what I thought you'd say. I knew it the moment I laid eyes on you. I thought, there's a woman who could use a good fuck and by someone who knows how."

I nearly laugh. "Are you always this arrogant?"

"Get on that counter, spread your legs, and I'll show you why I have a reason to be."

Heat flushes over my entire body. "You better close that door," I tell him, nodding to the door that's been ajar this whole time.

He turns around and quickly shuts the door, and before I have time to try and sit back on the counter, his large hands are wrapping around my waist and hoisting me up. He then puts them at my thighs and spreads them as far as my dress will allow.

"Hike up your dress," he tells me. "I want to see how wet you are."

Good lord.

I feel the blush creep on my cheeks as I do as he says. I hitch my dress up over my thighs until it's gathered around my waist.

He presses his hands against my thighs until they're open wide.

"Move your underwear to the side," he says, stepping back to get a better look. "Show me."

I reach down and move my panties to the side, until I'm completely exposed.

I want to feel embarrassed or ashamed or vulnerable. I want to look away.

Instead I'm completely fascinated by his expression. I've never been looked at like this before, not even by my ex-husband. Prince Orlando's intense gaze between my legs is addicting, mesmerizing, like watching the flames in a growing fire.

Even so, I manage to quietly say, "I've never done this before."

His magnetic gaze reluctantly lifts away from my pussy and meets my eyes.

"Spread your legs for a prince?" he questions.

I nod. "Yes. And I don't normally . . . do this sort of thing."

He squeezes my thighs and stares at me curiously. "Do you feel the need to explain yourself to me? As if I'd think you were a whore otherwise?"

I give a shy shrug. "I don't know."

"Listen, Stella, princess," he says to me, taking his hands away and stepping in closer between my legs. One of his hands goes to his fly. "You don't owe me any sort of explanation and I don't owe you one either. I don't need to know your past. You're allowed to just be a woman who wants a good fuck, okay? And I'm allowed to be a man who wants to make you cream yourself on my cock. Got it?"

Oh. I got it.

For emphasis, he undoes his zipper with a sound that seems to fill the bathroom and then his pants are coming undone and dropping to the floor.

He's going commando.

I was not prepared for that.

His cock juts out, bobbing in front of him, capturing the space between us. It's even bigger than I felt against my palm, thick and dark and long. It's as beautiful as a penis can get. No wonder he's so arrogant.

"We have a saying in Monaco," he says, wrapping his fingers around the base of it. "Let the cock go free."

"Is that really a saying?"

He gives me a crooked smile before he places his other hand at the back of my neck. "It's *my* saying. Along with, never trust a man who hates cats, and the day isn't over until I've made a woman come."

I give him an incredulous look.

He laughs. "Just kidding about that last part but in this case, this day isn't over until you've had at least three orgasms."

"Before we talk orgasms, let's talk condoms."

"I don't have any on me," he says, hesitating. "I'm clean though, I have to be."

I raise my brow at that. "Royals got to stay healthy?"

"Something like that."

"Then same for me. And I'm on the pill."

"So..."

"So..." I give him a coy smile.

But before the smile even has a chance to fade on my face, his grip on my neck tightens as he positions his cock at my entrance and drives himself inside.

The wind is knocked out of me.

I gasp, my legs automatically wrapping around his waist like a reflex as his cock sinks in deeper and deeper.

I was not prepared for this. I don't think anyone would be prepared for this.

Holy.

"Fuck," he moans, as he pushes himself in to the hilt. My

body is so tense that I can barely take in a breath, all I feel is him and there's a *lot* of him. Thank god I'm as wet as I am.

He slowly pulls out and stares at me through hooded eyes, and I can feel him drag along every nerve inside me. "You're fucking incredible," he says, and then he slides his hand up into my hair and makes a fist. He pulls my head toward his, his mouth capturing mine.

The kiss is searing and sweet and wet and I groan between his lips as he starts thrusting back into me. There's so much hunger building through me that the only way out is through our probing tongues and clashing teeth, this need to consume him. The need for him to consume me.

Usually, I have a first kiss and then that eventually leads to sex but this time it's all been backwards. And yet I wouldn't have it any other way. This chaotic, messy, almost crude way of coupling feels like the only way to get what I want, what I need.

"How do I feel?" he murmurs into my mouth, his voice thick. "Tell me how good my cock feels."

Another thing I'm not used to. With my ex, I could barely say the word cock without giggling like a schoolgirl. But now, with this dirty prince, I feel like I'm a different person, just for tonight.

"You feel amazing," I tell him, my voice taking on a husky quality that would give Scarlett Johansson a run for her money. "How do I make you feel?"

"Like a fucking king," he says without missing a beat, kissing me again, wet and chaotic and wild. With his grip in my hair tightening and the other ripping my other breast free of my dress, he dips his head and sucks my nipple in between his teeth. Hard.

"Oh fuck," I cry out, my words melting into intelligible moans as my hands fly to his shoulders, gripping him tight. For a moment I'm reminded that he's still injured but he doesn't seem to give a shit at this moment. Honestly, neither do I. His bluntness has rubbed off on me and now all I want is to come, to feel that wild release.

I'm not far off either. His hips keep pumping into me, enough so that my head almost smashes back into the mirror, his hand softening the blow.

Lips and teeth suck and bite at my breast until I'm nearly coming just from that.

I feel swollen and bruised and beautiful.

Fingers reach down between my legs and slide against my clit and that's when the world starts to open, spreading and building along with the pressure inside me.

"I'm going to come," I gasp, surprised, nearly betrayed by my body for having such an instantaneous reaction.

"Good," he grunts, hips pistoning until I'm sure we might be black and blue, and then his fingers are stroking me steadily, his lips sucking sharply along my neck.

"Fuck!" I cry out, the wave reaching me before I have a chance to prepare. My body quakes and shudders and I'm trying not to yell because I know this has to be secret but at the same time I am screaming inside with my release.

I bite into his shoulder, tasting the fabric of his shirt and the sweat beneath, and I'm coming over his cock, squeezing and riding him until I can't remember my name or who I am or where I am and why I'd ever care about anything but this.

My god.

The world doesn't right itself right away. It tips over and over on its axis and then I'm dragged along wave after wave of bliss and pleasure until the next thing I know is Prince Orlando is pulling himself out of me, placing me back down on the ground, and then turning me around so that I'm bent over the sink.

My knees are shaking. I barely have enough time to reach out with my hands to keep myself steady against the tiles before he's gripping my hips, pulling my bare ass toward him. He pushes my underwear back to the side and tries to push his cock in but gets stuck.

With a hungry growl of frustration, he grabs the underwear and rips them right off of me. It's just a cheap thong that could barely contain my hips as it was, so it tears with ease. The sound echoes off the walls.

"Fuck that was hot," he says through a groan, before he digs his fingers into the flesh of my hips and thrusts back inside.

I'm beside myself, stretched to the brim again and already needing more of him. All of this, again and again. His groan deepens as he pumps into me and I'm back to gasping. Even though I'm soaked and still raw and throbbing from earlier, he still fills me until there's no more room.

"God you feel so good," he says thickly, his body slapping against mine as he drives deeper and deeper. "We look so good. Look at yourself. Look at what I'm doing to you."

I look up at the mirror which is just inches from my face and see our reflection.

We look good. I mean, if this was a high-class porno. I barely recognize myself. My hair is down and in knots, my cheeks red, my pupils dilated. Both my tits are hanging out of my dress, looking pink and full as they sway from each thrust.

Then there's *him*. The prince in the mirror. God, he really is sex on a fucking stick. His white shirt is sweat soaked as it sticks to his massive shoulders, and half unbuttoned, showing a glimpse of hard, tanned chest. The rolled-up sleeves that show off the bandages on his forearm only make it hotter. The fact that he wanted to fuck me this badly, that being injured didn't even matter to him.

His face is what makes it though. Such a beautiful face contorted in a beautiful way. With eyes pinched shut, his mouth is open and wanting, and I can hear the ragged breaths as he struggles to contain himself.

I'm making him feel this way.

Then his eyes fly open and strike mine in the reflection that's being fogged up by our heat, by my gasps for air. They spark, like there's a livewire between us. I feel more captivated by the lust in his gaze than I do by the relentless pounding of his cock.

"Come again for me," he says, and before I have a chance to tell him to make me, he makes me.

His hand slips between my legs and finds where I'm swollen and drenched and greedy and that's all it takes.

"Oh, god," I cry out, and I have to look away, the top of my head pressed against the mirror as he slams into me and as my world explodes once more. "Oh god, oh god!" The words spill out and the lights behind my eyes turn to pinks and blues and stars, swirling like a galaxy and I have that feeling that I'm no longer in my body anymore, I'm somewhere else entirely.

"Fuck, fuck, fuck." The staccato flow of Orlando's grunts and groans fill my ears and his fingers tighten so hard around my waist and hips, it's almost violent. His hips thrust into me once, twice, his cock driving in deeper than ever before, the breath pulled out of me, and then I feel him coming, the shaking and the quivering as his body releases inside me.

Dear god.

I can't even think. Thoughts try to build but they float away as quickly as they appear. All I know is that my heart is trying to break through my rib cage and that being breathless has never made me feel so good. Every part of me aches and throbs in complete satisfaction.

Reality slowly returns.

The fact that I'm bent over the bathroom sink in the

royal palace, my dress hiked around my waist, my hair tangled.

Face pink.

Delirious.

Happy.

Prince Orlando of Monaco behind me, his handsome, flushed face looking both smug and sated at once. He meets my gaze again in the mirror and then slowly pulls out.

I immediately feel empty without him inside me, like he filled some need, however brief, that I didn't know I had.

He quickly tucks his cock back into his pants and zips them up, then grabs a hand towel and runs it up between my legs, cleaning me off.

My legs themselves feel unsteady, so he reaches over and helps me straighten up and turn around. I laugh as I attempt to shove my boobs back in my dress, while he pulls the dress down over my hips.

Then he looks at me and smiles.

"Are you going to keep your hair down?" he asks, reaching back and brushing it over my shoulders. "Or will it be too obvious that I just fucked you?"

"I'm not sure what your family is used to," I tell him, turning back around so I can see myself in the mirror. "But mine would never even imagine such a thing."

"Because the single mom is never allowed to enjoy herself? Be a sexual being?"

I pause for a moment before I pull my hair back off my head and start twisting it around into a quick updo that I hope no one will inspect. I don't have anything to say to that, probably because it's true.

"How old are you?" he asks, as he hands me my diamond hair clip.

"Thirty-four," I say with a frown. "Why? How old are you?"

"Same damn age."

"Isn't that lucky."

"It is. We're young. Younger than the world seems to think we are. I don't know if it's society or if it's being a royal, but this isn't the end, it's only the start. You don't have to play the role of the single mom who has given up on getting what she really wants, just because you think you have to at your age."

I study him, nearly giving him the stink eye. "Might I remind you that you don't know me."

"Maybe not," he says. He licks his thumbs and then smooths back the loose hairs from my hairline. "But I know what you feel like from the inside and I know what you sound like when you come. That's good enough for me."

He leans in close, his breath hot on my cheek. "I like you. I liked this. So I'm just reaching out and telling you the truth. We both have roles to play, roles that were handed to us. But they don't have to define us. And they don't have to contain us." He places a slow kiss at my cheek. "Believe me, Your Highness, when I say that I know."

Then Orlando pulls back and flashes me his carefree smile. He picks up his suit jacket and slings it over his shoulder as he opens the door. "Come on. We have a dinner party to return to."

And just like that, he's walking away from me and down the hall.

When I step back out, it feels like the whole world has changed.

I take a deep breath in, pat down my hair, and follow Orlando back to the dining room.

CHAPTER 4
ORLANDO

I wake up in pain.

At first, I thought it was all in my dream. I was running down the halls of a palace lined with red velvet walls and black floors, chased by a herd of wild pigs with blood running down their tusks. They meant to kill me and as I ran and ran, I yelled for help, not sure where to turn.

Finally, I turned a corner into a ballroom and saw my father standing in the middle of it with a rifle, dressed in his ridiculous safari hunting gear.

But instead of helping me, my father turned the gun on me, and I had to run back.

The pigs got me right on the arm, which hurt and throbbed and ached until the dream spit me out.

Except now that I'm awake and staring up at a strange ceiling with gold and white mouldings, I realize that my arm actually hurts like a motherfucker.

I stare at it all bandaged, lying on top of the lush teal quilt. It looks okay. Not bleeding much, not swollen, but it definitely aches.

Fucking pig.

Snarf Snarf?

What the hell kind of a name is that?

And what the hell was I thinking playing hero, thinking I could just tackle a pig and be okay? I hadn't at all been prepared for how huge and strong that fucker was and how hard he'd fight back.

All to impress a fucking lady.

Well, actually, a princess.

Not that I was going to let anyone get trampled by that runaway hunk of bacon, but I definitely wasn't going to let that happen to her. I also wasn't going to let it run around the King of Denmark's palace and tear it to shreds. So I stepped in.

I don't regret it.

It ended up in the best fuck I've had in a long time.

Maybe ever?

I don't know, but it was definitely something.

When I stepped into this palace, into that stuffy sitting room filled with portraits of high-cheek-boned miserable people, and saw Stella, standing there, looking beautiful and uncertain, I immediately felt something for her. Nothing emotional, nothing sweet, though perhaps not as crude as what I voiced to her, that she was a woman that needed to come on my cock.

Oh, that thought passed through my head for sure. But it was more than just some lustful twitching in my pants. It was like I knew her in some strange way. Or maybe it was just the feeling of relief to see someone like her there. Someone I could maybe relate to for once.

She was looking at me like she immediately disliked me, which is hot. I've always loved a challenge. Especially when I saw that it wasn't coming from the usual place, the way that most other royals and aristocrats look at me and my family. She wasn't being a snob; she saw something that rocked her foundations a little. Made her a little uncertain, maybe a little scared.

As gorgeous as she looked with her regal posture and hair piled on her head like strands of silken wheat, begging to be let down, and her pouty lips, delicate features and beguiling blue eyes, I could tell that this wasn't the place for her. She didn't belong in a palace where she had to watch everything she did and pretend to be king for a day. She belonged out there in the real world.

Of course I knew about her before I came here. When my mother announced she wanted to do a tour of the Nordic kingdoms, I did a bit of due diligence and researched the countries, the families and their backgrounds. After all, I'll be the head of Monaco one day. We never get the title of king, yet as princes we wield more power over our kingdoms than any other monarchy. And a good future ruler prepares for everything.

I learned that Princess Stella is King Aksel's only sibling.

Their father died a few years ago, thrusting Aksel into the role as King.

He had a wife, Helena, who later died tragically in a car accident. I remember that very well since Helena had a Princess Diana vibe about her, beloved and beautiful and always doing charity work (in fact my sister, Matilde, was inspired by both of them).

Aksel has two daughters from that marriage. He then fell in love with his Australian nanny, which caused a great scandal, even though they now have twin sons together and she's become the queen, while his sister Stella is divorced with a young daughter.

With all that research in the back of my head, I thought I knew what I was getting into when I first went to Copenhagen, but Stella threw me for a loop. It wasn't just that I knew some things about her, it's that when I looked in her eyes, I thought I knew her. Deeply. Like we were cut from the same cloth. Maybe just by the press, or maybe by our families, but I knew that she knows exactly what it's like to be tied to a role in such a way that you can't remember the person you once wanted to be.

I also knew she wanted me. That was apparent. And if the tabloids had been true, she deserved a damn good fuck. I wanted to show her a good time, let her hair down—literally. Push her buttons a little. Yeah, so maybe I was a bit of a bastard with her at times, leading her on and then pretending I wasn't interested, but I like to have fun too.

I groan, both from the throbbing in my arm and the throbbing in my dick. Just the thought of her sweet perfection has me horny as hell. I could have gone all night with her. I wanted to. Fucking her like that in the bathroom—as hot as it was—wasn't enough for me. But this wasn't something we could flaunt in the open or even around our families. So we went back to the dining room and finished up the rest of the night, with everyone making a fuss over my pig-tackling and subsequent injuries.

When the night was winding down, Stella excused herself, not meeting my eyes. And just like that, she had gone to bed early and I wasn't about to start roaming the halls of the king's palace, looking for her bedroom (though the thought did briefly enter my mind).

Now we're supposed to push off somewhere else today. Sweden, I think, though I'm dreading that considering the gross things my stepmother was saying about the prince. We're better off going to Norway to see Prince Magnus, who I consider a friend of mine since we sometimes race cars against each other, but he'd probably welcome her attention since he's an attention-whore.

I groan at the thought. To be honest, I would rather stay here. I might act like my family isn't strange or embarrassing, but I know they can be a bit much. Here, it feels safe. Stella and her aunt have seen the worst, plus there's the fact that I was injured. Anything that could have gone wrong last night for our first tour of the Nordic royals did in fact go wrong, and if I've learned anything, that usually means it's just going to get worse.

I contemplate going back to bed but a quick glance at my phone tells me that it's past nine a.m. I've slept in. Plus the pain is getting worse.

I get out of bed, taking quick stock of the room. The guest room is nice, full of teals and dark wood, a little more updated than I would have thought, especially compared to the palace in Monaco. My bloodline has been occupying the same palace for 700 years, so while it's often being rebuilt in certain places, it's just not the same. It's old as fuck.

I get dressed and head down the ornate and sweeping staircase to the first level. Thinking that there might be some royal breakfast, I'm starting down the hall toward the dining room, noting that some servants are cleaning the carpet where Snarf Snarf tracked in dirt last night, when I hear someone behind me.

It's my stepmother.

"Orlando," she says. Even though it's early, she's dressed in a flowing black dress that would be better suited on Matilde. "How are you feeling?"

"Honestly? I need some meds. Do you have any?"

Penelope basically carries an arsenal of all the best pain killers. I steal from her stash more times than I like to admit.

"Of course," she says, patting my bad arm and then wincing. "Oh, I'm sorry. Why don't you go sit down and have breakfast, and I'll go get some."

"Don't worry about it, I'm sure we have to push off soon."

She grins at me. "Didn't you hear? We're staying a few more days."

What?

I watch as she runs up the stairs and then I turn and head to the dining room. Didn't I hear? I just got up and no one tells me shit.

Also, did someone run this past Stella? Because I'm pretty sure she wants us the fuck out of here.

Once in the breakfast room I discover the rest of my family already sitting down and eating from a spread of eggs, cold cuts, cheese, rye and crispbreads, and what I assume is pickled herring.

"Nice of you all to start without me," I tell them, pulling out a seat and sitting down next to my father.

"We didn't want to wake you," he says to me. "I know how dangerous those boar attacks can be. Exhausting." He spears a piece of ham with his fork and shakes it at me. "This is what I ought to do to that bastard. I need to avenge my son."

Sometimes I wonder how on earth he's in charge of a whole country, but then I remember he was born into it. Not chosen.

"He's someone's pet," I remind him. "Two little princesses. What would you do if Matilde had a beloved pet that misbehaved? Eat it?"

"He did!" Matilde yells with wide, angry eyes. "Don't you remember when I was seven and had Mr. Bunny Buns and then one day he was gone? They said he disappeared but then the cooks served us rabbit a few days later. Coincidence? I think not."

My father's mustache twists with his smile. "World is full of coincidences, darling."

I switch the subject before things turn into a yelling match again. Matilde and my father don't see eye to eye, never have, and they normally don't spend this much time together. I'm not sure how they're going to survive the next week.

"So what's this news of us staying here longer?" I ask.

And I ask this just as Stella walks in the room and comes to a halt.

"I beg your pardon?" Stella asks, staring at me incredulously.

She looks fantastic dressed down, like this is the real Stella. She's in a striped blue and white shirt that knots around the waist and full white skirt, her hair pulled back in a messy bun. It makes me want to walk over there and undo it, run her silky strands through my fingers and give them a tug. Make her moan again.

But she also looks vaguely horrified, especially as Penelope appears behind her.

"Did you hear the news?" she says to Stella, smiling brightly while clutching a few prescription bottles in her hand. "We're going to stay a few extra days."

Then Penelope comes over to me and places the pill bottles beside my plate. "I have Percocet, codeine, Vicodin, anything you want, darling."

"Thanks," I say to her uneasily, watching Stella. She does not look happy. I mean, she's trying. She's put that stiff smile on her face, but I know she's probably freaking the fuck out. I feel bad, even if I'm actually pleased that I'll be around her a little longer. "Perhaps we should probably clear this all with Princess Stella, hmm?" I tell Penelope. "Would be the polite thing to do."

She waves at Stella as if she's not standing by the door. "Oh, it's fine. This is part of her royal duties, you know. Entertaining us. We do the same when royals come to visit us."

That's true, but not that many royal families seem to pop by anymore.

Three guesses as to why.

"It's fine," Stella says, though she doesn't say it to me. "You're welcome to stay as long as you'd like."

I know she doesn't mean it and I wish she didn't say it because who knows what wavelength Penelope is operating on. We might be here indefinitely.

"I'll go let the staff know," Stella says to us, before turning and leaving the room.

I get out of my chair and everyone looks to me in surprise. "I better go see if she knows a doctor, just in case my arm gets worse."

I stride out of the room and jog down the hall after Stella who is stomping away.

I reach out and grab her by the arm.

"Hey," I say.

She stops and whirls around, looking at me with an expression I can't read. Surprise? Worry? Disgust?

"What?" she snaps.

I try not to let her attitude rile me up. "What nothing," I snap back. Well that didn't go so well. I give her a quick smile and start over. "I'm sorry about my stepmother. I didn't know we were staying longer."

She exhales hard through her nose and looks away, her jaw tense. "It's fine."

"It's not. I know you want us to be out of your hair." I pause, studying her face, that manages to look sweet even when she's angry as hell. "And I know I'm just a complication."

She frowns and looks back at me. "You're not a complication."

"Well, you seemed to go to bed pretty early and pretty fast last night. A headache, was it? Almost as if you were afraid I'd offer my company."

Her frown deepens and she sucks her lip into her mouth.

I wouldn't mind doing the same. "I did have a headache. And I was tired."

"I wore you out, did I?"

A small smile creeps on her lips. "Entertaining guests is a lot of work."

"I see. Can't admit that you needed that fuck, can you?"

"You're so crude."

"Only because I like seeing you blush. I know it turns you on."

"You don't know me."

"You've said that quite a few times, I'm afraid you're starting to sound like a broken record."

She looks away and down at my arm. "How is it?"

I wave it at her. "Oh this old thing? It hurts like a bitch."

"I was wondering about all the painkillers. Starting to think I might need them too if you guys are overstaying your welcome."

"Yes, well, perhaps we can all pop them and have a fucking blast. In the meantime, I think I might need you to hook me up with a doctor because the last thing I need is a fucking infection and die of swine flu."

"That's not what swine flu is."

"Well thank you, boar expert."

She rolls her eyes. "Okay, well I'm not really sure what to do. I mean, I'll make sure we get a doctor over here, that's not a problem. But what does your family expect from me?"

"You mean what does Penelope expect? I guarantee Matilde and Francis would be happy exploring the streets of Copenhagen, getting a little drunk, and doing a little shopping. My father should be kept well away from Snarf Snarf, and Penelope, well, don't be surprised if she wants you to give her a more in-depth tour of the palace. Outside. Where the paparazzi can take their pictures."

She purses her lips together for a moment. "And what do you want?"

I open my mouth to tell her exactly what when a voice calls out from down the hall.

I look around Stella to see her prim Aunt Maja coming toward us.

"What time should I arrange for the cars to take them to the airport?" she asks her. Then she sees me and does a curt-sey. "Prince Orlando. I hope you're feeling better."

"I am . . ." I say slowly.

"They're staying a while longer," Stella informs her.

"What?" Maja asks harshly, then she eyes me. Puts on a smile. "Well, that's certainly unexpected but we will make arrangements. I'll let everyone know."

I watch as Maja walks away.

Stella quickly turns and starts going in the opposite direction.

"Where are you going?" I yell after her.

"To call the doctor," she says, disappearing down a corridor until I find her around the corner in a small library, the wall shelves stacked with books with a large desk in the middle and a plush loveseat tucked into one corner.

"Nice room," I comment. "This your office?"

She stops at the desk and picks up her mobile phone that was resting on it. A hardcover book is face down, but the title is in Danish. "Kind of. Aksel has his office upstairs but it never feels right being there."

"Are you close with him?"

A thoughtful look comes across her pretty eyes. "Yeah. We are now. Maybe not when growing up."

"Age difference?"

"Not really. I mean he's eight years older so yeah. I guess that's the same with you and your siblings, right?"

"You pay attention. I'm impressed."

She shrugs and leans back against the desk, toying with the phone in her hands. "I did some research on you last night."

I raise my hands. "I don't want to hear it. None of it is true."

"Maybe not. But since you're staying longer and you're going to be loopy on painkillers, I might just get to the bottom about some things. Such as Zoya."

I stiffen at the mention of her name. Sometimes it's easy to forget. "Zoya is a nice girl but I'm not with her like people would have you think."

"I sure fucking hope not or you'd be a total asshole to fuck another woman when you have a girlfriend."

I swallow hard, not liking where this is going. "I was honest when I said I have no commitments." I pause, bringing the conversation back to her. "So, if it wasn't the age difference, why weren't you and your brother close?"

"I guess . . ." She trails off and stares at the bookshelves in thought. "I guess because he was always groomed to be king. From day one, he was the heir, the chosen one, if you will. And I was kind of . . . brushed to the side and forgotten about."

"Did you want to be queen?"

"When I was little, yeah. Absolutely. But as I got older, I realized it was a trap."

"This is all a trap, you know."

"Adulthood?"

"Being a royal."

"Well, I suppose you're in Aksel's shoes. You've been groomed for the role from the start. Maybe not king but it's semantics, right? You're the heir, the future ruler." She looks at me curiously. "Is that something you've always wanted?"

"Who even says I want it right now?"

Her brows raise. "You don't want it?"

"You're making me sound like Jon Snow," I tell her. "I want it. I just . . . it's normal to want what you don't have and what I don't have is freedom."

"I don't know about that. My brother has been able to do a lot of the things that he wants. Freedom to fall in love with a young nanny and make her his queen. That's something."

"It's different for me," I tell her, but I don't go into specifics. There's a time and a place for that and it's not right now.

No, right now I have other things in mind.

I walk over to her and she stiffens up slightly at my approach.

I stop right in front of her and stare down at her lips, her nose, her eyes. She gazes up at me through long, dark lashes.

"Why do I feel like I have unfinished business with you?" I murmur. I reach out, running my thumb over her cheekbone, feeling the warmth of her skin. "Oh, I know why. I told you I'd give you three orgasms and I only gave you two."

I watch as she swallows. Clears her throat. "Two was good enough for me. I wasn't even expecting one."

"Don't turn away what's owed to you, princess," I tell her. "Especially when there were so many other things I didn't get to do to you."

"I don't think this is a good idea."

"Why not?"

"Last night was last night."

"You're afraid of me hanging around you for the next few days?"

"It might complicate things."

"Complicate what? Listen, little star—"

"Little star?"

"You're named after the beer, right?"

She rolls her eyes.

"Listen," I repeat, sliding my hand down her back, "you're

going to need a bit of stress release with my family, with your duties. When this is all over, you'll go back to your daughter and the life you have there but, until then, I can get you off, again and again, and if that doesn't happen, it sounds like a fucking shame to me."

"I need to call a doctor."

"Then call a doctor."

She gives me a wary look, probably because I'm not backing out of her space. Just like last night, I have her cornered, this time against a desk. I think she likes it. She hasn't once tried to walk away.

With a sigh, she looks down and starts scrolling through her phone until she finds the number. Brings the phone to her ear.

I hear the muffled voice on the other side as someone answers.

"*Hej?*" Stella says, her accent thickening as she starts speaking to someone in Danish. I don't understand a word. While French is my main language, I'm fluent in English, Italian and the language of my people, Monégasque. Danish seems like a whole other world. Luckily, everyone here speaks perfect English, but even if she didn't, we could communicate in other ways.

I'll see if she picks up what I'm trying to communicate right now.

While she's talking, saying who knows what, I let my hand slide around her waist, over to the front of her skirt. She stiffens up, sucking in her stomach. I grin, letting my fingers slip beneath the waistband, feeling her soft skin underneath until the tips of them tease the lacey trim of her underwear.

She gives me a look, wide-eyed and warning, and yet she doesn't move. She clears her throat and says into the phone. "*Ja? Jeg er her.*"

"Keep talking Danish," I whisper to her, leaning in to place a kiss at her neck. "It makes me hard."

I feel her swallow against my lips. Her pulse is rising, skin growing warm. I love what I'm doing to her.

And as my fingers slide underneath her underwear and I feel how drenched she is, it's obvious she loves it too.

"Already wet for me?" I murmur, slowly licking up her neck until she's practically shivering. Her breath shortens and she's trying desperately to retain composure, even as my forefinger strokes along her flesh.

"*Ja* . . ." she says again into the phone, breathless. I have to wonder what the receptionist on the other end is thinking. "*I dag.*"

I watch as she closes her eyes and lets out a breath of air, her mouth open, her phone pressed against her chest as I push my finger inside her. She clenches around me, greedy, hungry and I slowly insert another finger, then another.

"Shit," she swears, gasping, her back arching. Then she composes herself just enough to quickly say into the phone. "*Nej. Jeg venter.*"

If she keeps this up, they're going to think the doctor is for her.

"I'll stop if you want me to," I say hoarsely. "Just say the words." I keep my fingers swirling around her clit, making her grow slicker, her breath sharper. "Or I can keep going."

Her eyes are closed, head back but she's nodding. Whether she's nodding in regard to something on the phone or saying yes to me, I'll take my chances. It won't take long, at any rate.

Testing her, I start sliding my finger out of her, letting them make wet trails up to her stomach. She lets out a little moan of disappointment.

"You want more?" I slide my fingers back down. "Tell me. I need to know."

"*Ja*," she whispers huskily, nodding. "Please."

"Please? Such good manners. It's almost like you're begging." I can't help but grin, loving how undone she's becoming. "You want to come for me? You feel like you're seconds away from coming as it is," I whisper into her ear, my voice hoarse and ragged. "Like if I drop to my knees and place my lips on your pussy right now, you'll immediately start writhing. I'll pop that hot clit of yours into my mouth like candy, suck your sweetness, have you melt onto my tongue until you're all I can taste."

The phone slides out of her hands at that and she makes a quick fumble to catch it before it falls to the ground. She gives me the most incredulous look and as she meets my eyes, I see the wildness in them, like watching grey-blue storm waves crashing against the shore.

I could drown in them.

"You better take that call." I nod at it. "I'm a sick, sick man."

Her cheeks flush pink, and I give her a quick grin before I do exactly as I warned.

I drop to my knees, slide my hands under her skirt and up her thighs until they grasp the sides of her underwear and then pull them down and off. Then I lift her skirt and stick my head under it until my mouth is at her inner thigh. I hook a leg over my shoulder, spreading her open, and inhale her scent.

I've been hard this whole time but her musky, sweet, intoxicating scent is like a straight shot to my dick. It strains against my fly, aching, making me groan. She's close to coming, but if I keep this up, I'll be letting loose in my own fucking pants.

My lips go together, and I blow lightly on her clit, enough for her body to tense and quiver and then spread her with my finger before I place my tongue on her.

I can hear her whimper, know she's gripping the edge of the desk, and I slowly begin working my tongue back and forth, lapping up her sweet cream.

"Oh god!" she cries out, and that's when I feel the phone hit me on the head and hear it fall to the floor. Guess that phone call is over.

I go at her, a man starved and feasting on a buffet. My mouth and lips and tongue probe and lick and suck until she's squeezing my head between her legs, needing more, wanting me deeper, harder, faster. It's messy, and she's dripping, and no woman has ever tasted so good.

"Orlando," I hear her gasp, and then she's coming, her body stiffening before shaking like an earthquake. I feel her pulse onto my tongue, her wetness melting into my mouth. "Don't stop, don't stop!" she calls out, her voice breaking.

I don't. I assault her with my lips, sucking her into my mouth before I thrust my tongue inside her, over and over again, until the pressure of her legs around my head starts to lessen.

"Oh god," she says breathlessly.

I grin to myself as I pull my head away and wipe my mouth with the inside of her skirt before I pull her underwear back up. Then I lift my head out of her skirt and grab both sides of her hips, staring up at her while I'm still on my knees.

She glances down at me, looking hot and bothered, her eyes glazed. "The doctor is coming," she manages to say.

"Seems like you came first," I tell her, getting to my feet.

CHAPTER 5
STELLA

I stare at Orlando for a moment, not really sure what's going on, my heart pounding heavily in my head, my body hot and flushed and on fire.

Did that actually happen?

Did he just go down on me while I was calling the royal doctor?

Did I just come harder than I've ever come in my life?

What kind of person is he turning me into?

This is getting ridiculous.

"You don't have to worry about returning the favor," he tells me, as he stands in front of me. I'm barely holding onto the desk and I know if I let go, I'll fall, my knees feel *that* weak. He's reduced me to jelly.

I glance down and can't help but notice how turned on he is. Despite what he says, I know I'm going to have to do something about his massive erection, though I'm not even sure I could fit it all in my mouth. The new me might be up for the challenge, though.

"Stella?" I hear my aunt Maja's voice echo from somewhere in the palace.

Shit.

She's everywhere, all the time.

I clear my throat and smooth out my skirt, trying to look composed. "You might have to take care of your problem yourself," I tell Orlando, giving him a sweet smile before walking out of the library.

Holy shit.

I can barely walk.

My legs feel boneless and my underwear is soaked.

And yet I can't help the cheeky grin that I know is spreading across my face as I stagger away from the room. I might not be acting like myself lately but there's a part of me that's reveling in it. I feel naughty and I don't think I've ever felt naughty in my whole entire life. I've always behaved, always done what was asked of me. At thirty-four, perhaps I'm finally rebelling.

I don't hear Orlando behind me, which either means that he's staying back as to not raise suspicion or he's actually jacking off in the library since I wasn't able to give him a hand. Damn. The thought of that is so hot I almost turn around and go back to look, but I know I have a job to do today.

And it's a doozy.

I sigh as the reality comes back. Entertaining Orlando's family. Maybe he was right, I do need him for stress release.

It can't hurt.

Right?

I go and find Maja, who is pacing in the hall beneath the main staircase. She's not worried that the Monégasques are staying longer than expected, but she's annoyed and when she's annoyed, she gets impatient and snippy. I know she wants this palace to go back to normal as soon as possible too. So we quickly make a plan for the day and then find the family, who are still finishing up breakfast, and get their input.

Penelope and Pierre want to do a photoshoot in front of the palace. I'm not sure where that came from, but apparently, it's already been arranged in the time that their son was going down on me in the library. I'm not even supposed to be in the photo, which is more than fine by me since I don't want to get dressed up, and they made it clear that their children can do whatever they want (Matilde and Francis want to go shopping in Copenhagen, much like Orlando predicted).

Though I don't know half the things I was saying on the phone to the doctor, I do know he's coming by just after noon to give Orlando a check-up and administer some antibiotics if needed. I certainly don't have this "doctor on call" service back at home but it sure is a nice thing to have here. I'm sure the last thing Aksel needs is for the news of Snarf Snarf's "attack" getting out. This way it can all be kept a secret.

Speaking of secrets, I'm finding it harder and harder to be around Orlando after all of that. And by that, I mean orgasms. I'm fine when his family is around—I can just pretend he's not there and they're distracting enough—but when we're more alone, well, it's like he's a black hole of sex. I keep getting drawn into his orbit and with his father and Penelope doing a photoshoot and his siblings out shopping, there isn't much to stop me from jumping him.

Thank god for Dr. Bonakov. He's the doctor for both the Swedish and Danish royal families and bounces around between us. When he arrives he takes one look at Orlando's arm and dispenses antibiotics and some painkillers, which I'm sure Penelope will be swiping from him at some point.

"You need to get some rest," Dr. Bonakov tells him, as we're gathered in the sitting room, Orlando lying down on the couch. "You're starting to get a fever but that should go down in time." The doctor glances at me. "It might be best if you take him to his room, draw the shades. Make sure he drinks plenty of liquids . . . non-alcoholic. And keep people from pestering him."

The way he says pestering makes me think that perhaps he's dealt with Penelope before. I wouldn't be surprised.

I thank the doctor for coming on such a short notice and then, after he leaves, glance down at Orlando who is staring up at me with a smirk on his face.

"What?" I ask.

"He thinks I have a fever," he says. "He doesn't know I'm just hot for princess."

"Quoting Van Halen now . . ."

"It's my own song. About you."

Damn. Those painkillers kick in fast, don't they?

I cautiously approach him and then reach down and lay my hand on his forehead. I think the doctor is right. He is warm to touch.

Orlando reaches up and grabs my wrist. I expect him to do something lewd with it, like put it on his crotch, but instead he gently pulls it to his mouth and kisses the back of my hand.

His tenderness catches me off guard, like the room starts to tilt.

Jeez, that feels . . . *nice*.

"Are you going to help me to bed?" he asks.

"You can't do it yourself?"

"I already did once. Don't want to do it alone again."

Always with the innuendo. I help Orlando to his feet, and we head down the hall and up the stairs. At this point I don't know where anyone is, so without the doctor here, there's nothing keeping us apart, nothing to stop me from climbing him like a tree.

Except the fact that he's drugged, I remind myself as we walk down the upstairs hall to his bedroom. *And he's an injured man.*

And he's The Royal Rogue and you're Princess Stella and nothing good can come out of this.

I tell my brain to shut up.

"Here we are," I tell him, attempting to linger in the doorway, but before I can he wraps his arm around my waist and yanks me inside, simultaneously shutting the door behind him.

Then his lips are on mine, both hands grabbing the sides of my face and holding me as his mouth draws me into a long, passionate kiss. I feel it in the form of lightning strikes and birthday sparklers, rushing all the way down from my lips to my toes.

Jesus.

He's an incredible kisser. I don't know if it's the medication spurring him with extra desire or that I feel more comfortable with him or what it is, but the way our mouths and lips and tongue move together is like living poetry.

"I've been wanting to do that all day," he whispers against my lips, his hands going back into my hair and making a mess of it.

"I think you already did that."

"Different lips," he says with a salacious grin. "Both hungry just the same."

"The doctor said you need rest."

"The doctor thinks I have a fever," he says, sucking my lip into his mouth. "Do I have a fever? Put your hands on me and see."

He doesn't have to tell me twice. He's wearing a light-grey button-up shirt that makes his eyes seem even icier, and I'm quick to unbutton it as he starts to shrug it off.

The shirt is thrown to the floor and I'm left with my first good look at his body. Yeah, when I did some internet spying last night, I stumbled upon some images of him when he was younger and into pro surfing, so I've seen him shirtless before.

But that was on a screen and when he was young. This is so, so different.

He's still lean and tanned from the Mediterranean sun, but he's got muscles popping absolutely everywhere, I don't even know where to look or how to take him in. His rock-hard rounded shoulders, firm, expansive chest, ripped six-pack, and sharp V hip dips. His arms. Oh god, his arms. I'd felt their power before, know what his hands can do, know the feel of his forearms but now, in front of me, I see their real strength, the veins and the thick ridges of muscles and how much brute force they hold.

"Your face is worth every hour in the gym," he says.

"How are you even real?" I ask in awe, tentatively running my hands down his shoulders.

"I'll tell you it gets harder to maintain as I get older," he admits.

"You're doing a good job," I say breathlessly. I sound like some dumbass who has never seen a real man before, but in some ways, it's like it's true. I've never seen a man like *this*. It's not even my fault, this body would make *any* woman question herself.

My fingers coast down over his chest, reveling in the feel of his taut muscles, pausing at a tattoo on one pec.

"What does this mean?" I ask, peering at the tattoo. It's cursive, written in French.

He glances down. "*Tu me manques*." He gives me a quick smile. "It's French for 'I miss you' but the English translation doesn't capture the depth of it. What it really means is that you are missing from me."

"That's . . . beautiful," I say softly. "Who is missing from you?"

His smile morphs into something bittersweet and thoughtful. "My mother."

Oh. His mother, Princess Selene, who died from breast cancer when he was a boy. I feel bad for even asking.

"I'm sorry," I tell him. I look to the floor.

"Hey," he says, placing his finger beneath my chin and raising my face up until he's looking into my eyes. "Don't be sorry at all. I wanted to honor her and while there is no real way to explain the void she's left in my life, this is the best I can do. We all do our best, don't we?"

I feel like there's extra meaning in those words but I just nod.

"Now," he says. "Let's get back on track. I don't think my examination is over yet."

I laugh and bring my hands down to his pants and start to undo them.

Definitely not over.

PRINCE ORLANDO AND HIS CRAZY FUCKING FAMILY END UP staying at Amalienborg Palace for two more nights.

Two nights of dealing with Penelope's drunk ramblings and outlandish ideas (such as inviting Danish male models over and having our own private fashion show, which, thankfully, Matilde nipped in the bud), as well as Pierre's horrible hunting stories and dad jokes.

Two nights of Matilde and Francis getting drunk in the streets of Copenhagen.

Two nights of Orlando screwing me senseless.

After we had sex in his room, causing his actual fever to spike briefly, we pretty much didn't stop the entire time. You name the room, we had sex in it. You name the position, we did it. You name the dirty things he said, well, the man definitely doesn't need a dictionary.

With all the filthy coupling, I wasn't sure what I was going to feel when the day finally came that they pushed on their way.

Relieved, yes. I mean, even with all the sex, having guests in the house—especially when it's not your house—was stressful. I got used to having them around but because they were all so unpredictable, I could never quite let my guard down.

Plus, Maja and the staff were never quite relaxed either. Always on the go, always cooking, cleaning, making sure everyone was happy. They're used to getting a break when Aksel goes on vacation, but this time was different.

Yet, when it was time to actually say goodbye to everyone, I felt bereft.

Perhaps not at the moment they left but the hours after.

Orlando and I shook hands and that was it. He gave me a wink and then he was on his way. It's like he was already a stranger to me, no more different than the cocky man who first entered the palace.

We didn't even exchange phone numbers or emails or anything. While we were fucking and the few tender moments after, there was no talk of the future. Or the past. It's like we only existed in the moment. Just a snippet of time. And that was all.

And I was okay with that. I still am. I knew what I was getting into.

But sex can fuck with your feelings. The intimacy of the body sometimes confuses the intimacy of the heart. Sex can make you see things that weren't there before, feel things that should remain in the bedroom. I started to feel something for Orlando in a way I couldn't really explain.

Not to mention the loneliness that settled in.

I like being alone. Other than Anya, I don't really need anyone. My company is enough, and I almost think it's romantic that it's just me and my daughter against the world.

That said, when you go from being alone to being social and surrounded by people and then back to being alone, a sadness and a loss creeps in like you wouldn't expect. It doesn't happen right away; it takes a few hours. After you've relished the peace and quiet. That's when you start to miss the company. It's like they've distracted you from yourself for a good while, made you forget about the bad bits about life.

I actually started to *miss* them.

Most of all, I missed Orlando.

Obviously, the sex was fantastic. I think I came more with him than I ever did with my ex during our entire marriage. But I missed his presence, too. He was surprising. I thought of him one way and he always proved me wrong. We had good dialogue, we had chemistry. I liked just talking to him about anything, even if the sex sometimes took precedence.

Now he's gone off to Stockholm and Oslo and I have no idea when I'll see him again.

Or if I will at all.

"They're coming back."

Maja's words make me jolt in my chair, nearly spilling my glass of red wine.

"What?" I ask, craning my neck to look at her as she comes into the living room, looking agitated. "Aksel?"

He's supposed to be back in four days, and at this point it couldn't happen any sooner.

"No," she says pointedly. "The Monégasque royals. They're coming back."

"What? Why?" Orlando is coming back? I hate how giddy I feel. "When?"

"Tonight."

"Tonight?" I nearly spill the glass of wine again. It's

already five p.m., which, according to Jimmy Buffet and men with red Mount Gay hats, is an acceptable time to drink, but in hindsight I thought I was just doing this tonight and going to bed. "But, but . . . what will we eat?"

"I've already alerted the cooks. They're going to do fish, I think. They can handle it. But you better get changed."

I swear there's a bit of a twinkle in her eye, which is very unlike her.

I look down at my outfit, which is just black leggings and a long denim shirt. Good for lazing around inside all day, not so good for entertaining. With one gulp I finish the wine, pour another glass for courage and then take it upstairs to change.

They've been gone for four days and I honestly didn't expect to see them again on their way down but what I've learned from that family is to expect the unexpected.

I haven't brought a lot of clothes here and I don't fit into Aurora's stuff (not that I would try anything without her permission anyway), so I put on the same dress I wore the first night. This time though, I wear my hair down and put on a touch more makeup. My reflection shocks me but I don't hate what I see.

"You look lovely, Stella," my aunt tells me, as I hurry down the stairs to join her.

"I wore this last week," I remind her, tugging down at the dress.

"But you look different in it somehow," she says, looking me over. "Must be the hair."

Her words seem to hold a lot of weight in them.

Does she suspect something happened between Orlando and me?

It doesn't really matter, though. There's no time to think about it.

The both of us head to the sitting room to wait for them when Henrik suddenly storms out of the kitchen toward us.

"I'm not sure we have enough fish," he says, looking worried. "They just pulled up and there's an extra guest."

An extra guest?

I glance at Maja who looks just as confused. "Who is the extra guest?"

He shrugs. "I'm not sure but she looks familiar."

She?

Maja glances at me. "Well, this could be interesting."

But I don't think it's interesting at all. In fact, I have a bad feeling about this.

A really bad feeling.

"The mystery guest can have my fish," I tell him.

He looks like he's about to protest but then the air fills with the sound of Penelope's high-pitched chatter. There's no proper entrance, no introduction this time. They're just suddenly *here.*

I take in a deep breath, trying to calm my nerves about seeing Orlando again, plus the mystery guest. Maja pats my shoulder affectionately.

And then they appear from around the corner, dressed in their Sunday best.

Penelope and Pierre.

Matilde and Francis.

Orlando and...

Zoya.

Zoya the Destroya, the Russian tennis player.

Zoya Ivanov, the six-foot-tall, honey-haired, super tanned supermodel.

That woman.

Standing in front of me, wearing a neon yellow dress that I swear I saw J-Lo wear to the Met Gala last year.

And she's holding Orlando's hand.

Holding.

His.

Hand.

I blink. I smile. My smile shakes but I manage to keep it up.

Oh my god, oh my god.

"So lovely of you all to pay us another visit," I tell them, after I manage to tear my eyes away from Zoya and her spell-binding beauty. I can't even look at Orlando.

Penelope says something in return and laughs but I don't hear her. I don't hear anything except the whoosh of the blood in my head, and I don't feel anything except the tight-ness of my smile, like it's being held in a vice, and the skin of my palm where my nails are digging in.

I should have known.

Oh, I fucking should have known.

Before I met Orlando, one of the things I knew about him was that he had been The Royal Rogue, the hard-party-ing, surfing, drinking, playboy prince. He had been all of those things, famously, until he met Zoya Ivanov. They started dating and even though reports had them on and off from time to time, they had been together for at least four years. The last I had heard were rumors they were off again, and I wasn't paying that much attention. In fact, I didn't even think about it until after we had sex in the bathroom.

Then I asked him about her.

He told me he had no commitments.

I believed him.

And yet here he is, with her.

"Princess Stella," Prince Pierre says, gesturing to Zoya. "Allow me to introduce Zoya Ivanov, Orlando's girlfriend and future princess one day."

"Oh come on," Zoya says, acting bashful. She does a quick curtsey to me and then beams. "It's a pleasure to meet you, Your Highness. I've heard so many good things about you."

Her Russian accent is thick, her teeth are so perfect and white that they have to be veneers, and her smile is genuine. She actually sounds like she's happy to meet me.

"Likewise," I tell her, and my smile feels faker than ever.

Because . . . what the fuck?

I mean, seriously, *what the fuck?*

I glance over her shoulder at Orlando and he's just smiling politely at me.

Smiling.

Politely.

As if I knew he was bringing her all along.

You know those cartoons where the person's head gets redder and redder until it goes off like a train whistle? Well, I'm pretty sure that's what's happening right now.

Maja clears her throat and shoots me a nervous glance. "How about we make our way to the dining room. Dinner is almost ready."

Perhaps I look like I want to murder him.

Because I do.

Oh, I do.

Everyone starts walking to the dining room like they all live here now and Zoya falls in step beside me. "I love your dress," she says to me. "Who makes it?"

I blink at her, so damn confused. "Uh, this thing? I don't know. Maybe Valentino."

"I thought so," she says. "So flattering to your figure. And your hair is gorgeous. All real? No extensions?"

I nod absently. What's happening? "All real."

"Mine is real too," she says. She's currently wearing hers in a high Ariana Grande style ponytail. She tugs at it. "All the papers say it's fake, but I know it's not. But sometimes I think maybe I could sell my own line of hair extension accessories. You know, in case the tennis thing doesn't work out."

I have to say, I'm rather charmed by her at the moment, so charmed that I've momentarily forgotten why I feel so horrified. "I'm pretty sure the tennis thing is working out for you."

"Not forever," she says in a low, almost sad voice.

We sit down at the table and Orlando happens to be across from me, Zoya beside him.

I don't know where to look. I can't really look at either of them.

I'm livid that Orlando was still seeing Zoya this whole time, that he lied to me. No commitments? Is that why she's here, now, in front of me? I mean, what the hell? You don't bring your girlfriend to the house of the girl you just cheated on her with! Even if they had been on some sort of break, it wasn't quite a break if she came back in the picture days later.

And I feel embarrassed and ashamed for Zoya. I'm the other woman in this situation. I'm sitting across from her at this dinner table while the servants place tuna carpaccio in front of us and the champagne is flowing and meanwhile, last week, he had fucked me all over the damn house.

Last but not least, I'm mad at myself. I should have known he was a liar. I should have known he was a smooth-talker and too good to be true. I should have kept my walls up, my guard up, I should have ignored my hormones the moment he walked in that door.

I'm pathetic. A real pathetic excuse for a woman. And even though Anya isn't here and wasn't involved in this at all, I feel like a horrible mother to boot.

"Princess Stella," Zoya says to me, and I glance up at her, suddenly remembering where I am. Everyone at the table is looking at me curiously and I have a feeling that I totally missed something.

I'm also clenching my fork like I want to stab someone.

I relax my hand and smile. "I'm sorry, I was somewhere else."

Zoya tilts her head and gives me a sweet look. "I was just asking about your daughter. Orlando told me about her. How old is she? Nine?"

Orlando told me about her.

What the fuck else did Orlando tell you?

Did he tell you how he made me come so hard I had a religious experience?

Did he show you the nail marks I made on his back?

Didn't you wonder?

"Anya. Yes, she's nine."

"Such a fun age," she says warmly. "I have a niece who is nine and I love her to bits. She's obsessed with pigs right now and I think she would love Snarf Snarf."

"She won't love him so much when he nearly bites her arm off," Orlando comments ruefully.

"That's nothing," Pierre injects, as he chews. "When I was in Zimbabwe, I had a friend who got a boar tusk to the shin."

"And totally deserved it," Matilde adds cheerfully.

I glance at Orlando's arm. He's wearing a black dress shirt that fits him like a glove and, from what I can tell, he doesn't have a bandage on. Any other time I would ask him how his arm is doing but right now all I can think about is stabbing that arm with my fork.

But that wouldn't be very becoming of me and I have to remind myself that no matter what, I have to keep Aksel's best interests in mind. I'm representing him at this moment. Any personal issues I have must be shoved to the side.

"Well Anya is obsessed with horses," I manage to say, even though making small talk is an effort with all the rage surging through me and such. "She's been obsessed since we moved to England. She's been doing horse camp and pony clubs and lessons and begging for a pony every day, but so far I'm waiting to see if it's a phase or not."

"Good for you," Zoya says. "You would think being a royal and all that you would just be handed whatever you want, but it's good that you're making her wait and not spoiling her." She makes a funny face at Penelope. "Not like the princess here did with her children."

Penelope rolls her eyes. "I had nothing growing up. I say, spoil your kids while you can."

"I agree," Francis says. "Which reminds me, I need a new car."

"Oh you do not," Pierre says, which then launches them into an argument about cars.

I don't pay it any attention. In fact, the whole dinner and dessert go by in a haze. By the time it's over, I already have my exit strategy.

"If you'll excuse me," I say, as I get up. "I'm going up to bed. I have quite a headache that's not going away."

Pierre narrows his eyes. "You had this same headache last week."

"I must be allergic to something in the champagne."

"Tannins," Penelope says, nodding vigorously.

Sure. That's it. Tannins. Not your asshole stepson.

I bow to the guests and then quickly get my ass out of there. I'm just getting to the second floor, breathing a huge sigh of relief that I can finally process all this by myself, when I feel someone behind me.

I whirl around to see Orlando.

I don't have time to think.

I just go right to him and place my hands at his chest, giving him a hard shove back.

He's immovable but I don't care.

"Fuck you," I sneer. "Fuck you and your fucking face."

"I can explain," he says calmly, but I just shove him again.

"And fuck you for bringing her. And fuck you for sounding so calm."

"Because I can explain, if you just listen to me."

"I'm not listening to you. There's nothing you can say to me that will ever make this right."

"It's not what you think."

"What do you mean it's not what I think?" I snarl, trying hard not to yell. "I saw you kiss her during dinner, multiple times. You held her hand. Her hand was on your knee. The damn tabloids say she's your girlfriend. Are you going to deny that you're together?"

He sighs and rubs the heel of his palm into his forehead. "No."

Even though I knew it, it still hurts to hear. My heart drops a little.

Which makes me mad, because I really shouldn't be this mad.

He's an asshole. A liar. A cheater.

And I had sex with him.

This is all his problem, not mine.

"It's complicated," he says after a moment.

"It's not complicated, you fuckface," I say to him. "You're just a dick. You want to have your famous tennis superstar girlfriend and fuck a princess on the side. Well, congratulations. You did just that."

"Will you just sit down with me and hear me out?" he pleads, his voice hard. If I wanted to get caught up in believing the soulfulness in his blue eyes, I could. But I don't. I'm better than that.

I'm angrier than that.

"Sit down with you? Listen to you? Fuck right off. I hope I never ever see you again."

And with that I turn away from him.

"Stella," he says and grabs my arm, but I shrug it out of his grasp and march down the hall to my bedroom.

Once inside, I lock my door.

I plan to stay here until everyone is gone tomorrow.

I'll probably stay in here until Aksel comes back.

And then I'm going back to my daughter.

Back to my usual role.

My normal life.

Back to where I belong.

And all of this will soon be nothing but a bitter memory.

CHAPTER 6
ORLANDO
MONACO

Two weeks later

"O ver here, Prince Orlando!"

"Zoya, show us that pretty smile for the camera."

"Your Serene Highness, will you address the rumors about your brother?"

Normally I don't pay any attention to the multi-lingual shouts that the reporters and photographers fling at us during these events. It's always the same and you learn from a young age to just ignore it. But when they start to question me about my brother Francis, then I can get a bit prickly.

I stop halfway up the steps, tugging my hand out of Zoya's tennis racket grip, and try to find the face of the reporter who asked me that. My eyes scan the bunch of camera-toting fuckers dressed like penguins, as if they'll be allowed in the casino if they dress nice enough, and then see a man with balding hair, tiny beady-eyes and a befuddled look on his pale face, as if he never expected me to look at him.

And this is him. I've seen him before. I've seen all of them before, but I'm pretty sure he reports for one of the shitty tabloids up in the UK. He might have even been the one who came up with The Royal Rogue nickname back when I was young.

"What about my brother?" I ask him, squaring off. There's a red velvet rope keeping the photographers away from the gala guests, but that doesn't mean anything to me.

Whatever shock is on his face vanishes. I expect him to cower a little—I'm a big guy and people like him know very well what I'm capable of—but instead he raises his brow, a cocky motherfucker.

"I asked if you will address the rumors about your brother, Prince Francis," he says, raising his chin.

"And what rumors are those?"

The man glances behind him at the other photographers who seems to step away, not wanting to be involved in this. My family has been tabloid fodder since as long as I can remember but there are still some questions and comments and stories that seem a little personal. Anything that has to do with Francis, Zoya, or my real mother tend to be off-limits. Stories about my stepmother's plastic surgery or my father's bloodlust are accepted as normal.

"Before you say something that's going to piss me off," I quickly add, "why don't you start by telling me your name and who you work for?"

"Mancel Thereuax," he says. "French correspondent for the Daily Mail."

Of course. The Daily Mail is notorious for being the breeding ground for bottom feeders.

I can hear Zoya clearing her throat from behind me, coming back down the steps. I know she doesn't like it when

I start to get involved with the press like this since it could put her at risk. "Orlando, they're waiting," she says brightly, though I hear the tension in her voice.

I don't even have to turn around to know she's aiming her blinding smile at the reporters. Even more camera flashes go off and they start yelling at her again to pose. She's wearing a glittering silver gown that's low-backed, skin-tight, with a slit that goes to her hip and, just like that, she's brought the attention off of me and Francis and back to her.

We're all in this royal mess together.

I give Mancel one last hard look. "If you want to talk about Francis, I'd be happy to give you a private meeting and tell you everything you need to know."

There's no mistaking what I mean by this. AKA, I'll fuck him up.

He stares at me for a moment and then presses his lips together, looking away.

I exhale internally in relief and then turn around to see Zoya posing for the photographs, sticking out her tanned leg that is shimmering with bronze powder. I give her a grateful smile for her distraction. She probably prevented me from punching Mancel out. I'd done that once before when I was young, and it still haunts me. Fucker deserved it, though.

I take her hand and pull her up the stairs and into the Monte Carlo Casino.

It's not unusual for us royals to be going to all sorts of events and fundraisers and galas, but this one is important because Matilde is putting it on. She works with a few humanitarian groups in Botswana and Mali and once a year tries to raise public awareness in Monaco. Her belief is that this is the wealthiest and most expensive country in the world, and we could do a lot by giving more to others.

I agree, and in some ways, I wish I had the kind of

passion and focus that she has. Matilde knows exactly what she wants out of life and she goes for it.

Zoya is no different. She knows what she wants. But she also knows that what she *really* wants seems impossible at times. I'm just her happy medium. I used to think perhaps I was her steppingstone but sometimes I wonder if this is it. Is this my future?

"Why do you bother responding to them?" Zoya whispers to me, as we're walking through the casino arm in arm, smiling and nodding and greeting various public figures and local aristocrats. Everyone is dressed in their black-tie best. There are musicians scattered around the corners of the casino, playing orchestral ballads. Champagne glitters under the low lights and some guests have gathered around the blackjack tables, watching others play. "You know the press are vultures. They just want a rise out of you so they can write about it."

"I don't like the way they go after Francis," I admit. "I'd rather they go after me."

"They have gone after you. Your whole life, since your mother died, all the way until now."

"And they've stopped because of you," I point out, keeping my voice low as I smile at the Mayor of Marseille but keep walking. Maybe he was the Mayor of Nice? It's hard to keep track. "You give them the illusion that I'm grown up and respectable," I add. "A royal rogue no longer."

"And you give them the illusion that I'm not-at-all madly in love with a woman," she says. She smiles broadly at the faces as we keep walking but there's a lot of anguish in her heavily accented voice. If only everyone could hear what we're saying.

The truth that only my siblings know about.

"So we help each other out," I say. "But there's no one to help Francis."

"He can help himself, Orly," she says tiredly, using a nickname she doesn't use much anymore. I glance at her and her smile is just starting to falter. After Zoya joined us for the back end of the Nordic tour, we've been on the go ever since, making appearance after appearance. Since tennis—and her secret lover Emily—had taken her for most of the summer, I know it's overwhelming for her to be thrown back in the deep end of our very fake relationship, back in the public eye and living an elaborate lie.

"He's twenty-six-years old and he can handle his own truth," she goes on. "If the press wants to spread rumors that he's gay, let them. Don't fight his battles for him."

"Let them say what they want? That's easy for you to say."

She looks at me sharply and though to the naked eye it may seem like she's smiling at me adoringly, I can see the fury in her eyes. She's frightening when she gets mad. Times like this I know what it's like to be her opponent on the court and why she so often wins.

"It's not easy for me to say. Okay?" she says in a harsh whisper. "If Francis comes out, he's not going to lose what I have to lose. I'll lose my career. I could even face death. You have no idea what it's like back at home, no idea at all. I have no rights there. Perhaps your father will be deeply disappointed in him and maybe the tabloids will be invasive, even cruel, about his sexuality. But he would survive it. I wouldn't."

I know better than to argue with Zoya. She's right.

I'd always figured Francis wasn't straight, so when he pulled me aside, drunk and crying, at his twentieth birthday and admitted to me that he was gay, I wasn't shocked. Matilde knew, of course, as twins do. Penelope did as well. But he wanted to keep it a secret from our father. As amiable as he is, our father is very old-fashioned and can hold a grudge like no one's business. Just ask the King of Spain. Plus, this would mean that Francis could never give him a legitimate heir to the throne and that would throw our whole family into turmoil.

Which is why all the damn pressure falls on me. If I don't give my father an heir to throne—a legitimate one, through marriage and all—the fate of the entire country is at stake. The Franco-Monégasque treaty of 1918 states that without an heir, all of Monaco reverts back to being part of France. In addition to that, if I settle down like I'm supposed to and become a father, the pressure is lifted off of my brother, letting him be free to be whoever he needs to be.

I nod at Zoya and squeeze her hand. The truth is, I love her, and I need her, just as she needs me. I don't love her in a romantic or sexual way—that stopped a long time ago—but I feel about her the same way I feel about my siblings. As such, I want to protect her. Yeah, she gives my father peace of mind, thinking that the two of us are in love. But without me acting as her front, there's no way Zoya could continue her relationship with her girlfriend and not raise suspicion.

It's about as fucked up and complicated as it can be. Whoever thought being royal meant having a simplified life had obviously never met my family before.

"There you are!" Matilde yells at us, Francis right behind her as they walk over. She's wearing a gown that's white and draped in a way that wouldn't look wrong on a Grecian statue, her hair pinned up in a million braids while looking very fresh-faced. Francis looks dapper, as usual.

"No date?" I ask her, as she pulls me into a quick hug. I like to bug her about her perpetually single status, mainly because it pisses her off. It's nothing new though. She and Francis tend to stick together like glue.

"A date? Here? And how would I entertain him? I don't feel like babysitting," she says, and then gestures to the crowd gathered in the casino with us, sipping champagne and gambling. "I'm working."

"Always working," Francis says with a roll of his eyes. "Sooner or later, you're going to find the urge to babysit *someone*."

She glares at her twin. "And where is your date? Hmm?"

"He's over there," Francis says, taking a sly sip of his champagne while eying someone across the room.

"Well you better take it easy, for Orlando's sake," Zoya says to him. "He nearly punched a photographer for asking about you."

Francis rolls his eyes again. "What happened now?"

I shrug and pluck a champagne glass off a passing waiter. "Just someone that needs to mind his own business."

"I don't need you to be a hero," Francis says, squaring his shoulders.

"That's what I said," Zoya tells him.

"You know I'm not hero material," I say gruffly, as I quickly down the champagne. This was meant to be a fairly easy evening. Put on a tux, come to the casino with Zoya, smile for the cameras, support my sister. Yet, somehow, I'm feeling this immense pressure, more so than normal. That feeling of being trapped in your own life, with no escape.

It must be showing up on my face because later, while Zoya is talking to a Grand Prix racer and Francis is off somewhere, Matilde pulls me aside.

"How many glasses of champagne have you had?" My sister asks accusingly, her bracelets shaking together as she points at the glass I'm currently gulping down.

"Not enough," I admit, letting the empty glass dangle by the stem.

She studies me for a moment and then purses her lips together. "What's wrong?"

"Nothing."

"Orlando," she repeats. "You're usually Mr. Devil May Care. Now it's like the devil is right on your shoulders."

"I don't know," I admit. And what I do know, what I feel, I'm not about to get into it here on the night of her fundraiser, surrounded by my future subjects.

"You haven't been the same since we got back from Scandinavia," she says. "To be more specific, *Denmark*." She squints at me thoughtfully. "What exactly happened between you and Princess Stella?"

I blink at her. Hearing Stella's name feels like cold water being splashed in my face. Not that I haven't thought about her. I have. A lot. So maybe that's why it feels weird to have it voiced like that, not just living in my head.

In my fantasies.

Every night.

"She did a number on you, didn't she?" Matilde goes on, folding her arms across her chest. "The single mom from Copenhagen got under your skin."

"Oh fuck off," I tell her.

She grins at that. "Defensive! I see how it is. Jeez, Orlando, I thought maybe you just screwed her a few times. It's not like you to give a girl any more thought after that."

"You make me sound crass."

"You *are* crass. Just because the entire world thinks Zoya is the love of your life, doesn't mean we all buy this version of you." She pauses. "But judging from how the Princess was acting toward you that last night, I have a feeling you never told her the truth."

I sigh. "What would the point have been? I won't see her again. Let her think I'm a cheating, lying bastard if she wants to."

"She liked you," she says. "I could tell."

"She hated me most of the time," I remind her.

Which is why fucking her was so damn hot. Every time I made her come, every time she gave into me, she was at war with herself. Hating that I could make her feel such a way and yet loving it at the same time. I'd never had my cock so deep inside someone who made me feel like she was a battle I needed to win.

Even though my time with her at the palace was brief and somewhat tumultuous, with my overbearing family and her kiss-kill attitude toward me, I have to say that I hadn't felt such freedom in a long time. It's not that I haven't had one-night stands here and there, but they've been so distant and cold. With all of them I have to have the woman sign an NDA so she won't report to the press that I'm "cheating" on Zoya. In the end, I get off, yeah, and the woman does too. But I'm left with an emptiness that wasn't there before.

With Stella I didn't have to do that. Because I knew she wouldn't tell. Because in so many ways, she was just like me. A royal. And a misunderstood one at that. She's actually the first woman of nobility I'd ever had the pleasure to screw, and there was something so right about it, like gears clicking into place. She understood me in a way no one else has.

Which is maybe part of the problem.

"Well, I'm sure the Princess definitely hates you now," Matilde muses, a sparkle in her dark eyes. "But there's no reason why it couldn't have gone further."

I give her a pointed look. "Yes. There is." My eyes flit to Zoya in the crowd and back to her.

Zoya. It's always Zoya.

Matilde exhales through her nose and gives me a sympathetic smile. "Is this really going to be your future? Are you really going to marry Zoya? Is she going to be the mother of your children? All while the both of you are living a lie, forever? You'll just both have affairs until you die? That's no life to live."

I don't say anything to that because I don't know what there is to say.

My sister puts her hand on my arm. "You're my brother. I

care about you a lot. You know that. I just want you to be happy. And honestly . . . I don't think I've ever seen you happy, Orlando."

I think I know the last time I was happy. But it was a long time ago. Back when I had my mother.

"Then what's the difference?" I eventually say. I don't want to talk about any of this anymore. There're too many layers to unravel, too many ways to fall into the abyss.

"The difference is, it's never too late. Look, I know what it's like. I've been there. I grew up being your step-sister and somehow feeling illegitimate that way, that my mother wasn't *your* mother."

I shake my head. "Don't be silly."

"I'm not being silly," she says. "I'm being honest. Your mother was sweet and elegant and kind. My mother is . . . well, everyone thought she was a joke. People were so angry that father married her and so soon after your mother died. I know you were angry, too."

I rub my lips together. She's right. I was only ten when my father remarried and yet I don't think I ever hated anyone more. I hated the both of them, especially for seeming to forget about my mother so soon.

She goes on. "Then I grappled with knowing that I'd never be up for the throne, because I wasn't a man. I spent a lot of my life looking for answers, trying to figure out who I was and what I wanted. It wasn't until that trip to Africa that I realized my purpose in life. To help as many people as I can. Your purpose is out there, too. It's just not what you think it is."

"And what do I think it is?" I ask, challenging her.

But she just smiles. "What your bloodline is telling you it is. Your purpose isn't to pretend to be the man that father wants, that the monarchy wants, that history wants. It's to be the person that you are deep inside." Her smile fades a little and she frowns. "I'm just worried that you won't be able to keep up appearances forever. I think both you and Zoya deserve to be free of the bullshit that holds you together, and the sooner that you both realize that, the better you both will be."

But it's all easy for my sister to say. Zoya's parents are famous Russian athletes with ties to the Russian government, a government that might severely punish her for her sexuality. At the very least, she would lose sponsors and the support of the national team. She could lose it all.

As for me, well, my bloodline has me in a chokehold I don't think I'll ever escape from.

CHAPTER 7
STELLA

"Can we get a cat?"

I close my eyes for a moment, mid-buttering of bread, and breathe in through my nose.

Anya had just asked me that last night as I tucked her into bed.

She asked me that in the morning too.

And the day before that.

And now, again, after saying no . . .

"Mom?" she says louder, standing behind me in the kitchen. "Did you hear me? Can we get a cat?"

I grip the butter knife and pray for sanity. My patience has been non-existent these days and my temper has been short. To be honest, I've felt like shit this last week, just tired and crabby and achy. My breasts hurt like hell, like someone has been using them as punching bags and even the butter I'm attempting to put on her toast is making me feel nauseous.

There's also the fact that my period is four days late.

I'm trying not to think about it. I really am.

"We could rescue one from the shelter," Anya adds. "I think it will look good for your public image."

I nearly snort at that. I slowly turn around and look at my daughter.

She's wearing her pink, glitter-framed eyeglasses, dressed in a denim apron dress with a pink tee underneath and high-top sneakers. Also pink and glittery, a child's knockoff of the expensive Golden Goose brand. I've been letting Anya dress herself all summer without any input from me and it's been the season of magenta.

"My public image?" I repeat. "Really?"

She shrugs and grins, showing the gap between her teeth. "You complain about it all the time. So, can we get a cat?"

I roll my eyes and quickly finish up her bread, sliding the plate on the kitchen table next to the herring, cheese and cold cuts. Even though we've been living in England for many years at this point, I still haven't embraced the English breakfast. Instead, we eat the traditional Danish style.

"Sit and eat. And no cat. Okay? I don't want to talk about it anymore."

She frowns at me and goes over to the chair, slumping down with a face of absolute resignation. "Boy, you sure are grumpy these days."

"Anya," I warn her, shaking the butter knife at her. "You know better than to talk back to me."

"I'm not talking back. I'm making a statement," she says, before taking an angry bite of her toast. "Why can't we have a cat?" Crumbs shoot out of her mouth.

Some princess she is. Like mother like daughter, I suppose.

"Eat with your mouth closed," I remind her. "And it's because I don't like cats."

"You like cats," she says, covering her mouth with her hand as she chews.

"I'm allergic."

She swallows. "That doesn't mean you don't like them."

"I'm allergic," I repeat, heading over to the fridge. I haven't felt like eating anything lately, but my stomach right now is churning in a big queasy mess.

"Do you die?"

Feel a bit like dying right now, I think to myself as another wave hits. I rest my head against the door of the fridge, my hand on the handle. "No," I say slowly, breathing in and out. "I just sneeze a lot."

"What if you were allergic to me? What would you do?"

I'm used to Anya's way of questioning, but I'm not sure I can handle this right now. The room feels like it's filling up with water, making everything seem swimmy.

"I'd take a pill," I finally manage to say.

"Then you can take a pill for the cat. I mean, why do Freja and Clara get a pig and I can't get a cat?"

"Anya, please," I say, my voice breaking. Oh god, I'm going to be sick, aren't I?

There's a long pause and then she asks, "Are you okay?"

Before I can even answer her, come up with some lie, tell her I'm fine, the contents of last night's dinner come rushing up through me. I barely make it to the sink before I'm puking Chinese food everywhere.

"Ew! Gross! Gross!" Anya yells. "Now I'm going to throw up!"

Right. As I'm vomiting my guts out, my face red and hot, tears streaming down my face, I remember that Anya always throws up when she sees someone else do the same. I can't even yell at her to make it to the washroom. Instead I hear her throwing up all over the kitchen table, followed by wailing, since the poor girl always cries after she gets sick.

Somehow, I manage to pull myself together, splash water on my face, and then proceed to clean up Anya and the kitchen table. Of course, during the ordeal, as I'm leading her to her bathroom so she can shower the puke out of her hair, she manages to ask between sobs if she can have a cat.

The answer is still no.

But Anya's cat obsession is the very least of my problems right now.

The fact that I was sick means that the thing I've been trying so hard to ignore is rearing its ugly head. I told myself it was impossible, that it couldn't be true. Even now, I'm convinced it could just be a giant coincidence. After all, maybe I caught a flu from somewhere. A stomach bug. Those are always going around, right?

I mean, just because my period is late doesn't necessarily mean the worst, right? Periods are often late because of stress, and if I've been sick then that could stress me out, right?

I can't possibly be pregnant.

I'm on the pill, for one, to help my endometriosis.

For two, that very same endometriosis makes getting pregnant extremely hard, so I'm told. Anya took forever to conceive.

And for three . . . well, normally, I would have to chalk this up to immaculate conception but since I did have sex about a month ago, then I guess I know who could be to blame.

Shit.

Please, please, please let this all be a huge coincidence.

I can't be pregnant, and Prince Orlando, that sex-on-a-stick rat bastard, can't be the father.

But I know what I have to do.

I need to be responsible. I need peace of mind.

Yet I can't just pop into the chemist and pick up a home pregnancy test, because lord knows some paparazzi is going to catch me doing that. So I make an appointment with my doctor and then the next day, while I get Margaret, the nanny, to watch over Anya, I head on over to the clinic.

I'm still feeling sick, though I think my nausea is increased because of how nervous I am. Thankfully the clinic I go to in Cobham is very hush-hush and used to dealing with wealthy, famous and even royal clients such as myself, so I go in the backdoor and I don't have to wait in the waiting room.

"What can I do for you, Your Highness?" Doctor Bradshaw says to me, smiling his dorky grin. Doctor Bradshaw is old, with nose hair that's long enough to braid. He enjoys calling me Your Highness, as well as princess. I used to think it was charming but now, considering the severity of the situation, I don't think it's cute at all.

"I think I might be pregnant."

He raises his brows and seems to think about his reaction. "Oh? Are you back together with your ex-husband?"

That thought also makes me sick. I shake my head, grimacing.

"Oh," he says again. "I see. Well it's none of my business who it is. But when was the last time you had sex?"

"About a month ago."

"And how many times did you have sex?"

Even though it shouldn't, a small thrill runs through me at the thought. I try and think. "Probably ten times. In three or four days."

His eyes widen. "I see. And your period?"

"Should have been here five days ago."

"You're still on the pill?"

"Yes."

"You haven't missed any?"

"Missed? No." Have I been taking it at the exact same time every single day? No. But then again, I didn't see all that sex in my future. How could I have?

"No condom?"

KARINA HALLE

I can't say it didn't cross my mind that we didn't use one. "No," I say, feeling ashamed, like I'm sixteen again and about to get lectured. I should be better than this.

"Are you feeling sick? Sore?" he asks.

"I want to vomit right now."

"Well then," he says briskly. "Let's get you tested."

He brings me into the washroom and gives me a similar test to the one I'd taken when I was pregnant with Anya. Everything was so different back then. Back then, I was deeply in love with my husband, I was hoping that I'd get pregnant, I felt scared of course but also hopeful and secure. It was all I wanted.

Now, it's just pure fear.

I pee into a cup and slide it through to a technician.

I don't have to wait long before the doctor comes back out to see me, holding a dressing gown in his hands.

That is not a good sign.

"I'm glad you came in to see me today," he says to me in a grave voice, though his mouth is lifted in a soft smile.

"I'm pregnant. Aren't I? Aren't I?"

He nods and my heart freefalls in my chest. "Never sure whether to express my congratulations or condolences sometimes," he says gently. "But yes. I'm going to need you to put on the gown so I can perform a vaginal sonogram so we can get a better picture of all of this."

"But I'm on the pill!" I blurt out, shaking my head. "And I have endometriosis. Which is why I'm on the pill! I'm not supposed to get pregnant."

"Nature has a funny way about her sometimes," he says. "Now please, put on the gown."

He leaves the room and I'm left there, stunned.

I'm beside myself, having an out of body experience.

How could this happen?

How could I be pregnant?

And how could I feel so wildly different about being pregnant now versus being pregnant with Anya? How can the same biological function cause such different reactions? Utter joy and excitement with Anya, and complete dread and disappointment now.

That's what's getting me the most of all.

The disappointment in myself.

I never let my guard down. I try hard to provide the best life for me and my daughter. I've shunned as much of the royal life as possible so that she can live a normal life, the life I never got to have when growing up. I've been careful. It took me ages to decide to leave my ex-husband, longer than it should have. After all, I discovered he was cheating on me when Anya was four years old and yet I decided to deal with it, ignore it, swallow it down and put on the brave face for her, so she wouldn't have to deal with a split family. I did it until it started to take a toll on me, and I stopped being the good mother I tried so desperately to be.

I tried to do everything right for the both of us, and yet all it took was one smirk from one rogue prince and suddenly I was bending over for him.

Literally.

But as much as I want to blame Orlando, I can't. It's not his fault. It's mine. I'm the one who gave into him, I'm the one who traded her carefully controlled life for a couple of good fucks. I'm the one who risked it all for orgasm after orgasm.

I thought I was protected.

I wasn't at all.

And now I have to face the consequences.

I'm in that same daze throughout the sonogram, when the doctor tells me I'm about three weeks pregnant.

He tells me my options.

Says that an abortion would be discreet and painless at this stage.

It's more than tempting.

I've always been pro-choice. I'm still pro-choice. I believe in a woman's right to choose what is best for her own body.

And I know that, on the surface, what's best for my body is probably to terminate. To choose Anya's future. To do it and pretend none of this ever happened. Women do it all the time. They don't regret it. They go on to live the lives they choose to live, doing what's best for them.

But even knowing that, even with how I always thought I would approach something like this . . . I don't know if that's the answer for me. Not right now, not at this age.

And yet, if it's not the answer, then it means having this baby.

Alone.

If I thought I had been totally screwed before, I'm completely and utterly screwed right now.

I tell the doctor that I need to think about things and of course he understands. I think he'd understand either way. After all, it's hard enough for a normal single woman to raise a child alone—it's even more scandalous when you're royalty.

When I get back home, Anya can sense something is off. I ask Margaret to stay and help with dinner and she does so gratefully. She only lives down the street from us. She's in her 70s and used to have a huge family, seven children, though they've all flown the nest a long time ago. I think Anya thinks she's like her grandmother, which I don't mind. It fills the void while her real grandmother is in the hospital, not remembering that she even has a grandchild.

Margaret senses something is wrong too, but she's respectful enough not to ask me about it. Or maybe she can just read it on my face, that if she does ask, I might turn into a blubbering mess.

But if I don't talk to Margaret, I don't really have anyone else to talk to. You don't make a lot of real friends as a royal and you never quite know who to trust.

When dinner is over, I take my phone outside in the backyard, which faces a deep forest, and I give Aksel a call.

"Stella?" he answers on the third ring, sounding worried already. "You never call."

"I always call," I remind him. "You just never answer. How are the girls? How are the twins?"

"Good, good," he says quickly, and then let's a pause hang in the air. "How are you?"

Hold it together. Don't cry on the phone.

I take in a sharp breath and blurt out. "Do you think Anya and I could come visit this weekend?"

"Yes. Of course. Why?"

"I have some news . . . "

A deeper pause. His voice lowers. "What? Is it mother? Is it you? Anya?"

Before he can get carried away, I say, reassuringly, "Everything is fine. Really. They're all good. I just . . . I need to see you and Aurora. I need someone to talk to. I need some advice . . . I need my family."

"Then I'll arrange the jet for you. We'll be waiting."

༒

THE WEEKEND COMES SLOWLY. NORMALLY I WOULD JUST head right on down but since Anya has a couple of riding lessons this week (her first time doing cross country), I don't want to pull her away from it.

It does remind me though that if I choose to go through with the pregnancy, it's going to completely disrupt the life I have with Anya here. I don't want to be pulled away from her,

I don't want to give her any less attention, I don't want her to resent me or the baby.

If you have the baby, I remind myself as the limo pulls up outside the Amalienborg Palace. *Don't make any decisions until you've talked it through.*

Henrik greets me and Anya, surprised to see me again so soon, and then we're whisked inside.

It feels totally different here now that I'm not the royal regent. In a way, I have a chance to just relax, even though the secret I'm carrying with me does nothing to put me at ease.

It also doesn't help that as the two of us walk down the hall to the living room, we keep passing by places that remind me of Orlando.

Orlando. How does he even play into all of this? What do I tell him, if anything? Yet another thing to figure out.

"Anya!" Freja and Clara cry out the moment we step into the room. They leave their father's side and run over to us, both of them grabbing Anya's hands and pulling her in different directions.

"Let's go dress up Snarf Snarf!" Clara tells her.

"Let's go make paper dolls," Freja says.

"Clara, leave the pig alone," Aksel chides her.

"Why don't you three play with paper dolls," I tell them, patting the girls on the head. "Have a contest, who can make the craziest dress."

"I'll obviously win that one," Clara says, with a roll of her eyes, completely serious, before the three of them run off down the hall.

"Oh and it's nice to see you girls!" I yell after them sarcastically. "So much love for your dear aunt."

"Sorry about that," Aksel says, coming over to me and giving me a quick kiss on the cheek. "They've been wild lately. I think the weather has been too hot here, it's been melting their brains."

"It's doing the same to Anya," I admit. "She won't stop bugging me about getting a cat."

"Well, let's just hope the girls don't become an enabler," he says, smiling softly. "If they can come back with a baby pig in their backpack, they can surely come back with a cat."

"Let's hope not," I say, and then look him up and down. Though I just saw him last month after they *finally* came back from vacation, he looks even more tan and sun-kissed. "Do you have any royal duties at all, or do you just lounge around in the sun all day?"

He grins and his teeth are bright white against his skin. "Blame Aurora. She says the sun does me good. Something about my mood."

"Where is she anyway?" I ask.

"Upstairs with the twins," he says. "She'll be down in a minute."

"You know that's what a nanny is for," I remind him.

Another smile from him. "What do you think Aurora is? Just because we're married and she's the queen, doesn't mean I ever relieved her of her position."

"Very cute," I tell him.

His smile starts to fade as he peers at me closely. "So now you're here. Are you okay?"

I shake my head slightly, eyes dropping to the ornate pattern on the blue carpet. "No."

"Do you want it to be between you and me or . . ."

I give him a quick glance. "No. Aurora too. She's my sister now and if anything, it's her advice I might need more."

He raises his brow. "Okay." He takes my hand and gives it a squeeze and then gestures to the couches. "Let's sit down then."

I take my seat and he goes to his bar and pulls out a bottle of Scotch, even though it's about two in the afternoon.

"Am I going to need this?" he asks me, holding it in the air.

"You might."

He pours himself a glass. "Will you?"

I can't help but give him a sour smile. "That's part of the problem. I wish I could."

And that's all I needed to say. He freezes in place, glass of Scotch in his hand, just as Aurora comes in the room.

"Stelllllaaaaaaaaaaaa," she cries out dramatically, doing her best impression of Marlon Brando in *A Street Car Named Desire*, by way of Elaine Benes from *Seinfeld*. Her Australian accent has not been softened by Denmark or by her new-found royalty.

I still manage to smile at her impression, even though she literally does it every time she sees me, sometimes more elaborate than others. But Aksel is still motionless, quiet, stunned.

"What?" Aurora asks him as she walks over to us. She then stops and looks back and forth between us. "What happened? Did that stop being funny?"

I shake my head. "It's always funny," I assure her. "I just have some news and I think Aksel already knows what it is."

"My god," he finally says, voice quiet and hushed. "You're serious."

"What?" Aurora asks him, louder. She plops down on the couch beside me and twists to face me, a deep line between her groomed brows. "What is it? Are you okay?"

"I'm not sure," I say slowly. I close my eyes for a second and take a deep breath. I keep my eyes closed while I say, "I'm pregnant."

"Oh my god!" Aurora cries out. "That's huge! That's amazing! Congrats!"

I open my eyes to see her beaming at me in shock.

"I'm not sure congratulations are in order," Aksel says

quietly, then he gives me an apologetic look. "Unless Stella says otherwise."

I sigh again and shrug. "Honestly, I don't know. I'm confused. So fucking confused. I need someone to talk to. I don't know . . . I don't really know what to do, what to think. What to feel. I'm just so scared."

"Oh," Aurora says, and then grabs my hand. "It's okay. That's what we're here for."

"Who is the father?" Aksel asks stiffly, as if he's going all protective big brother. "Your ex?"

I make a face. "No. What kind of person do you think I am?"

"Well, this is quite the surprise," he comments.

I suck on my teeth for a moment, knowing that he probably won't be happy about the answer. He's not a fan of that royal family, and after spending too many days with them, now I know why.

"It's Prince Orlando."

"What?" Aksel practically spits out. "The Royal Rogue?"

"Oh my god," says Aurora, hand at her chest. But she's smiling. "Damn girl, he is fucking fine."

"Aurora," Aksel says sharply. "Come on. This is my sister here and this isn't funny."

"I didn't say it was funny," she says to him, fire sparking in her eyes. "I said he was fucking fine. As in hot. As in good for her, getting laid by that guy." She grins at me. "I know this is a big deal, but I just think you needed to get laid." She throws her hands up in the air innocently. "That's all."

"How could you?" Aksel asks me, and then a look of recognition comes over his eyes. "Stella, what the hell? You had sex *here*, didn't you?"

I can feel my cheeks going red. They shouldn't. I'm thirty-four years old, a mom, I shouldn't blush at something like this, but sometimes those sibling relationships really send you back a few years.

"Don't worry, we didn't use your bed," I tell him.

"I can't believe you're pregnant," Aurora says. "When did you find out?"

"Last week," I tell her. "I was feeling sick, missed my period. Went to the doctor and he confirmed it."

"What are you going to do?" Aksel asks quietly, before taking a sip of his drink and sitting down across from me. I'm grateful he didn't automatically assume I'd get an abortion.

"I don't know," I say slowly.

"I suppose you do have some time to think about it, don't you?" Aurora asks. "And you know whatever you decide, we'll support it."

"You've always been very pro-choice," Aksel points out. "I remember you being very vocal about it growing up."

"I still am."

"Good."

"But I'm not sure what to do. I think . . . I always thought that if I found myself in this position, I'd get rid of the problem. But something in me has changed. Maybe it's because I have Anya. I can't really explain it."

"You don't have to explain to anyone," Aurora says. "These are such personal decisions and they're personal for every woman. You don't have to answer to anyone but yourself."

"And Orlando," Aksel says. "You will tell him, won't you?"

I slump against the couch and put my head in my hands. "I'd rather not."

"Stella," Aurora says. "I think you should."

"I know, I know. It's just . . . things didn't end well between us. He had a girlfriend that whole time."

Aurora nods. "Right. The hot Russian tennis pro."

"And judging by the late-night stalking I've been doing on his Instagram, he's still with her."

"It doesn't matter," Aksel says. "It's as much his problem as yours. You need to tell him, no matter what you end up deciding for yourself, he should at least know."

He's right.

My brother, the King, is often right.

It's just funny how the idea of telling Orlando, a man who was inside me, a man whose child is inside me, a man that I barely even know, might just be the scariest thing of all.

CHAPTER 8
ORLANDO

I'm sitting outside on the terrace of my penthouse and smoking a cigarette, watching the super yachts pull in and out of the marina, when my phone rings.

"Orlando, darling," Penelope says over the phone. "Are you available for dinner tonight?"

I sigh internally. Ever since we got back from Denmark, even though it was well over a month ago, she's become pushier than ever. My stepmother and I have never been that close, but lately it seems she's really trying.

Which isn't necessarily a bad thing. I'm not a monster. I know that things have been rocky between us from the start, especially since she came into my life so soon after my mother died. I was young and it happened so fast. I hated her, hated my father, hated God for taking my mother away. It wasn't until I was out of my teens that I started to see how unfair I was being. I went to university in Milan and there I was with people my own age. They didn't really care who I was; there were people from all walks of life, people who lost loved ones, who lived through tragedies like me. It made me see everything with new eyes.

After that, I made an effort to be nicer to Penelope, even though she drives me crazy all the time and I often wonder if she has a sincere bone in her body. But she is a good mother to Matilde and Francis for the most part, and father somehow seems to love her, despite how very obvious it is that she has several lovers on the side.

"Orlando?" she repeats herself. "We haven't seen you all week. I'll make sure Matilde and Francis will be there. Oh, and bring Zoya."

"She's out of town," I tell her, taking another drag.

Truth is, Zoya is behind me inside, sitting on the couch and watching Netflix.

"Where is she?" Penelope almost sounds accusing.

"She's in Paris for a fashion thing," I say. Which is almost the truth. She's going tomorrow morning to meet with someone from the Louis Vuitton company in hopes that they'll pick up her sportswear like they've been doing to a lot of brands lately.

"When is she coming back? We'll have to do dinner then."

"I don't know." Probably a week, since Emily will be meeting her there and they'll hole up in a private estate somewhere.

"Orlando, is everything okay between you two?"

"Yes, why?"

"It just seems like she's been traveling a lot."

"She's got a career, Penelope," I remind her. "That's a lot more than I have. I'm just a professional louse."

"Oh you're not a professional louse, Orlando. You're the future ruler of this land." She pauses. "It may not be a lot of land, but it's something." She always jokes that she should have married the King of Spain, not because she's Spanish herself, but because he has a lot of land. Monaco, aside from the Vatican, is the smallest country in the world.

"Anyway," she goes on, "I hope things are good between

you two because your father and I were talking the other day about the future."

This again.

"And, well, you know you're not getting any younger and neither is she."

"She's twenty-nine," I remind her.

"I had the twins well before that," she says stiffly. "I know in the real world it's normal for women to have babies late, but we don't live in the real world. We're royals. And she needs to start popping them out soon because you need an heir or . . . well, you know what will happen."

Yes. Our country will become a part of France and the 700 years of rule will come to an end and the nationality of the Monégasque people will cease to exist.

"Don't you think we should get married first?" I ask dryly.

"Yes, of course! Get the ring and ask her to marry you and let's get this started. The fate of our country is in your hands Orlando. Don't you forget it."

As if I've forgotten it for a second.

I think the only time it's slipped my mind, this mind-crushing pressure, is when I was with Stella. Our days together were brief, but it was only when I was tasting her skin, feeling her touch, that I was somewhere else.

But that was obviously never meant to be. I don't know why I still keep thinking about her, it's not doing me any good.

"So you're coming over for dinner?" she adds hopefully. "Be here at seven."

I sigh and hang up the phone, taking in a deep drag of my cigarette and letting the smoke fall from my mouth. It's hot, but never too hot here thanks to the sea breeze. The sun is hanging in the sky, glittering off the waves in such a way that it makes my eyes hurt. I have nothing to do today except this dinner plan now. I have a penthouse apartment, a gorgeous girlfriend, and all the money in the world.

I should be happy.

I'm anything but.

The sliding door opens and Zoya sticks her head out.

"Who was on the phone?" she asks.

"Penelope," I tell her. "She wanted you over for dinner, but I said you were already in Paris."

She lets out a sigh of relief. "Thank you."

"I wasn't so lucky."

"You handle them so much better than me. You know I get . . ."

"Anxious? Crazy? Yeah."

"I just can't handle a lot of socializing," she says, as she comes out and sits on the chair across from me. "I don't get *crazy*."

"Yes you do. It's why you're so good on the court."

"Phhfff. Yes, that's why. Not the fact that my parents have been training me to be the best tennis player in the world since I was two years old. My first word was *tennisnaya raketka*."

I laugh. "Let me guess. That's Russian for tennis racket."

"Well, yes," she says. I take another drag and blow the smoke away from her. She peers at me thoughtfully. "Are you okay?"

"Why wouldn't I be?"

"You only smoke when you're stressed. Why are you stressed?"

How do I explain it to her? That I'm stressed because of her? That because we made this arrangement, because we've fallen into these roles, that this is now my life. A life I actually chose—can't blame anyone but myself—but not a life that makes me happy.

I shrug. "Must be the changing of the seasons."

When Zoya and I first started dating, everything was legitimate. I was attracted to her, obviously, who wouldn't be? I liked being around her. I had feelings for her. I . . . loved her? I'd never been in love before, so I still assume that's what it was. Whatever I felt, though, it was strong, and it was real.

She said she felt the same for me. I believed her at the time. Now, I'm not so sure. It's not because she's bisexual. But the spark and the passion she has with Emily, I don't think she ever felt that for me.

Our relationship started to drift apart after the first year and a half.

She told me she met someone else, that she was desperately in love with a woman, a Slovakian tennis coach.

But she didn't want to break up.

At this point, I thought I was on track to marry her and then that curveball was thrown my way. She asked me for a favor. A promise. Said that I needed to be her cover until she figured out what to do. And because my father was insanely happy that I was finally getting serious about someone, I thought it was best I go along with it.

Now we've been in this for four years and I honestly don't think there's any way out. Breaking up with Zoya wouldn't ruin her life, but it would mean that she could never be with Emily, that the chances of them getting caught would be too high. If that happens, she would lose everything she's worked her entire life for.

As for me, well, I know there's no one out there for me. If I'm going to have to marry someone and produce an heir, it might as well be Zoya, someone I care for deeply anyway.

"It's the pressure, isn't it?" she asks me. "Penelope. She's been pressuring you to propose."

I nod.

"I can tell."

"She says we're getting old."

Zoya rolls her eyes. "Well she's going to have to wait a bit longer. I know, I *know* that I'm so close to winning the U.S. Open. Wimbledon. My first Grand Slam. I can't have a baby now; it would throw everything off."

"She knows that."

"Does she? She keeps bringing up how Serena Williams did it."

"She's a superhero and so are you."

Zoya gives me a grateful smile. "Still, I know the pressure is getting to you . . ." She chews on her lip for a moment. "Have you, you know, even thought about the ring?"

It's such a complicated situation. We both know we need to get married, but both of us wish we didn't have to.

"I should look into that, shouldn't I?"

She sighs and reaches out, taking my hand in hers. "You're a good man, Orlando. You're loyal to the bone. I can't tell you enough what all of this means to me. But . . . I do think the time is coming. The papers are already starting to talk, wondering why we're not engaged yet. I think, maybe before Christmas, that would be the best."

My chest starts to constrict but I manage to take another drag, my lungs filling with smoke. "I agree." My words echo with finality.

"Good," she says, and then gets up. She's a formidable sight. She's only an inch shorter than me and her limbs seem to go into other time zones. "I'm going to go pack."

She heads inside and shuts the door.

I let out a sigh of relief, tilt my head back, and close my eyes. I need a drink. I need something. Perhaps one of the painkillers the doctor had prescribed me. I still have one or two left.

My phone rings and I expect it to be my stepmother again, but when I pick up the phone, I see it's from a number

I don't recognize. Normally I wouldn't answer but I could use the distraction.

"Hello?" I say.

There's a pause, then, "Orlando?"

It takes me a second to recognize the voice.

"It's Stella," she says with her light accent. "Princess Stella," she adds awkwardly.

"Hi, Stella, hi," I say, completely taken aback. "H-how are you?"

"I'm fine," she says. "Listen, I know I'm calling out of the blue but I, uh, I really need to see you again."

"Okay . . ." I'm shocked. I thought she hated me. I'd hate me for sure, too, since I never got a chance to tell her the truth. "That's fine. I mean, yes. Where? At the palace?"

"No, Aksel is there."

"You could come here?"

"I don't think so. How about Cyprus?"

"Cyprus?"

"We have a compound there, it's lovely. Or so I'm told. Regardless, it's completely private."

Private. Okay. So this is, in fact, an elaborate booty call, isn't it? Perhaps I had more of an impact on her than I thought.

"That sounds great. When?"

"As soon as you can."

Wow. Okay. So I guess she's really got it bad.

"I can leave tomorrow," I tell her. "How did you get this number, by the way?"

"We have ways," she says. "Tell your pilot to take you to the Paphos airport and I'll have someone come meet you at the plane. I'll see you then."

She hangs up and I'm left staring at the phone for a moment.

Shit.

I think I'm going to need another cigarette.

෴

THE NEXT MORNING I'M BOUND FOR CYPRUS, SITTING alone in the royal private jet with only a stewardess for company. I stare out the window and watch Capri and the Amalfi coast of Italy fly beneath us before the plane jaunts over Greece and the Aegean Sea.

I've never been to Cyprus before. Living on the Mediterranean means that we are more likely to go to the Caribbean or even the South Pacific before exploring other places so close to home.

The land here looks dry and barren as the plane swoops in over the sparkling sea, the water startlingly clear against white beaches. I have zero idea what I'm getting into here, but as long as Stella is there, it has to be good.

Right?

At least Zoya seemed to think so. I'd filled her in about Stella and everything that happened between us in Copenhagen. Zoya seemed pretty happy about it. I don't often have affairs because of the whole NDA thing, so I think it weighs on Zoya a bit to always be "stepping out" on me. I guess with Stella it felt like it evened things out a little.

It's fucking weird, I'll say that much, to have your girlfriend be happy that you're jetting off somewhere to have a sexfest with someone else. But she also really seemed to like Stella as a person, too, so that definitely helps.

Soon the plane is landing and I'm heading down the jetway at the far end of the runway where a tall, overtly tanned man in a dark suit and sunglasses is waiting for me. He's a man of few words as he takes my duffel bag and I get into a Suburban with tinted windows. It's so hot outside that even the aircon on full blast seems to do nothing, and for a second I'm hoping Stella sent him and this isn't some sort of kidnapping.

Twenty minutes later though, we're pulling off the two-lane highway and heading down a narrow-paved road through scrub and stunted trees until we come to tall gates and a massive wall bookended by the sides of two converging cliffs. The gates open and we drive on through.

It's not a huge house—two stories, white stucco, red-tiled roof—but the landscape is something else. A terrace spans the space between the house and the cliffs and beyond that is the sea, shimmering brightly.

I get out of the car and head up the steps, practically sweating through my dress shirt as the sun bears down on me.

Halfway up, Stella opens the door and leans against the doorway, peering at me.

I stop where I am and take her in. She looks completely different here, her vibe, her energy. Her hair is long and blowing lightly in the breeze, she's wearing little makeup and, though her skin is pale, I can see a few freckles poke through, making her look like the sexiest girl next door. She's dressed in just a white cover-up with blue pom-pom accents, the cheap kind you'd pick up from a seller on the beach, with the straps of a bikini showing through. She's barefoot.

"Hi," I tell her. A bead of sweat drops off the tip of my nose, and I wipe my brow with the back of my arm.

Fucking smooth. I feel like an idiot standing in front of her and I don't know why. I have so much explaining I need to do here; I need to set things right and clear my name a little.

"Glad you could make it," she says. I expect her to make some small talk, but she just turns around and heads back into the house.

I follow her and as soon as I'm inside, the driver comes up behind me, places my duffel bag on the floor and then exits, closing the door behind me.

I watch as she walks through the tiled foyer and around the corner.

"So it's just us here?" I ask, following her through the house. There's something so different about her now and I don't know what. Not that I knew her well to begin with, but she seems like more of a stranger than before.

When I turn the corner and find myself in the kitchen with blue-tiled walls, she's standing by the counter holding a glass of clear liquid. She holds it out to me.

"Here," she says, meeting my eyes briefly. "This is for you."

"Okay . . ." I sniff it and grimace. It fucking burns my nose and smells like raisins.

"It's local. Zivania."

It smells like a hangover.

"Are you not having any?"

She shakes her head.

"Are we saying cheers to something?" I ask, lifting the drink to my lips and taking a tepid sip. It's not that bad. "Because I've got to be honest with you, I'm getting the impression that you're not in a celebrating mood. Which makes me wonder why I'm here."

"We're not celebrating anything," she says and winces. She exhales loudly. "I need to talk to you about something important."

Oh no. My first thought is that perhaps Aksel found out about us and wants to kill me for some reason, like I've insulted his honor and he's going to invoke the Danish tradition of the King beheading his enemies, or something like that. Or perhaps it's that other people found out about us and now it's making the headlines in Denmark and I just don't know it yet.

"What?" I ask warily.

Her smile is sharp and sour and strikes fear in the heart of me.

"I'm pregnant."

The words come out of her mouth like a blunt instrument, but the blow doesn't take me down right away.

"What?" I repeat dumbly.

I blink at her.

Why is she telling me this?

She gives me an incredulous look.

Oh.

Here comes the blow.

"You're pregnant," I repeat, the words finally sinking in.

Holy *shit.*

"Are you sure?"

She nods. "Oh, I'm sure."

"How . . . how long? I mean when? I mean . . ."

"Obviously since I last saw you," she says sharply.

"And you know for sure it's mine?"

If looks could kill, I'd already be dead.

"Of course it's yours!"

I throw my hands out feebly. "Well, I don't know. That was over a month ago. You could have had a million lovers since then."

"That's not how I operate, but it's obvious that's how you operate."

"Hey, that's not fair."

"You had a fucking girlfriend!" she yells at me, eyes blazing, nostrils flaring. She's terrifying and beautiful and oh my god, she's pregnant with my baby. "You probably still do!"

"We aren't together!"

"Stop lying to me!"

"I'm not!" I try and calm down. I don't want to yell at my baby mama. "It's complicated."

"Stop saying that."

"Zoya is a lesbian," I confess, and that's enough for her eyes to go wide. "Okay? Well, she's bisexual. Or something. Regardless, she's in love with a woman named Emily. They've been together for years."

She doesn't say anything. I'm not even sure she believes me.

"It's true," I go on. "Yeah, when we first started dating, that was real, and then after a while she told me she was in love with a tennis coach."

"So, if that's true, why are you still with her?" Stella folds her arms, raising her brow as she watches me.

"Because it's safer for her that way."

"Safer?"

"She's Russian. It's not accepted there. More than that, it's actually dangerous to come out. She says her parents have ties to the government, some shady shit. I don't know, I've never actually met them. But I've looked into the LGBTQ rights, hell, even the human rights, situation over there and it's horrible. It's non-existent. Her parents would disown her, she'd lose her sponsors, she'd be kicked out of the Russian league. She could even lose her sportswear line. Anything is possible. Most of all, she might be made an example of for coming out. It's a fucking big deal."

She nods slowly, seeming to mull it over. "That doesn't explain why you're with her."

"She needs a front. A beard, if you will. If I'm not with her, covering for her, it'll be harder for her to be with her girlfriend."

"Again," Stella says, "why are *you* with her?"

I lick my lips and shrug. "I made a promise to her. I keep my promises."

"You mean to tell me you're that loyal? That you'd be in a fake relationship just for the sake of someone else?"

I stiffen at that, feeling my hackles go up. "Why is that so unbelievable to you? I may not be *in love* with Zoya, but I love her like family, and I made a promise to her." I clear my throat and look away. "Besides, it's not just her sake. It's mine too. If I don't marry and produce an heir, the country of Monaco reverts to being part of France. I don't want that on my shoulders."

"The agreement of 1918," she says.

"You know it?" I ask, surprised.

"I may have done some more research after you left," she says. "And then some when I found out I was carrying your child."

Jesus. There it is again. It's just too fucking unbelievable. Like I'm being pranked.

"I guess you do have an heir after all, just not with the right person," she says lightly, but I know she's taking this anything but lightly.

Fuck. This is messy. So very messy.

"I think I need to sit down," I tell her, and quickly finish the drink. It burns and I have the urge to finish the whole bottle, drink until the world makes some sort of sense again.

"I figured you would."

She leaves the kitchen and I follow her out to a small shaded part of the terrace, caught between the grey-white cliffs, a clear infinity pool, and the startlingly blue sea.

Stella sits down in a wooden chair and stares out at the waves, not facing me. I take the chair beside her. It almost feels like we're two vacationers who have just arrived at their sunny destination and don't know what to do with themselves.

I don't know what the fuck to do with myself.

I've never gotten anyone pregnant before. I've been careful, too. It's a well-known phenomenon that women will seek out royalty and give birth to illegitimate heirs, so I've been extra cautious when it comes to this.

But I clearly wasn't that cautious when I was with Stella. She said she was on the pill and I really should have insisted on a condom, especially since I always use them. I guess the moment blinded us. And then all the hot and sweaty moments after that. Being with her in the palace was like being in some other world where neither time nor consequences existed.

Except there are some very big, very real consequences right here beside me.

"I know it's a lot to take," she eventually says, keeping her focus on the horizon. "I've had a hell of a week trying to figure things out and I'm not sure if it's ever going to feel . . . real." She quickly glances at me, her brows knitting together. "Aksel insisted I tell you. Said it was the right thing to do, even if I hadn't figured out what direction I was going to go in."

"Well, I'm glad you did," I admit.

"Even if I end up getting an abortion?" she asks. "Though I suppose that would be the easiest for both of us. You wouldn't end up with a bastard heir and I wouldn't be trying to raise another kid alone. I could have not told you and you would have never known."

"I'm glad you told me," I tell her again. "If anything, it's just nice to see you again."

She lets out a sharp laugh. "Right. Well, these aren't the best circumstances."

"So are you . . . you know, not keeping it?" She raises her brows and I quickly add. "Keep in mind, I will support you no matter what your choice is. And I one hundred percent understand that it's your choice here, not mine. I mean that."

She rubs her lips together and nods, her expression wary. "Good. Thank you."

"Take all the time you need to decide, and I'll be here for you."

"I've already decided."

I sit up straighter. "Oh."

"I'm keeping it," she says. "I've decided to keep the baby. Can't really explain why but this is just the way it's going to be. I don't expect you to be involved, and for your sake, I won't ever reveal who the father is."

This is all so much to take, I don't even have the thoughts or the words, though I know I don't like the idea of having a child who will never know me as a father.

"I want to be involved," I say, when I've finally found my balls. "I really do."

"Your life is complicated as it is, Orlando. You don't need this. I didn't even think you'd be this supportive, and the fact that you are, just saying that you're okay with this decision, that's all I need." She closes her eyes to the sun, tilting her head back, and lets out a deep breath. "This is so weird. With Anya it was so different. She was such a struggle, you know. I have endometriosis, which means it's hard to get pregnant, among other things. It's why I was on the pill to begin with. To think that not only did the pill fail me but I got pregnant on top of it . . ."

"It's like it was fate," I fill in. "It was meant to be."

She opens her eyes and squints at me. "Do you believe in fate?"

I never did. But here, now, with this bombshell that's been dropped in my lap, I feel like I should start believing in something.

CHAPTER 9
STELLA

I wasn't sure what to expect from Orlando. I figured he would have freaked the fuck out, probably blamed me or something. I know that didn't seem in character with the man I slept with, but I've heard more than enough stories from women about how the man completely changes when they find out their partner is pregnant. They're usually so quick to leave.

But Orlando didn't act that way. He was shocked, for sure, and I could tell he was scared. Can't blame him for that. Yet, the way he told me that he'd support me no matter what I chose, it was so damn sincere that I knew he meant it. Especially, when I told him my decision.

To be honest, I had been on the fence about it for days. I was sort of waiting until I met with Orlando to find out how I truly felt. I thought maybe I would have changed my mind once I saw him. Maybe he would have tried to convince me one way or another.

And yet, even before he had a chance to react, I knew.

I saw him coming up the stairs to the house, the sun glinting off his hair, the concern in his azure eyes, the beads of sweat on his determined brow, and I knew that I wanted his baby. Maybe it was something as primal as the way his shirt clung to him, seeing those muscles again, his height and strength, some cavewoman response to a caveman who she knows will provide for her and protect her.

Either way, if I'm the cavewoman, then that caveman is the baby daddy.

Prince Orlando.

"So, what now?" he asks me. We've been sitting out on the terrace for hours it seems like. Not saying all that much. He's asked me a lot about technical things, medical things, and seems genuinely interested. I only have my pregnancy with Anya as a comparison, but I tell him everything that we should expect.

We. Sounds funny, doesn't it. Other than me and Anya, there hasn't been a 'we' in my mind for a very long time.

"I guess we wait," I say.

"For?"

I glance at him and shrug. "I don't know. I didn't plan this far."

"To be fair, I don't think any of this was planned," he says. "What I mean is, tonight. Did you want me to go back to Monaco? The plane is still at the airport . . ."

Oh. Right. "Sure," I tell him. "I guess it was kind of silly to make you come all this way, but I felt like I had to do it in person. I don't think things like this should be done on the phone."

"When are you going back?" he asks.

"I'm not sure," I say slowly, gnawing on my bottom lip. "It's hot as stink here but it's beautiful. I might just need to clear my head." She pauses. "Then again, I should go back to be with my daughter. I hate leaving her."

"And I hate leaving you," he says. "You shouldn't be here alone. And I have no place to be."

He actually wants to stay? I look at him curiously. "You don't have any public engagements with Zoya?"

He shakes his head. "No. She's gone to Paris to be with Emily. She won't be back for a week." He twists in his chair to face me and I'm struck by how beautiful he is. It's going to be one hell of a good-looking baby. "Let me stay with you."

I tense up automatically. "What do you mean, stay?"

He gestures to the sea, to the pool, to the house. "Here. With you. In Cyprus. What isn't there to get?"

"I'm not sure that's a good idea," I say after a moment.

I'm speaking the truth. As much as I actually like the idea of him staying, of not being alone, I also know that things are going to get infinitely more complicated with him here. I'm still attracted to him like bees to honey. I don't trust myself around him, not with that cocky smirk and those dangerous hands and those muscles that can go all night. I'm afraid that if he stays, I'll fall back into bed with him and the whole situation will do a number on my heart.

That's the one thing I have left to protect. Being pregnant, I've never felt more vulnerable and insecure in my life. I feel like I'm barely tethered to this world as it is and that all he has to do is cut a few strings and I'll never be grounded again.

This man, this gorgeous prince, he could break my heart. He seems like the type who does it in his sleep.

Just because he stays, doesn't mean you're going to fall in love with him, I remind myself. *You can have sex without feelings involved.*

But I know that's just my wild hormones trying to play tricks on me. They got me in trouble last time. They can't be trusted.

"Is anything a good idea?" he asks me. He gives me a charming wink. "I promise to keep my hands to myself."

And what about my hands?

"You'll have to sleep in one of the guest rooms," I tell him, sitting up straighter and clearing my throat. Time to start being on my best behaviour.

Starting now.

"That's fine with me. I can sleep on the couch if you want. You just tell me what to do."

"Okay," I say. I hold back a smile and look at the sea instead.

Since it's fairly early in the day still, I show him to his room, which is down the hall and as far away from my room as possible, then we decide to go out to get something to eat. These plans were so last minute that I had no time to arrange for any staff for the place. There's just Cristos, the driver, and that's it. And even if Cristos happens to be an amazing cook, there's no way I'd ask him. Every time I try to talk to him, I just get grunts and one-word answers. I know he speaks English, but apparently, he just doesn't want to speak it to me.

Or to Orlando either. When we get in the car and have Cristos drive us into the town of Paphos for dinner, Orlando starts playing a version of twenty questions with him and every single question he answers with either a yes or a no or a grunt.

"Sure is Mr. Personality Plus, isn't he?" Orlando asks me, as we walk away from the car and start strolling along the boardwalk along Paphos Harbour, looking for a place to eat.

"Pretty sure he works for the mob," I admit. "But at least we'll be protected."

"Hey, I can do a pretty good job of protecting you," he says, and then shows off his bicep which pops nicely against his black t-shirt. "Remember these muscles?"

"I remember," I say softly. I look away, keeping my focus on the passing shops so he doesn't see the flush on my cheeks. I don't know if it's because I'm pregnant or because the memories are that ingrained, but I still can't help but fantasize about him. Every night. It's been frustrating to say the least, yet another reason why I know I have to keep my distance from him.

I automatically put an extra foot of space between us as we walk.

"Do I smell?" Orlando asks, raising his armpit and taking a sniff.

"You smell good," I tell him. Too good. "But just in case there is paparazzi around, I don't want anyone to get the wrong idea. Especially now."

I'm actually not too worried about that. Aksel and Aurora were just here, and they didn't have any sort of photos taken of them and they hadn't appeared in any magazines either. To be safe, both Orlando and I are wearing dark sunglasses and hats and are extremely dressed down. He's got his black t-shirt, jeans and a newsboy cap, I'm wearing jean shorts and a plain white tank top with a mustard-colored ball cap that says Cyprus on it. We seem to fit in with everyone else.

We keep walking along the promenade, watching the sun go down on the horizon, pausing every now and then to read the menu of a restaurant or watch the paddleboats come in for the day.

"Hey, look at that cat," he says, pointing at a cat on the side of the path eating some cat food that's been strewn on the ground. Guess someone fed him. "And that cat," he says, as another cat comes and joins the other one. "Maybe they're the neighborhood pets."

Except as we keep walking past all the big hotels, we keep seeing more and more and more cats. Literally, everywhere you look, there's a cat.

"This is heaven," he says, staring in awe at the copious amounts of scrawny wild felines.

"Heaven?" I repeat. "You're a cat person?"

"I'm a dog person, too," he says defensively. "But yeah. All my youth I always had a cat. I just love how they don't give a fuck."

"I can see why you'd relate to them."

He shrugs. "It's true. They follow their own rules, they do their own thing. They're independent and when they love you, you know it's love. You know you've earned it."

"Well, I hate cats."

He gasps, over dramatic. "No."

"Yes. I'm allergic."

"Doesn't mean you hate them though."

"Uh, yes it does. It means when I'm around them I sneeze and turn into a miserable, snippy bitch."

He cocks a brow.

I point at him accusingly. "And don't you dare finish that thought."

He grins at me. "I don't know what you're talking about. But anyway, you could just take a pill for that."

"You sound just like Anya," I grumble.

"She wants a cat too?"

"Yes. All day long, that's all she talks about. A cat or a horse, and honestly, I think a horse would be so much better. I wouldn't have to see the horse at all, it could live at a stable far away and someone else can take care of it."

"Geez, you're starting to sound like an animal hater," he says.

"I'm pregnant," I tell him. "I'm starting to hate everything."

"I guess I should be pretty grateful you're not hating on me right now."

"Right at this moment? No. As the pregnancy moves along? I'm going to be cursing your name all day long."

"I'm looking forward to it," he says.

"I'm sure you are."

"I mean that, by the way," he says, stopping on the path so I come to a halt along with him. "I hope you know that about me at this point. I mean what I say."

"And you keep your promises."

"That I do. And I promise you, Stella, you're not going to be alone through any of this. You might hate me, you might push me away, but I'm always going to be there for you."

My heart does a little skip in my chest.

The emotion behind his words, the sincerity in his eyes, tells me he means it in a big way.

Keep your head on straight, I remind myself. *Don't start falling for pretty lines.*

But I'm not so sure it's a line.

Then again, I'm not so sure of anything these days.

"We should find a place to eat," I say after a moment, gesturing for us to keep walking. "I'm getting tired."

He watches me for a second and then nods. "Sure."

I can tell it's bothering him, the way I'm shrugging off his words like this. Part of me wants to reach out and grab his hand and tell him that I'm grateful he's being supportive. Tell him that it means a lot to me.

The other part of me is scared. Scared of being pregnant, scared that he's the father, scared that in the end, even after all the kind words and promises, he'll just break his promise to me in order to keep a promise to someone else. I just can't trust him, not with the pregnancy, not with my body, not with my heart.

I can only hope I keep my wits about me.

The sun has now dipped beneath the horizon, bathing the sky in the most magical colors I've ever seen. Lilac and pink and tangerine reflecting off the dark metallic blue of the sea. We stop and watch the color spread from the horizon to the clouds, just as everyone else has seemed to. It's like the entire world has paused for just this moment, to take it all in. To connect. I take my phone out and snap a few pics. It's so vibrant in real life that it actually shows up in the photo.

"That was something else," he says to me, after the last cotton candy cloud fades to blue. He turns to face me. "You're something else, too."

"What did I say about trying to hit on me?"

He rolls his eyes and folds his massive arms across his wide chest, and wow, that's such a look. "Okay, you've never said anything about me hitting on you. And also, I wasn't hitting on you." I stare at him. "What? I wasn't. I was trying to pay the mother of my child a compliment."

I scrunch up my nose.

"Oh no," he says. "That was weird, wasn't it? Too soon?"

I nod. It was too soon and weird and yet it also felt right.

Have I mentioned yet how complicated this all is?

"Let's just get some food," I say, for what feels like the millionth time.

We end up eschewing the restaurants in favor of a little surf shack bar by the sea. There's nothing but French fries to eat, but they have good non-alcoholic mojitos, so I'm happy. I also like that it feels so absolutely normal to be doing this. We could be tourists from anywhere, just having a drink after sunset on a sandy beach.

"This must be what it's like to be normal," Orlando comments, taking a French fry and putting it underneath the table.

"You read my mind," I tell him.

"I have to admit, it feels good." He takes another fry, this time breaking it into a few small mushy pieces and then does the same again. "Slumming it and all."

"What are you doing?" I ask, looking down to see a pile of fries by his feet and a tabby kitten happily munching away on them.

"Oh my god, you're not."

"I am," he says smugly. "And I'd like to point out that you haven't sneezed once."

"That's because I'm outside. I don't have a problem with outdoor cats."

"Good," he says, as I take a sip of my drink. "Because I'd like to take this cat back to the house."

I stare at him for a moment, the mojito straw dangling from my lips. "*Hvad?*" I say, reverting to Danish.

"This cat," he says, leaning over to scoop up the kitten and place him on top of the table. "I've named him Mokey."

"Mokey? When the hell did you manage to give him a name?"

"Just now," he says. "Look at the way his hair stands out behind his ears. He kind of looks like Mokey from Fraggle Rock."

"Fraggle what?"

"It was an American show. Like the Muppets."

"Orlando, you can't just bring a cat back to the house."

"Why not?"

"It's not your house! It's technically a palace!"

"What makes it a palace?"

"I don't know, but it is. And it's not even my palace, it's my brother's."

"You know what I think you need?" he asks, smiling at the cat as it explores the table.

I clutch my drink to my chest. "Please don't say a cat."

"You need a place of your own."

"I have a house."

"But is it a palace? You're a princess. A pregnant princess. You deserve your own palace. The palace of Princess Stella."

"Listen, I've got enough on my plate right now, I'm not going palace shopping."

"But you could. You have the money. You are royalty.

Really. You are. I get the feeling that you don't believe it half the time."

He's not wrong about that.

"I think it's better to believe you're lesser than you are than it is to believe you're more than you are," I admit.

He bursts out laughing, which makes the cat jump into his lap. He scoops him up and holds him to his chest, and while it's extremely cute, seeing the little orange cat buried in his muscles, I can't help but think about fleas. Thank god he's not sleeping in my room tonight.

"What's so funny?" I finally ask.

"I just can't believe you said that," he says.

"Why?"

"There's humble and then there is just stupid. You're not stupid Stella, so don't act like it."

"I don't know about that. I'm pregnant, aren't I?"

He narrows his eyes at me for a second until the cat starts to bat its paw on his arm.

"You should always believe you're better than you are. In time, you might become it. It's dangerous to go the other way." He reaches over and plucks the straw from my drink. "You shouldn't use this. Think of the turtles." Then he starts to tease the cat with the straw.

"Anyway," I tell him, ignoring the loss of my stolen straw. "I don't need a palace."

"Will you just admit you're a princess?"

"Of course I'm a princess. It just doesn't mean that's something that I feel like I am, or something I even want to be. I'm just . . . normal."

"You can be both." He wiggles the straw at the cat who captures it in its tiny paws. "Hey Mokey? You want to become a royal cat?"

"You're still thinking of bringing him back?"

"I already made a promise to him and you know how I feel about promises."

I grumble and then finish the rest of my drink, sans straw, the ice bumping against my face. "Okay, but then he's going back to Monaco with you." I pause, wondering if I should press on. "What will Zoya think?"

"She won't care," he says. "She's so busy, she's never there anyway. And you don't have to get all weird and cagey when you ask me about her."

"Well, it's hard not to. It's just so weird. I feel like . . . like a mistress or something."

"You're not a mistress."

Maybe not. But I'm something. If he ends up getting married to Zoya, I'll definitely be something. Makes me wonder how naïve I'm being in thinking we can keep this all a secret forever. I know I told him I wouldn't tell the baby who the father was but I'm starting to wonder if that's even fair. Doesn't every child have a right to know exactly where they came from?

"No one is getting hurt from this," he goes on. "I promise."

Not yet, I think. *Not yet.*

CHAPTER 10

ORLANDO

"What was your saying again?" I hear Stella yell from the kitchen. "Never trust a man who doesn't like cats?"

"You remembered," I comment. "I'm very impressed."

She grunts something in response, and I go around the corner into the kitchen to see coffee grounds spilled absolutely everywhere. On the floor, on the counter, in the sink.

"What the hell did you do?"

"Me?" she snaps, angrily wiping away the hair that's fallen in her face. "This is your damn cat's fault."

"Sir Mokey did this?"

"Oh, it's *Sir* Mokey now?" she comments, shaking her head. She tears off paper towels and attempts to clean up. "The cat got knighted?"

"Hey baby mama," I say, coming over to her and taking the paper towel out of her hands. "You go relax. I'll take care of this. And the cat."

She makes a feeble sound in response and then walks off to the living area where she collapses on the couch in a huff.

We've been at the compound in Cyprus for three days

now and have plans to go back tomorrow. I'm not really sure what's on our agenda, other than I'm going back to Monaco (with Sir Mokey) and she's going to England. The last few days we've talked about everything under the sun, but the complexity of our personal situation doesn't seem to be any clearer.

All I know is that I don't want to be apart from her. I would rather go back with her to England and meet Anya and help her with every step of this pregnancy.

But I also know that's going to be tricky when it comes to me and Zoya—I'm not even sure if I'll ever tell her the truth at this point. On top of that, I don't know if Stella even wants me in her life after this. She seems so adamant that she can handle it all herself, without any help or input from me, and while I respect and admire how strong she's being, she doesn't realize how much I *want* to be there for her and the baby.

It's surprising even to myself.

Maybe this is just what happens when you become a father (or future father or baby daddy or however else I'm supposed to describe myself these days). Your instincts kick in. You want to be involved; you want to be able to watch over the mother to protect the baby. Either way, I'm feeling drawn to Stella in an even more magnetic way than before.

I just want to take care of her, be with her, as much as I can.

And I'm not sure our lives will let that happen.

I exhale loudly through my nose, trying to work through it, then I clean up the kitchen. I'm really not sure how the cat managed to get inside, let alone tear apart the bag of coffee. I've been pretty good about obeying Stella's wishes regarding Sir Mokey.

When I'm done cleaning it up, I go back to the sitting room.

"All clear."

"Well, where is the cat?" she asks, looking around her warily.

"I'm sure he's somewhere. I'll find him. You just relax."

"I'm allergic, you know."

"Uh huh. I don't think I've heard you sneeze once."

"Cat litter is bad for the baby."

"We're not keeping him inside. Jesus."

I swear I see a tiny smirk on her lips.

"What?"

"Nothing."

"You enjoy busting my chops, don't you?"

She shrugs and looks at her nails. "It's good to have hobbies."

I walk over to her and stand at the side of the couch, looming over her. "If you weren't pregnant, do you know what I would do?"

She glances up at me, a little fearful. "What?"

"I'd tickle the fuck out of you."

She laughs. The sound of her gorgeous laugh strikes me right in the heart.

I *feel* it.

Shit.

Shit, what is happening here?

"Okay," she says, sitting up and holding out her hands in a truce. "Normally I would be the first to remind you that I'm barely pregnant—"

"You just told me about kitty litter!"

"But I will have to say, you're right. Tickling me would be very dangerous right now."

"I think you might be asking for it," I say, holding out my hands and making the tickle motion.

"This is how boys flirt in middle school," she says, with another laugh.

"Maybe some boys don't grow out of it," I tell her, taking another step until I'm right up against the couch, inches away, my fingers wriggling.

The most determined, wild look comes across her face as she quickly reaches out and grabs my wrists with an iron grip. "If you tickle me, I will knee you right in the balls," she says through grinding teeth. "I don't care if I do any damage. I already got your sperm."

Now I'm laughing. "Say sperm again, it was incredibly sexy with that Danish accent of yours."

"Shut up," she says.

I make the move to tickle her but then her knee comes up and I have to think quick, blocking my junk just in time before she makes contact.

The movement causes me to fall over onto her.

"Ahh," she cries out and starts to squirm, but I press my weight on top of her and pin her hands behind her on the couch.

"Gotcha," I tell her, my face inches from her.

It takes all of my strength, not to keep her pinned, but to keep myself from kissing her.

Those lips.

I know what those lips taste like, what they feel like.

How they make me feel.

I don't know how it's even possible at this point, but I've missed her.

She's been by my side here on this island for a few days, and yet I've missed her in the deepest parts of me.

Mainly my dick, but other parts too.

"Get off of me," she says, the words come out rushed and soft. Her eyes keep flitting between mine and my lips. I like it. This push and pull. The way I can tell that she still wants me but is doing everything she can to keep her needs at bay.

"Let me guess, this is dangerous too?"

"Yeah, for you," she says, and makes an attempt to knee me in the balls.

She manages to just graze me. It's enough.

Fucking hell that *hurts*.

"Ow," I cry out, rolling to the side and onto the tile floor with a *thunk*.

I try to keep my wails to myself and suck it up, but even so, she's giving me an assertive look as she lords over me from the couch. "You know that pain? Now multiply it by a million and that's what it's like to give birth."

I manage to get to my feet and groan. "So what you're saying is, you're going to do that a million times over the next nine months?"

"It depends if you deserve it or not."

"So I take that as a yes?"

"We'll see," she says. I reach down and grab her by the elbows, hauling her to her feet. "Don't you have a cat to go find?"

"I've got a pussy right here."

Her eyes roll to the back of her head. "So that's why you like cats. All the pussy jokes you can handle."

"Trust me, I can handle a lot of pussy."

She giggles and places her hands on my chest. "You need to stop," she warns me, a lazy smile on her lips. It's like for a moment she's forgotten that she's been trying to keep her distance from me for the last few days.

But then her expression changes. Brows come together; jaw grows tense. She remembers.

"I think I'm going to get changed and go for a swim," she says, clearing her throat.

Her hands drop away from my chest and she walks away, up the stairs to her room.

I watch her go and then feel a pang of disappointment. I'm normally a lot smoother than this. My seduction tactics worked on her the first time around, but now it's like she's immune to me. I know she's still attracted to me. I can see it in her eyes, the way she bites her lip, I can practically smell it on her. She wants me just as badly as I want her.

But she doesn't want to act on it and I'm not about to convince her otherwise.

Then again, it's me.

Of course I'm going to try and convince her otherwise.

Mew.

I turn around to see Mokey sitting in the doorway to the kitchen, staring at me curiously and mewling.

Speaking of pussy.

"There you are," I say, going over to him. I scoop him up in my hands and hold the little orange rascal close to my chest. "You funny little thing."

We managed to take him to the vet yesterday where he was given a flea bath and some shots. When I get back to Monaco, I'm supposed to get him neutered too. Apparently, Cyprus has a huge stray cat population—1.5 million, which is half a million more than the people who live here. Every cat that gets taken out of here and given a home is for the best.

I take Mokey through the French doors and to the terrace outside. I bought a travel kennel at the vet and replaced the cardboard box that was previously his home. Inside is lined with towels and he has his food and water dish outside. He's free to roam wherever, but at this point he keeps returning. As long as he's around tomorrow morning, then he's coming with me.

Tomorrow. Just like it did when I was at the palace in Copenhagen, the last few days here on Cyprus have felt like a dream. A dream in which I'm not tied to my duties and my future, a dream in which I'm allowed to just be me.

And I'm allowed to be with her, even if it's just to be in her company.

Tomorrow that dream comes to end.

If I had her in my life in the way I want, it would become a dream I'd never have to wake up from.

You don't even know what you want, I tell myself. *You're as messed up as she is. Listen to yourself.*

I *am* listening to myself.

Maybe for the first time ever.

I place Mokey down by the kennel and he goes straight over to the cat food.

I look over to the sea. The sun is starting to set. It feels like the sun is always setting here. I keep getting Elton John's "Don't Let the Sun Go Down on Me" in my head on repeat.

"It's always so beautiful." Stella's voice rings from behind me.

I look over my shoulder to see Stella walking toward the pool.

I'm stunned.

I blink.

I'd say she's the one who is always so beautiful, but in this case, I would be lying because the word beautiful isn't enough to describe her.

She's wearing just her bathing suit, a turquoise string bikini that leaves very little to the imagination. I'm not sure if she bought that here or what, because I always pictured Stella wearing something a little cuter and more modest, but right now she's working it and my jaw is on the ground.

She glances at me and gives me a shy smile before hurrying to the pool.

"Where's the fire?" I ask her, and I'm totally aware that I'm leering at her. Aware but unwilling to change.

She shoots me another look over her shoulder, one I can't read with her backlit by the orange glow of the setting sun, but I'm sure it's a look that's telling me to mind my manners.

You know what? Not sure that I will tonight.

We leave tomorrow. I don't know when I'll see her again. I don't trust that she's actually going to keep me in her life.

Tonight might be all we have.

And there's no time for boyish flirting and all the games.

There's no time for anything but the truth.

I watch as she gets in the pool and swims to the end of it, where it drops off into infinity and there's nothing but beach and sea and sky beyond, currently turning molten.

Then I strip.

Take off my shirt, my shorts, kick off my sandals until I'm completely naked. It's still so hot out that it actually feels better this way.

She's not watching me. Her back is to me, her eyes on the horizon.

I walk over to the pool, my cock already hard, betraying me, and slowly sink into the water.

She finally turns around, surprised to see me.

I give her no room to move out of the way. I'm tall and broad-shouldered and I'm a fast swimmer. I cut through the water like glass and then I'm at her, my arms on either side of her body, bracketing her in as she stares at me.

"I'm not sure what I'm doing," I tell her, my voice coming out low and rough. "But I just know that tomorrow we're both leaving, and I don't know what that's going to bring."

She swallows, watching me with eyes that dance between desire and determination. "I don't know either," she says softly. "I guess we'll have to find out."

I frown at her, at the way she keeps playing it so cool, as if she's not carrying my child, as if there isn't so much at stake here. "What do you want?" I whisper. "Tell me. Talk to me."

She takes in a deep breath and stares at my chest, at my tattoo. "I want . . . I just want everything to be okay."

"It's going to be okay," I tell her, cupping her chin with my hand. "I promise you that."

"How can you promise that when you've made a promise to someone else?"

Fuck.

"I'm going to try and make it all right. You deserve that."

"But doesn't Zoya deserve it too?"

"This isn't about her. This is about you and me. I . . ." I reach over and brush a strand of hair behind her ear, her hair that is glowing coral and pink in the dying sun. "I can't explain how I feel about you and I'm not going to try. But I'm strangely drawn to you, Stella. Your name means star and there's nothing more fitting. It's like when the sky is black and there's that one bright light shining above you. It doesn't matter where you look, your gaze is drawn to that star every time you look up."

She stares at me for a moment and I see the softness come over her brow, as if she's letting herself believe me. But then it fades. She frowns. "You're just saying that because I'm the mother of your unborn child."

She says it like a joke, but for once I'm not smiling. "It's not just that," I tell her, hoping she can see the sincerity inside me. "There's something deep inside me that sees something deep inside you. It sees we are the same."

"We are not the same."

I bring my face closer to hers, see the rounded glow of my reflection in her pupils. "We are the same. And we want the same things. We do. And most of all, we want each other." I brush my thumb over her lips as my body grows tight with need. "There's no use denying it. Wanting each other is what got us in this situation to begin with."

"You mean mess," she says against my thumb, her voice low.

"No, not a mess. This isn't a mess, Stella. This is life."

"It's complicated."

"And life is complicated already. So what's another wrench

thrown into the gears? At least this way, I get to make you come."

Her eyes go wide, and before she can say anything, I'm pulling her into me, my cock sticking straight up between us, my lips smothering hers in a long, hard kiss.

She whimpers into my mouth, seems to fight against me, against this, and I'm about to pull away when suddenly a growl seems to rip out of her. Her hands go to my shoulders, down my arms, to my back, her nails digging in as she holds me in place. Her mouth opens to mine, greedy and hungry and I don't think I've ever been so turned on in my life.

This is complicated.

So fucking complicated.

But it's also insanely beautiful.

"Stella," I whisper against her lips, my mouth moving down to the soft skin of her neck, wet from the pool and tasting faintly of sweat and chlorine. "You have no idea how badly I want you."

"Uh huh," she bites out through a groan, as her hand comes around to my cock, making a fist over it. "I can draw my own conclusions."

A deep moan spills from my lips as she squeezes me, and I'm left nearly breathless.

"Careful," I manage to say, my fingers deftly untying the straps of her bikini. "I'm not coming until you are."

"And I promise you won't have to wait long," she says, leaning back against the edge of the pool, her neck arching to expose her throat, her breasts pushed up as her bikini top falls away. Her breasts already seem fuller and the water dripping off of them reflects the orange glow of the sunset.

I don't think I've ever seen anything quite like this.

She's *transcendent*.

I bend my head and lick up and down her breasts, tasting her, flicking her nipple with my tongue, making her moan over and over again until she starts to shake with impatience, wanting more. Always wanting more.

She takes more.

She wraps her legs around me, holding me in place and I realize I've never felt this way before. Not just in my body, but in a place I didn't think existed.

These feelings aren't alone, though. My body is a battleground, the urge to come is frighteningly strong while the rest of me wants to drown in the pleasure. The world around us is being painted in a million shades of color, some I don't think even exist on an earthly spectrum.

"I need you," she calls out, her voice is desperate and soft and warm all at once. "I need you Orlando."

My name never sounded so sweet.

"You have me, little star," I tell her. "You have me."

"Then come inside me," she says, lifting her head enough so that I'm staring into her lustful gaze, her face shadowed and backlit by the sunset, but her eyes still blue and clear enough that they shine. I think I could see her eyes anywhere, even on the blackest, coldest nights.

I reach down and untie the sides of her bikini bottoms until they're floating to the bottom of the pool, then I grab her ass and haul her up higher so she's level with my twitching cock.

"I suppose I should be more of a gentleman now that you're pregnant," I remark. "May I please fuck your gorgeous brains out?"

"Yes, you fucking may," she says.

I grin like a madman before I slam my cock into her.

Thankfully, she's even wetter than the warm water around us, because I slide in to what feels like blissful silk.

"Oh god!" she cries out, her back arching, the sun disappearing behind the horizon as I drive my cock in deeper and deeper.

Oh god is right. This right here is a religious experience, the kind that you have once and it changes you forever. I'm being fucking assaulted from all angles as I fuck her. The colors of the sky, the roar of the waves, the weightlessness of the water, the slick silk of her cunt as I thrust faster, harder. My nerves are on fire, coiling inside me, begging for sweet release.

I'm not coming until she is though.

I'm not coming until I've brought her to another level.

Until she feels exactly what I feel.

The hunger surges through me again, fueled by a type of desire that seems to come from somewhere ancestral. Primal. I've already laid my claim to this woman and yet that doesn't stop me from trying to imprint myself even further.

She's carrying my child.

The feelings I have for her are so complex it seems almost unnavigable.

But here, right now, pumping myself into her, the water in the pool splashing around us in waves, the way that her mouth is open as she cries my name, the feel of her heels as they dig into my back, all of this is coming together in a way that shines with clarity.

I'd told her the other day that we were meant to be.

But those words sound so trite.

They aren't enough.

They don't convey what's real.

It's not just that we're meant to be. It's not even that this is fate. It's that this has always existed in some place, maybe inside us, maybe in the stars, but it's existed. That's why it feels like I know her, because I do know her, and she knows me.

Fuck, maybe this is all my cock talking right now, but this, us, together, it shines a light on something that seemed in the dark before.

Purpose.

She is my purpose.

This baby is my purpose.

And I'm going to do my best not to fuck it up.

I'll start by making her come harder than she has in a long time.

I slide my hand between her legs, but before I can even rub against her clit, she's already coming, just from my cock alone.

"Orlando!" she cries out, her hands gripping the edge of the pool until her knuckles turn white. "Oh fuck me!"

Her eyes pinch shut hard and she lets out a strangled cry as she starts to come around me, her body jerking in the water as she's taken to another place. With the sky on fire, the rest of her perfect body dark and reflective, I don't think I'll ever see such a gorgeous sight again.

It's enough to push me over.

I start pistoning my hips into her hips, faster, harder, undeterred by the force of the water. I just slam into her, over and over until I can't control myself anymore. The orgasm rips through me, going off like dynamite, wild and explosive.

"Fuck!" The cry is deep and straight from my gut and I almost feel like my spine is being ripped out of me, leaving me boneless and demolished and unbelievably high. It's like I'm among the clouds already, soaking in the colors, unable to come down.

Holy fuck.

That was . . .

I try to swallow, to breathe, to remember where I am so I don't drown.

I reach out and grab Stella, wrapping my arms around her and pulling her to me.

To my surprise there are tears in her eyes. Or maybe it's just the water from the pool.

"Are you okay?" I ask her softly, taking my thumb and wiping the tears away.

She nods ever so slightly. "I . . . I think so."

I lean in and rub the tip of my nose against hers. "That was something."

"Just something?" she asks quietly.

I smile. "No. It was everything."

She smiles back, but there's a tinge of sadness in it, like it's fading to night at the same time as the sky.

I kiss her softly on the lips, not wanting to pull away, wanting to keep her close to me.

"We're going to be okay," I whisper to her.

Her throat bobs as she swallows hard. I can see her pulse beating wildly, matching the beat of my own heart. "How?"

"I don't know. But I know we are."

"We're still strangers in a way."

"That feeling won't last forever. It hasn't for me. Deep inside, we know each other, Stella. Sometimes time isn't a factor at all. We're one and the same and I'm in this with you. I promise you I am."

I promise you I am.

CHAPTER 11
STELLA

Everything is grey.

September moved in with blustery, cold gales from the North Sea, pushing away the last remains of summer, the sun turning to cloud, and the memory of Orlando and me on Cyprus, caught in that heady heat, seems like nothing but a dream.

You know, except when you wake up from the dream, you're still pregnant.

I've been back for a couple of weeks now, and during that time, my life has changed immensely.

At Aksel and Aurora's urging (more like nagging), I decided to pack up some of our stuff and temporarily move into the royal palace with them. My brother said I'd need all the help and support I could get, and as stubborn as I am, I knew he was right. It would just be until after the baby is born, plus I get Dr. Bonakov on call and all the privacy I can ever need. That's going to come in especially handy once I start showing. Lord knows I wouldn't be able to go anywhere in England before the paparazzi finds me and starts writing one million articles about who the baby daddy could be.

On the other hand, I don't think they would ever in a million years imagine that it was Orlando. The Single Mom Princess and The Royal Rogue don't really seem to go together.

I'm still not sure if we do. That's something I've been grappling with ever since we parted ways, exactly how much I want to keep him in my life and how involved I want him to be. I know he said he wanted this to work, but I have no idea how that's possible when he's still with his fake girlfriend and his family still has the pressure on him to marry her.

I mean, even now, there's no denying that we have chemistry together and we're best when we're rolling beneath the sheets. But all of that isn't enough to sustain a pregnancy or marriage. I'm not expecting the two of us to be a couple or to fall in love. This isn't a romance. But it does make me wonder if what we have is enough to survive everything that's going to be thrown our way.

Because, believe me, I think things are about to get exponentially hard.

"Do you think the girls at school will like me?" Anya asks. We're in the back of the limo heading from Copenhagen airport to the palace. The moving truck already came and dropped off some of our stuff, we are the last to arrive.

I give her a sympathetic look and put my arm around her. "Everyone loves you Anya." I kiss the top of her head. "You know, we don't have to move here. It's never too late. We can always go back."

"But then I don't get a horse," she says. "And I really want my horse."

I had wanted to stay in England for Anya's sake, since she was so into her riding and I had no idea how I was going to explain why we were even moving to begin with. But when I broached the subject with her, she decided to turn into a supreme negotiator.

She didn't even ask why we were moving. She just wanted to know if this meant she could finally have a cat.

I told her no.

No.

Especially after seeing what a pain in the ass Sir Mokey of Monaco was and how often I was sneezing around him (I was).

She then asked if she could get a horse. Said it would help her when she got sad from missing all her old schoolmates. Help her cope with the stress of the move.

If she doesn't grow up to be a lawyer, I'm going to be severely disappointed.

So, I promised her a horse, and after that it was smooth sailing. Funny that.

"Is the horse worth it if you miss all your friends?" I ask.

She looks up at me and grins cheekily from ear to ear. "Yes. Besides, I didn't like anyone at that school. They all made fun of my accent. At least here I'll fit in. And I'll be going to the same school as Clara and Freja, so they'll know how to deal with a princess."

She's probably right about that, though I'm a little miffed she played that "I'll miss all my friends" card when it wasn't true. Future lawyer, indeed.

We get to the palace and are immediately greeted and fussed over by everyone—Maja, Aurora, the head maid Agnes, Henrik and Johan. They've all been informed about my "condition," though none of the children have. I'll obviously have the talk with Anya soon, and Clara and Freja, but not until I'm ready.

"How are you, Your Highness?" Agnes says, putting her hand to my forehead. "You seem flushed. That's not good."

"Stella, you really shouldn't be flying in your condition," Maja says. "A boat would have been safer."

"You're glowing," Henrik says to me. "I'll bring the guitar out later and show you this lullaby I wrote."

"Everyone, please," Aksel's deep voice booms, as he comes in and starts pulling people away from me. "Back away from my sister."

"I'm fine," I tell him, and then smile at the others. "I'm *fine*."

"What's your condition?" Anya asks.

I look down to see her staring up at me.

With my eyes I tell everyone to shut up about the whole thing and then give Anya a quick smile. "No condition. Everything is fine. Why don't you find the girls and the pig and go play?"

"Yaaaay," she yells out, and then runs off down the hall. That was easy.

"You do look glowing though," Aurora says, putting her hand on my shoulder. "Your *condition* really suits you."

"Thank you," I tell her. "The nausea has gone away too, so that's a start."

"Everything is going to be fine now," Maja says reassuringly. "You made the right move in coming back here."

I glance at Aksel. "Can't say I wasn't pressured into it."

"You know it's for the best," he says. "Come on, let's get you to your room. You must be exhausted."

"I'm, like, only seven weeks pregnant Aksel," I tell him. But he's right. I am exhausted these days.

He puts me in the same bedroom I'm usually in (same goes for Anya), so as far as moves go, this one is pretty painless. It's familiar and it feels like home, even more so now than it did when I was a child. Back then it always felt like I was running around in someone else's place, even if I grew up here. Here there's a lot of my boxes from England already in the room.

"You going to be okay?" Aurora asks me as she walks

around the room, tidying things that were already tidied. That's pretty much what palaces are, grand ornate places where people walk around tidying the same things over and over again.

"I think so," I tell her. "It'll be nice to have everyone around. As much as I fought against the idea, Aksel was right."

She gives me a quick smile, her eyes soft. "I don't mean about moving in with us. I mean . . . in general. With the baby. With Orlando. The future."

I sigh and sit down in the armchair by the window, suddenly feeling weak. If that's a sign that I'm actually not going to be okay, then I don't know what is.

"I hope so," I say in a small voice. I feel the tears teasing my eyes and I do everything I can to hold them back. I need to be strong. If I can't be strong now, how will I ever survive this?

"Have you talked to the prince lately?"

The prince. I can't believe I'm carrying the child of a prince. I know I'm a princess and all, but it sounds like a dream or a fairy tale when I think of it like that.

I try not to think of it like that.

"He texts me every day for updates," I tell her. It's true. Every morning he texts and asks how I am. The last few nights he's texted at night, asking about my day, wishing me a good sleep.

Under any other circumstances it would be completely romantic but now, while I think it's especially sweet of him, I know he's doing it because it's expected of him. He's the baby daddy. He's obligated. He's trying to fill a role, just like the other roles he has to fill.

"And Zoya?"

I scrunch up my face. "She's around."

"Do they live together?"

"Yeah."

"Do they . . . sleep in the same bed?"

I had asked Orlando that. I shake my head. "No. She has her own bedroom. He says that the last time they were intimate with each other was back when they were dating. Two years ago."

"And you believe him?" Aurora doesn't look like she does.

I shrug. "I have no reason not to. He really has been honest with me. If I ask, he tells. I've got a pretty good bullshit meter and I think he's a pretty decent guy when it comes down to it. Insanely loyal. Maybe to a fault."

"I'll say. To her and to his family. Imagine having the entire future of your country, not just as a country but literally existing as a country, on your shoulders? I almost feel sorry for him. All these royal lives can be majorly fucked up. It makes me even more grateful that Aksel eventually acted on his feelings. Could you imagine how my life would have gone if he hadn't taken that chance? If he'd chosen the status quo over me? Over us?" She gestures out the window to the palace courtyard. "I wouldn't be here. I wouldn't have this conversation with you. I wouldn't have known the joys of being a mother, of being married—"

"Of being a queen," I interject.

"Oy," she says, waving her hand dismissively. "Who honestly gives a bloody fuck about being a queen? I know you don't. What really matters is the human experience. That's what Aksel has given me. He's given me love in the purest form, and I wouldn't trade that for any throne." She sighs and sits on the arm of the chair. "I know this is really scary for you right now. I know you're afraid of what the press will say about it and I know you're really worried about Anya. But she's going to be okay. She'll be better than okay; she'll get to be a big sister. And you, well, you know that love in the purest form? The love you feel for Anya? You're going to feel that same love for this baby, and it's going to make it all worth it in the end."

The tears are welling. Shit.

"All right, I'm going to have to leave you for a bit," she says, getting up and stretching. "I don't trust the twins alone with Agnes for too long. She's always trying to feed them some Danish homeopathic remedy and I swear it always has booze in it."

I watch as Aurora leaves the room and then I'm left with my thoughts for a bit. Though her words were comforting, and I know she made a lot of sense, I'm still feeling unsettled.

I think I need to have a talk with my mother.

MY MOTHER'S HOSPITAL IS ON THE OUTSKIRTS OF THE CITY, the best place in the country for treating dementia and Alzheimer's, and one of the best in Scandinavia. My mother has been here ever since my father died. We all think the stress of losing him triggered a stroke and then, shortly after that, something changed in her brain and though the doctors do say that stress can certainly speed up the symptoms of Alzheimer's, they aren't inclined to blame it on his death.

But the truth is, they don't know much about the disease at all. My mother was a very active woman, always going for walks, and in the summer she loved rowing. She didn't drink much; she ate healthy and she was pretty sharp. They say the warning signs would have been there but it's hard to say now what they were. Was she forgetful? Of course. But she was a royal. She was the dowager queen (and in many hearts, she still is) and that's a stressful role to play.

It doesn't really matter though, all the evenings Aksel and I sat around trying to figure out what went wrong and how it happened. It doesn't change anything at all, it just brings pain into our hearts. I know that we both have a ton of baggage when it comes to our parents. He believes that his cold upbringing was because they were preparing him to be the king one day and he thinks that I got the mother who was warm and loving.

I never really had the heart to tell Aksel that it wasn't the case at all. Our mother was always very distant with me. Cold. It didn't matter that he was going to be king one day and I was second to the throne. It's just the way she was, and I guess I wanted Aksel to think there was something special about me. I don't know. Sibling stuff can be fucked up.

It was our father that spoiled me a bit, really played up his "little princess," whereas he was very brutish when it came to Aksel. You can really see how that affected him as he got older and why it's taken so long for him to open up to people and stop being such a grumpy bastard.

I'm not sure what my excuse is, though. Not that I'm as moody as Aksel is (though ask me again in a few months), but I've definitely got some "mommy" issues to work through. Having a mother that would rather hug the wall than hug you can do a real number on you.

Maybe that's why I'm so clingy with Anya, I'm so afraid I'll make the same mistakes my mother did. I never want my daughter to not feel loved and supported. The thought of her thinking she doesn't have my love absolutely terrifies me.

And that's one reason why this pregnancy is so scary. What if the attention I give the baby makes Anya think I don't love her anymore? What if I don't have enough love in my heart to go around?

I let those thoughts dwell in my head as Maja and I enter the hospital.

"Are you going to be okay?" she asks me as we get to my mother's floor. "Or do you want me to go in there first?"

Because Maja is my mother's sister and was very close to

her, she still visits her once a week, bringing flowers and freshening up the place. My mother doesn't know who she is the majority of the time but that doesn't stop Maja. She always says, "what if?" What if she recognizes her again? What if her brain comes back to the present?

But then she says that even if she never comes back again to the here and now, and Maja is always a stranger to her, she'd still come. She believes the heart will always recognize the heart of someone it once loved, even if they don't know it. The heart speaks its own language, deep, poetic, and often foreign to us all.

I've lost my nerve. "You can go in first," I tell Maja, gesturing to the door.

I don't know exactly what I'm going to say, I just feel like my mother needs to know what's happening to me. As rigid as she was, she really was a good grandmother to Anya.

Maja goes inside the room and I wait around the corner in a sitting area, reading a magazine from a haphazard stack on the table.

Not just any magazine.

Hello Magazine.

And guess who is on page two?

No, not me (thank god) but Prince Orlando.

It's a picture of him and Zoya outside the Monte Carlo casino. They're standing on the red-carpeted steps and he's holding her hand while they both wave to the crowd.

My heart sinks.

Like it actually hurts, like someone's taken it from my chest and put it in a vice.

With shaking hands I read the article. The picture was taken at Matilde's African literacy gala a month ago. After he, well, knocked me up. There's no reason for me to get upset over this photo. I know they aren't together, and I know that this all happened before he knew I was pregnant.

But it doesn't stop me from having these delusional feelings.

I'm jealous of Zoya, even though I shouldn't be.

Not just her body or her hair or, more importantly, her legendary plays on the tennis court. I'm jealous that she gets to be with him. Even if it's fake, she's the one who gets to go home with him every night. Hell, she'll probably be the one to spend the rest of her life with him.

That won't be me.

That can never be me.

You don't even want that, I tell myself. *You don't even know him.*

But I can't tell myself that lie anymore.

I *do* know Orlando.

And more than that, I'm starting to form some very real, very complicated feelings for the man. Feelings that I'm too afraid to dissect any further.

I hear the door close down the hall and look up to see Maja exit. I tuck the magazine back in the pile.

"How is she?" I ask, quickly getting to my feet.

Maja is smiling, which is rare. "She's time traveling again," she says, her eyes glinting with happy tears. "She knows me. Thinks I'm six years old and we're at our parent's cottage by the lake." She pauses to wipe away a tear. "But she won't know you. It's not that time yet."

I nod. "That's okay." I grab my aunt's hand and give it a squeeze. "I'm glad she knew you in some point in time."

"Me too," she says. "Okay, go in. I would be quick though. The memory seemed to have tired her out."

The funny thing is, before I saw the article with Orlando, I knew what I was going to say. What I needed to talk about. Rant about.

But the moment I step inside the room and see her sitting in her chair by the window, all of that disappears. It seems kind of inconsequential now to bring up my problems, especially when she thinks she's a young girl again. I'm just some stranger complaining about being pregnant and asking her for advice about a man, advice that she would never know how to give.

My mother turns her head and looks at me. She doesn't smile anymore—the damage from the stroke won't allow that —but her eyes at least seem a little sharper than usual.

"Who are you?" she asks. She's not scared, just curious.

"I'm friends with Maja, your sister," I say to her, slowly walking over to her. I stop a few feet away and my heart shatters some more when I look at her. Every time I see her, I realize it's not just her mind that's betraying her, but her body. She's aging so fucking fast.

"Maja?" she asks and then tries to think. "Oh yes," she says after a moment. "Tell her I'm mad at her for pushing me in the lake. She should watch her back."

"I'll tell her that."

I sit down across from her and give her a warm smile. This isn't about me right now. It's all about her.

"What else would you like to tell me, Liva?"

I sit back and I listen.

CHAPTER 12

ORLANDO

TWO MONTHS LATER

"How long are you going for?" Zoya asks, as I slide my diplomatic passport into my down-lined jacket. Though the weather is still mild here in Monaco, I've heard November is fucking freezing up in Denmark.

"I'm not sure," I tell her. "Maybe a week. Maybe more."

"What will I tell people when they ask?"

"Tell them I'm seeing a friend."

"What did you tell Penelope and your father?"

"Same thing. Seeing a friend." I hesitate. I decide not to share the next part, what I really told them when I said I was going to visit King Aksel in Denmark. I told them that I wanted to talk to Aksel about rally driving, since Monaco is famous for the Grand Prix and that perhaps a Monégasque rally driving team wouldn't be a far stretch.

But I also told them that I wanted another royal's opinion on marriage. Made my parents think that I was going there to get advice about proposing to Zoya, about getting a ring and planning a wedding, anything that would buy me some time.

All complete lies, lies I would normally share with Zoya.

But the lies now feel as sticky as the truth.

I haven't told Zoya about Stella yet.

I'd like to say I haven't had a chance, but the truth is I wanted to wait until I figure out what I want to do. What Stella wants to do.

It's been two months since I saw Stella on Cyprus.

Two very long months of me checking in with her every single day.

Wanting updates on how she's doing.

Wanting to be a part of her life.

Two months of not knowing where we stand with each other.

When we left each other in Cyprus, I said that I would be there for her every step of the way and I still am. I just don't know where the steps are leading us. In seven months, she's going to give birth to my child.

Will I be there?

Or will I hear about it via text? Or, god forbid, the news?

When she discovers the sex of the child, will I know? Or is that a surprise?

Do I get to hear the name?

Do I get to choose the schools?

Do I get...anything?

I won't if things continue the way that they are. As it is, it seems like she's going to have the baby, keep my involvement a secret, and maybe I'll see the child every now and then. The child will never know I'm the father. I'll have to keep that truth buried deep in my soul. And I'll go on with Zoya, marrying her and having children of my own, children I have no doubt I'll love deeply, but will be so different from the one I have with Stella.

Because what I have with Stella...that's maybe the most real thing I have.

I may have not spent that much time with Stella in total,

but we've talked every single day for almost two months straight. All that "I don't know you" bullshit is over. I know her. She knows me. And I don't just want this baby with her, I want her too. Body and soul.

So I'm going to Copenhagen indefinitely. At least until we come up with a plan.

I want to be a part of her life, of the child's life, and that's exactly what I aim to do.

"Are you in love with her?" Zoya asks as I grab my suitcase in the hallway.

The question nearly knocks me down.

"What?" I ask, dumbfounded.

"With Stella. Are you in love with her? I mean, I don't care either way. I'm happy for you if you are..."

But Zoya doesn't look that happy. It's not that she looks jealous, it's just that she looks worried. And I can't blame her.

"I'm not in love with her," I tell her. Though my words sound weak, they're true. I'm not in love with Stella. I'm in *something* with her and I don't know what that is, but I keep that part to myself.

Zoya narrows her eyes at me thoughtfully before swinging her hair over her shoulder. "Honestly, Orly, it's fine. I have Emily. You deserve to have someone too. And I really like Stella. I think she'd be good for you."

"I'm not in love with her," I say again. There's more conviction in my voice this time.

"Oh." Her brow quirks up. "So, she's just a friend?"

I swallow uneasily. "You know it's more than that."

"I know. It's much more. I've seen how you are with booty calls and casual sex. You don't go back repeatedly. You don't spend all day on your phone. You don't stare off into space for most of the day. And you certainly don't masturbate to them every night."

"Hey, you mind your own business there." If I was the

type to blush, I probably would. "Shower time is private time."

"I am minding my own business. You're the one who is horribly loud when he comes. My god, it's like listening to some strange animal mating."

"It's the acoustics," I grumble. "Speaking of animal," I say, grateful for a segue. "You sure you'll be okay with Mokey? Remember if you go away, you can just call Matilde and she'll take care of him."

She looks over my shoulder at Mokey who is curled up on the top edge of the sofa and sleeping. He's gained a lot of weight in the last two months and doubled in size, but he's still pretty cute and is acting more and more regal every day. He's the family mascot now.

"You don't have to worry about us. We're like two pees in the toilet," she says proudly.

"I think you mean two peas in a pod," I tell her. "That's the English expression."

She shrugs. "You have your saying; I have my own. Just keep in touch, okay?"

"I will," I tell her, and give her a quick kiss on the cheek.

I'd only told Stella yesterday that I wanted to come by and see her, as well as finally meet her daughter, brother, and sister-in-law. I'd expected that we'd make plans for later in the month but to my surprise she sounded as eager to see me as I was to see her.

So at least I've got that going for me.

Still, when the private jet lands in Copenhagen and I'm picked up by a tall, wiry gentleman named Johan, I get nervous. The kind of nervous that rarely befalls me, the kind of nervous that makes me crack my knuckles and start smoking. I start doing the former and am about to ask Johan if I can do the latter when I stop myself. I actually need to make a good impression here. I'm meeting her brother, the fucking

King of Denmark, and the last thing I need is to show up reeking like smoke. He'd probably declare me unfit to mix with their bloodline and then kick me out on the street.

The car takes me through Copenhagen and to the back gates of the castle. It looks different now, surrounded by low, grey clouds and gentle rain. Summer feels like another lifetime.

Yet, when I step into the palace, it all comes flooding back to me.

Suddenly, it feels like it was only yesterday.

"Your Serene Highness," Maja, Stella's aunt, says as she approaches me by the door.

"Please, it's Orlando," I tell her. "We're pretty much family now."

She doesn't smile. Not even a little. She lifts her chin an inch and says, "Come with me."

She's going to be a tough one to crack.

But as I follow her down the hall and realize she's leading me into the sitting room, where I see the royal family has gathered, I know the toughest nut is going to be Aksel.

"May I present you, Your Serene Highness Prince Orlando of Monaco to King Aksel and the Queen Aurora of Denmark," Maja announces, as I step into the room.

Aksel is sitting in a highbacked velvet chair, dressed in a sharp grey suit, a most formidable impression on his face. There's stern and then there's Aksel stern (not to be confused with Howard Stern). With his cutting cheekbones and Viking-esque jawline, he's not a royal I want to fuck with.

Even his wife doesn't seem as cute as I remember from seeing her in interviews. I mean, she's obviously young and pretty but that easy smile that you always see in photos is gone. She's dressed in a black sweater and black leggings, her hair pulled high off her face.

They're both staring at me, emotionless.

Silent.

And Stella is nowhere in sight.

I turn around to ask Maja where Stella is, but she's already gone, and I'm left alone with the King and Queen of staring contests.

I clear my throat and give them my most charming smile. It didn't work on Maja but maybe...

"Thank you for having me over, especially on such a short notice."

Aksel's eyes narrow.

Aurora tilts her head to the side, seeming to study me.

Okay...

I stick my hands in my pockets and rock back on my heels as I look around the room. "Nice digs you got here." I glance at them. "By the way, when I said thank you for having me over just now, I also meant that for when my family was here. I know you both were gone at the time, but I also happen to know we were a major pain in the ass. So, you know. Thank you. And sorry if we drained your liquor cabinet."

"So you're the man who knocked up my sister," Aksel says, his voice booming, his accent refined. "*And* drank all my Scotch."

"Technically, I'm a prince. But yes, that was me."

Aurora glances at Aksel, slowly raising her brow. "What do you think? Shall we behead him?"

"I'm sorry, what?" I ask.

Aksel nods slowly, steepling his fingers under his chin. "It's tradition. I suppose it would be easy to dispose of the body this time."

Aurora finally smiles, a big, almost creepy-looking grin as she eyes me. "You see, Snarf Snarf has acquired the taste for human flesh after your little accident. You'd disappear in a second."

I open my mouth to say something but feel a presence behind me.

For a second I think maybe this is the part where I'm beheaded by Danish knights but as I whirl around, I see Stella standing there, looking amused, arms crossed.

"You guys, knock it off," she says to them as she walks past me, giving me a little wink as she goes.

I haven't seen her in so long it's almost disorienting to see her in front of me like this.

She looks beyond beautiful. I know that they say pregnant woman have the glow of life about them and she definitely has that, but it's almost something beyond words. Like the sunset that soaked her skin as we had sex in that Cyprus pool, she's transcendent and radiating.

Like a star, I think. *A shooting star come down to earth.*

She's wearing a long white sweater that goes to her knees and jeans. She looks dressed down and comfortable, her hair in a bun, her lips slicked with gloss. She's not showing either, not as far as I can tell, which, I have to be honest, is almost disappointing. I want to see her belly. I want to get hit with that jolt, the physical evidence that she's carrying my child.

She walks over to Aksel and Aurora, puts her hands on her hips and stares down at them. "What are you doing?" she asks them. "Is that how you treat all your guests, let alone royalty? With threats of beheading?"

Aurora tries to keep a straight face but then her lips start to twitch and she laughs. "I'm sorry. I'm sorry, I was just taking the piss out of him." She points at me. "You should have seen your face!"

"*I* was serious," Aksel says gravely. "At least about the Scotch and the fact that he got you pregnant."

"Might I remind you that it takes two to tango, Aksel. Anyway, how about we start the introductions over again." Stella looks over her shoulder at me and smiles.

Her smile makes my chest ache.

She clears her throat. "Orlando, may I introduce you to my brother Aksel, AKA King Grumpy Old Fart and his wife, Queen Aurora, the Australian Ex-Con."

"Hey," Aurora drawls out. "That's not fair to bring up the past."

"Well if it makes you feel any better," I say as I walk over to them. "You can call me The Royal Rogue."

Aurora scrunches up her nose. "Ugh. No. I'd rather not. Did the tabloids *really* give you that nickname or did you secretly feed it to them?"

I laugh. I like her. "Believe me, I was trying to get them to call me *Le Cheval*."

"*Le Cheval?*" She thinks it over, translating it in her head. "Why would they call you The Horse?"

"Aurora," Aksel says sharply. "Don't walk into that joke."

"Not a joke, just the facts," I tell him with a grin, but my smile only seems to make him hate me more. "Very large facts."

"Okay," Stella says, pressing her hands together in what seems like a plea. "Now that we're all acquainted, Aksel why don't you go and find another bottle of priceless Scotch and let's let our hair down a little."

"Pretty sure that's frowned upon," I tell her.

"Not for me," she says, with a roll of her eyes.

"I meant letting your hair down."

The memory of our first night together comes back.

How badly I wanted to let her hair down.

How I wanted her to loosen up.

How I wished I could get under her skin.

And now, now we're past all that and at the same time, it feels like every time we see each other we're starting over.

I like the newness of it all, I like the excitement and the nerves that happen every time we meet. But what I want most of all is something stable. Something solid. I want to be able to see her and kiss her and not have it be weird or hesitant. To touch her and hold her and not need an explanation. To know where we stand.

I just want her.

From the way she's looking at me, I can tell the same memories are going through her brain too.

"You know what?" Aurora says, getting to her feet. "I think you guys have a lot of catching up to do. I should go and check on the twins." She looks down at Aksel who is still staring at me with contempt. She kicks him on the shin. "*Honey*. The twins."

"Right," he grumbles, getting to his feet. "See you both at dinner," he says, taking Aurora's hand and leading her out of the room. "Don't touch my Scotch," he throws over his shoulder.

"He's prickly," I say to Stella once he's out of earshot.

"He's a teddy bear underneath," she says.

"I'll take your word for it. He doesn't seem to like me."

"No, he doesn't. But I think he got a bad impression of you from the tabloids."

"Isn't he friends with Prince Magnus? The king of sex tapes?"

She shrugs. "Scandinavians stick together. And you're from the Mediterranean. It's...different."

"It *is* different. This weather you have up here is total shit." I make a face at the grey mist outside the large windows. "You should come visit some time. Get some sun. You know you haven't yet."

She pats her stomach. "Yes. Well, I'm pregnant with child and all."

"You can still fly. Or take a train."

She laughs. "Take a train."

"Then take a royal cavalcade."

"And where would I stay?" she asks pointedly. "In your penthouse with your girlfriend?"

I give her a shaky smile. "I'd put you up in the palace. I think you'd like it. It's very different from here but it has its charm. It used to be a fortress, you know."

"And what would your parents think?"

She's got me there. As far as I know, neither my father nor Penelope suspect there is anything between us. And why would they? They're not as astute as my siblings and only see what they want to see.

"See," she says after a moment. "But honestly, I'm glad you came."

"So am I," I tell her, taking a step toward her and grabbing her hand. It feels good to feel her skin against mine. She doesn't even flinch, which means she must feel the same. "And I'm sorry it took this long to invite myself over."

"To be fair, I wasn't giving you the signals."

"And I usually invent my own signals and barge through all the red lights."

"Maybe you were being a gentleman and giving me space and time to figure shit out."

"Maybe," I tell her, giving her hand a squeeze. "And I'll still be that. But...Stella...when I tell you I haven't stopped thinking about you since Cyprus, you have to believe me. I haven't. You're all I think about, all the time, and it's driving me mad that I've been so far away from you." I pause, gathering up courage. "I have no plans to go back home."

She was staring at her hand in mine. At my confession she looks up sharply. "What do you mean?" she frowns.

"I mean, I'm here to stay. I realize that I've just invited myself to stay in your brother's palace with you but even so, that's the truth. I don't want to do the long-distance thing with you. I don't want updates via text and only get snippets of your life. The last few months have been hell for me, all I can think about is you and the baby. I want you both and I want to be in both your lives. I mean it."

Her throat bobs as she swallows, licking her lips. "What about Zoya?"

"She's busy. I think it's about time that I was the one leaving."

"Have you told her about us yet?"

I shake my head. "No. No one knows. I don't know where we stand with each other, so I wanted to figure that out first. I wanted to come here and stay here and be with you and make this work. Stella, my little star," I say to her, cupping her delicate face in my hands. "I want to make this work."

She stares up at me, then at my lips. "I don't know what to say."

"Say yes," I tell her. "Give me a month. I might have to go back on weekends for some events but give me a month, please. I'll take more if you're offering but...let me be a part of this. A part of your life."

Her mouth quirks up in a soft smile, her eyes languid and warm. "Do you mean that?"

"I promise."

I lean in and kiss her. Sweet. Soft. A kiss made of promises and hope for the future.

I can tell she's hesitating, though. That's okay. I can't blame her. She's been on her own for the last while and suddenly I'm here, pretty much telling her I'm moving in with her for a month, maybe more. I haven't even figured out my own shit, but I know that's what I want to do, what I need to do.

She places her hands at my chest. She doesn't have to tell me that this isn't Cyprus and that we're not jumping in where we left off. I get that it's more complicated than that.

I give her a quick smile, tucking a strand of hair behind her ear. "So, how about you show me to my room then?"

She laughs and it sounds like music, a faint blush coming across her high cheekbones. "You're staying in my room, you idiot."

I raise my hands. "Hey, I'm a gentleman. I didn't want to make any assumptions."

"Yeah right," she says. Then she takes my hand. "Come on, let me introduce you to Anya."

"Is she going to be tougher than Aksel?" I ask as she leads me out of the room.

"Maybe," she says.

She takes me down the hall to the wing near the ballroom and we step into a large room, not too dissimilar from the rest except that it's quite obvious that a roving pack of young girls have left their mark on every single inch. There are posters of cartoons and there's glitter and drawings and plush toys and dolls and toy animals everywhere.

And there's a real pig in the corner, lying down on its side, its big belly rising up and down.

"So we meet again," I say under my breath as I stare at Snarf Snarf.

Then Snarf Snarf actually makes eye contact with me and I quickly look away. I still have a scar on my arm. I'm not about to tempt fate.

"Girls," Stella announces. "I have someone very special to introduce to you."

The girls are gathered in the middle of the room around a giant iPad and taking turns doing something on it. They all look up and stare at me, curious, yet also hostile. I could be imagining that last part, though.

"This is Prince Orlando of Monaco," Stella goes on, and I do a silly bow which emits a giggle out of them.

Except for the girl with the pink glasses. Naturally, I assume that's Anya. Like mother, like daughter, I don't do well on first impressions.

"Hello," one of the girls says, coming forward. "I am Princess Clara of Denmark and this is my sister, Princess Freja. Oh, and that's Anya."

"Princess Anya," Anya says, annoyed. She tosses the iPad aside and comes right up to me. "Are you my mother's boyfriend?"

"Uh," I say, glancing at Stella. She shakes her head oh-so-subtly. "No?"

"Oh," she says. "That's good. She doesn't need a man."

What the hell is with the sass on this girl?

I lean into Stella and whisper, "She takes after you. I like her."

"Anya," Stella warns. "Show Orlando here some respect. One day he will rule the entire country of Monaco."

"Monaco is built on gambling and cars," Clara says, speaking up. "I learned that in school."

"Well, it's also one of the best countries for investment into clean energy," I tell her.

Stella nudges me with her elbow, her way of telling me not to get into a pissing match with her eight-year-old niece.

"Do you like cats?" Anya asks.

"Do I like cats?" I repeat. "What kind of a question is that? I *love* cats. In fact, I have a cat. His name is Sir Mokey of Monaco."

Anya purses her lips and then looks at her mom. "Is that true?"

Stella laughs. "Yes, it's true. I've met the cat."

Anya gasps as if horrified. "You met a cat and you didn't tell me!?"

"We have a pig!" Clara says loudly, gesturing to Snarf Snarf in the corner. "He used to be really small but now he's big and fat."

"Yes, Snarf Snarf and I have been acquainted," I tell her, and my arm starts to throb with the memory of pain.

"I want to know more about your cat," Anya says, putting her hands on her hips. "Can I see him?"

"Sweetie, he's in Monaco," Stella interjects.

"With the cars and gambling and clean energy investments," I point out.

Anya still doesn't seem to believe me. "I wish I had a cat," she grumbles, and then she goes back over to the iPad and sits down on the floor.

I glance at Stella, brows raised. I don't have a lot of experience with kids and I'm not sure how that went but she just pats my arm reassuringly.

"She likes you," Stella says to me after we leave the room.

"She likes the idea of my cat," I point out.

"Just take what you can get, trust me."

Speaking of taking what I can get, what I really want now is to go upstairs and explore my new room—specifically the bed—but before I get a chance to try and seduce Stella, Maja interrupts us and tells us that lunch is served.

I sit down across from Stella and then the children come in, gathering around one end of the table and staring at me suspiciously, while Aurora and Aksel are at the other side. An older woman I don't recognize pushes in a crib playpen type thing on wheels, where the twins are standing. They're boys about a year old, looking around the room with goofy smiles on their faces, their eyes the same blue as Stella and Aksel.

"Twins, huh," I comment. "My siblings are twins." I look down the table at the girls. "You're all going to be in for some weird times. Twins have mutant superpowers."

"Orlando," Stella admonishes me with a dirty look.

I shrug. "It's true."

"Are your twins your real full siblings, because Emil and Lars are our half-brothers," Clara says.

"They're my half-siblings too," I tell them. "Matilde and Francis."

"Did your father remarry? Ours did after our mother died," Clara says, then flashes Aurora a sweet smile.

"He did. My mother died too," I tell them, and from the look Stella is giving me, I think she might be realizing for the first time how similar all our stories are. "But my stepmother is a lovely person, just as Aurora is."

Aurora gives me a grateful smile though Aksel doesn't seem all that impressed.

"But yeah," I add, because I don't know when to quit, "there's always a good twin and an evil twin, so be sure to figure out which one is which when they're young."

Everyone turns to look at the twins.

After lunch, when I'm attempting to steal Stella away, we're accosted by Anya. She takes my hand and leads me to the library room, the very room I did some pretty naughty stuff to her mother, and sits me down on the couch. She insisted that Stella let us have a moment alone, which makes me think she's going to give me the third-degree about being her mother's boyfriend or something, something I'll have to continuously deny. Unless she breaks me. She seems like the type of kid that could break you.

"I want to have a talk with you," Anya says, pacing in front of me.

"Okay," I give her a big smile and over her shoulder I can see Stella's shadow just lurking out of sight. I'm not sure if she can hear us or not. "Let's talk. I'm happy to talk to you, I've heard so much about you from—"

"I want to know about your cat. Sir Mokey."

I can't help but laugh. "My cat?"

"Yes. What color is he?"

"He's orange."

"Just orange or are there some kind of stripes on him?"

"Uh, well, he's got stripes. For sure. Orange with orange-ish stripes."

"I would have called him Michael Stripes."

"Like the singer from REM?"

"Who is that?"

"Never mind."

"Why did you call him Mokey?"

"I used to watch a TV show when I was young. I went to America for a few summers, there was a show with puppets called Fraggle Rock."

"Puppets or muppets?"

"You know who the muppets are?"

"Who doesn't?" she says with a roll of her eyes. "So Mokey was on this show and looks like a cat."

"Actually, Mokey on the show was grey and was a she. I just liked the name."

"You're terrible at naming animals."

I give her a defensive look. "I am not."

"Orlando, I need you to talk to my mother and get me a cat."

I knew this was where this was going.

"I can try but she's been very adamant against them."

"She says she's allergic. Is that true?"

"I did hear her sneeze a few times in Cyprus. Anyway, I shouldn't be having this discussion with you, though I am flattered that you think I have sway over your mother."

She stops pacing and peers at me. I mean, she like really studies me, her eyes working hard under those glasses, trying to figure something out. Finally she says, "I have faith in you, Prince Orlando. You'll do the right thing." She waves her hand at me. "You are dismissed."

I watch as she leaves the room, going past her mother with her head held high.

Stella comes back inside, looking awestruck.

"Wow," she says, flopping down on the couch beside me.

"I am sorry you had to go through that, but it was far too entertaining to stop."

"She's quite single-minded," I tell her.

"Believe me I know. At least this time it's just a cat."

"It's been worse?" I ask her. I put my arm around her, testing the waters. When I feel like I get the go-ahead, I pull her close to me and she rests her head against my chest.

This feels *nice*.

"Oh yes," she says. "After her father and I divorced, she was so set on getting me remarried. All she wanted was for me to have another boyfriend or husband. She was obsessed."

"Really? Was she being a little matchmaker?"

"The best she could. She was a lot younger, of course, but she would ask me every single day when she was getting a new father. Or when I was getting a new husband."

"Sheesh. That's got to hit deep."

"It did. And it was embarrassing since she would actually stop men on the street and ask them to date me."

I laugh. "That I would have loved to see. I'm sure someone took her up on the offer." I kiss the top of her head, breathing in her sweet scent. "I can't imagine dating being difficult for you."

She snorts. "Give me a break."

"I mean it. You're gorgeous, Stella. And smart. And funny."

"I'm a single mom."

"So? Why let that define you? It's just a part of you, not who you are as a whole."

"Well, maybe you're strange because you aren't bothered by it or maybe it's because I'm carrying your child, but most men do care." She glances up at me. "Dating sucked, it just did. It was hard for me to open up because my husband screwed me over so much. I became closed-off to the idea of loving anyone ever again. And men were running the other way, anyway. It's not like I could woo them and win them over before they found out about Anya. My status as a divorcee and single mom were splashed all over the damn world."

"I know a lot about that."

"But you were called The Royal Rogue. That's almost complimentary."

"It was until it wasn't."

"Well you're treated better than I am. Probably has a lot to do with being a male. It's easier to take cheap shots at women, especially mothers."

"If anyone else takes a cheap shot at you, I'll ruin them. I promise you that. And whatever men turned you down in the past because of your status, they're the world's biggest idiots and I owe them a lot."

"You owe them?"

"You wouldn't be with me otherwise. We found each other at the right time."

She seems to mull that over, thinking. "I know I said this earlier, but I'm really glad you came back."

"So am I," I tell her, pulling her in for a deep kiss. "So am I."

She kisses me back and our lips and mouths begin to move with hunger and urgency, a sharp current of need running through my body.

"Let's go to your new room," she says to me, getting to her feet and holding her hand out.

I take it.

We head upstairs.

CHAPTER 13

ORLANDO

I'm nervous.

I shouldn't be.

When it comes to sex, it's something I know I do well. While I've been callous with lovers in the past, I've always made sure the woman enjoys herself. But when it came to actual feelings, well, I looked the other way. It was never an issue, at least not for me. Sex was an act of pleasure, of release. But suddenly, despite the fact that I know what Stella feels like when she comes, despite the fact that she's carrying my child, as I lead her upstairs through the palace to the bedroom, I feel like it's my first time.

Okay, it's not exactly like *that*. But there's a lot of pressure that wasn't there before.

I squeeze Stella's hand as I lead her down the hall and she squeezes mine back. I feel like a lot, no, *so much*, is at stake now and the feelings I have for her are growing more and more complicated with each passing second.

The easiest feeling to manage right now should be lust. The longing and the yearning for Stella over the last few months, my body's desperate urge to be with her, connect with her, feel her skin, is more than palpable.

I have to remember to keep myself in check. If I let my lust and desire take control, I'll operate on a purely primal level and I'm not sure how Stella would feel about that.

In fact, as we step inside her bedroom and she closes the door behind me, I note the anxious look on her face, the way she's worrying her bottom lip between her teeth.

"Are you okay?" I ask her softly. I'm torn between wanting to chuck her on the bed and have my way with her, and also giving her all the space she needs while being as respectful as possible. I'm not about to make any assumptions about what she wants.

She nods, giving me a quick smile. "I am. I'm just..."

"I get it," I tell her quickly. "You know, we don't have to do anything but talk. I'm here for awhile. There's no rush at all, baby mama."

She purses her lips in such a cute way that it takes everything in me not to kiss her, not to devour her right here on the spot.

"Is that what you want?" she asks.

I can't help the grin spreading across my face. I am a terrible liar. "No. It's not what I want."

With a raised brow, she takes a step toward me, still nervous, still tentative, but curious. There's tension brewing between us, sexual and otherwise, and it seems to grow thicker with each passing second, making the air in the room feel heavy and fraught with complication.

All these desires, all these needs.

"Why don't you tell me what you want," she says. Her voice starts off soft and as each word follows, becomes louder and more confident.

I get what she's doing. She's putting the focus off of her and on to me.

"I can do that," I tell her. Already my dick is fighting against my fly, thinking of all the dirty things I want to do and say.

"But I want you to strip as you do it," she quickly adds and then lets out a little laugh. Like she's still nervous but now more empowered.

"Are you saying you want me to strip and talk dirty to you, while you remain fully-clothed, just watching me?"

She nods, biting that lip again. God damn it, this is going to be hard (no pun intended).

"I have to say, I feel a little exploited at the moment," I tell her, slowly unbuttoning the top button of my shirt.

"Too bad," she says. She turns in a sassy little way and goes over to the bed where she sits down on the end. With the crook of her finger, she beckons me over. When I get close enough she puts her hand out to tell me to stop.

"Slowly," she says playfully. I oblige, undoing each button deliberately, teasing her. "Tell me what you want to do with me. I mean, really want."

I swallow hard. Jesus. She's gone from demure to playing hardball in a few seconds. But I guess if she feels in control, then she feels less anxious about the whole thing.

And to be honest, I'm finding this hot as fuck. She can ogle me all she wants.

"What don't I want to do to you?" I say, reaching the last button on the shirt and letting it lie open against my chest before very slowly taking it off. This must be what a stripper feels like, and I don't hate it.

I give her a lazy smile. "I aim to make you turn pink from the the tops of your cheeks down to your pussy."

It works. She's starting to flush a beautiful pink.

"Get you all nice and wet," I go on. "Make sure you're creaming your panties before I even lay a finger on you. Don't think I can do it?" I pause, letting the shirt fall to the ground.

"Just watch me." I reach down and rub my hand over my cock, closing my eyes at the feel. Even through the fabric of my pants, it's setting me off like dynamite. I let a loud groan fall from my lips. I don't give a fuck if she's watching, in fact I'm *loving* it.

I open my eyes and glance at her as I slowly bring my hand back up over the thick imprint of my dick. She's breathing heavier now, biting her lip in such a way that I'm sure she'll make it bleed. Her eyes are glued to the outline of my erection.

I grin, feeling like more of a king than a prince.

"You like that?" I say through a moan. "You want to see it? See what you're doing to my cock? All the dirty thoughts I'm having of you, of flipping you over on that bed facedown, and pulling off your clothes. I'll start licking and nipping at the back of your legs, the back of your knees, up your sensitive, soft thighs until I reach that perfect ass of yours. You want to know what I'll do then?"

I reach for my belt, carefully unbuckling it.

"What?" she asks, her voice in a husky whisper, eyes on my belt.

"Use this," I tell her, whipping the belt out. "Spank those perfect cheeks until they're as pink as your pussy."

Her eyes go as wide as saucers.

I go on, enjoying this far too much. "I know the thought is turning you on right now. I know you're soaking the bed just sitting there, aren't you? That tight little cunt is just dying for my cock, needing to come around it, milk me dry." I begin to slowly, deliberately, undo my fly. "I can smell how desperate you are for me right now. Smells like heaven."

She doesn't say anything but that flush on her face keeps spreading, now to her chest in blotches, her chest that is heaving with each labored breath. I'm undoing her all right here, right now, without even laying a finger on her.

My pants fall to the ground. My cock juts out, thick and heavy, the tip shining with precum.

"But maybe you'll have to wait," I tell her, stepping out of my pants and taking a step toward her. I make a fist over my cock and start sliding it to the tip, before letting it run back down to the hilt, the precum making everything slick.

I moan loudly, my eyes pinched shut, my ass cheeks flexing as I slowly start to fuck my hand.

Back and forth.

In and out.

My fist gets tighter, my balls start aching.

I start to push harder, jerking off in front of her, prepared to come all over.

"Stop," she manages to say.

I open my eyes and look at her. Now I'm breathing heavily, my vision a bit blurred. My heart is thumping in my head and I want nothing more than to follow through and keep going, keep going until I'm coming right in front of her.

It takes great effort, but I manage to stop. "What?" I ask hoarsely.

"I want you to come inside me," she says.

"Oh really?" I raise my brow. "Maybe I'm not done telling you what I want to do to you? How I want to soothe the belt marks with my tongue. I want to spread those pink and tender cheeks of yours and lick up that heavy cream, eat you, devour you, suck you down until you're begging to come in my mouth. And then I'll stop. I'll make you wait." I take another step toward her so that I'm right in front of her. She could suck my cock if she wanted to and by the way she's looking at it, I think she does. She's a hungry one, this princess. I want to fuck all that hunger out of her.

I peer down at her. "Is that what you wanted to hear?"

Her breath is ragged as she speaks, licking her lips. "What happens after you stop?"

With a grunt, I reach out and grab the back of her head, pulling it toward me until her mouth is inches from my swollen tip. "How about you tell *me* this time?"

"How about I show you?" she counters.

Then she reaches out and grabs my cock, making a fist in front of mine, slowly pushing it through her very wet, full lips.

Fuck.

It feels like the wind is knocked out of me, just from her touch, the tension sizzling through me and I'm being unraveled. As she starts to suck me off, her lips and tongue sliding over the stiff length of my cock, teasing the hard ridge underneath and sucking my tip, I'm starting to lose control of my thoughts, of everything. All that's taking over is this primal need to come.

But I manage to pull myself in. As much as I would love to come inside Stella's gorgeous mouth, this is about her. This is about making her feel good, about strengthening that connection between us. I don't want it to be one-way, I want to get lost in her body the same way she'll get lost in mine.

"Wait," I tell her, placing my hand over hers and pulling my cock away. "Stop. I need to be inside you."

She stares up at me through her dark lashes, her mouth open and wet and wanting. "I told you that earlier."

"I thought you wanted me to torture you. You see, I take your commands very seriously. Like it's my job to listen to what Her Royal Highness wants."

"I want you. Now. Come inside me."

Fuck. That's all I needed to hear.

I bring her mouth to mine and I lose it. I lose all composure, lose all rational thought. I practically devour her, my mouth covering hers, messy, wet and wild, fucking her with my tongue.

"Your wish is my command," I tell her in a gasp, breaking apart enough to bring her sweater over her head.

She quickly pulls off her bra and leggings—no panties this time—and lies back, naked.

I take in the sight of her body. So beautiful, her fair skin, her curves, the way she fits with me, like she was made just for me.

But there's not enough time to let the sight sink in.

My urges have a mind of their own.

I pounce on her, my hands roaming over her naked body, her skin smooth under my palms, my cock begging for her.

"What ever you ask, I'll give it to you," I tell her, my mouth ravishing her neck, her chest, lips moving against her hot skin. "Say the word. It's what I'm here for."

She gasps, writhing beneath me. "You make it sound like it's your job."

"It is. I fuck like it's my job because I've taken it upon myself to make you, Princess Stella, come as hard as possible."

And with that, I'm spreading her legs and pushing inside her.

We both gasp at once. It's hot, tight, slick.

I know I had all these devious, dirty plans, all these things I wanted to do, but in the end it doesn't matter. I just want us to come together.

Now.

I start pumping into her, sliding in and out, a lewd wet noise filling the room and spurring me on, my ass getting a workout as I thrust into her.

She moans and digs her nails into my back.

I fuck her faster.

Slide my hand over her clit.

She's off like a bomb, crying out my name, her body jerking from the spasms, her words breathless and fevered.

It's enough to do the same to me. With a jagged cry that feels ripped from my lungs, I'm coming inside her.

I'm feeling...*everything.*

All at once. This woman, what she means to me, how she makes me feel. Our uncertain future, a future I want to try desperately to figure out.

It all comes through me in a cascade of pleasure and emotion until I don't know which way is up.

But I know she's the way.

By the time it's all over, I nearly collapse on her. Our bodies are hot to touch and slick with sweat.

I kiss her, tasting her, then roll over. Breathless.

"You sure know how to do your job," she says after a few minutes. My heart rate is starting to slow. I'm coming back to earth.

She's by my side.

🐾

A FEW DAYS LATER I CALL IN A FAVOR TO MATILDE.

The day after that, a man shows up at the palace door holding a small cat carrier.

I suppose I should have cleared this all with Aksel first but oh well.

"What the?" Maja says, turning around and holding the carrier. "Orlando, is this for you?"

I put my finger to my mouth. "Shhh. It's a surprise."

"I'll say." She hands the carrier to me and I can see Mokey's yellow eyes peering at me from inside.

"Hey Mokey."

"I'm not sure the King is going to like this," she says with a sniff, eyeing the carrier with disdain.

"It's not for the King," I tell her. "It's for Anya."

"Then I'm not sure Stella is going to like this."

"We'll see," I say, giving her a cocky grin.

Though most of my confidence is pure bravado. I don't know if Stella will like this at all and Mokey might be on the first plane back to Monaco.

I do know Stella is in the sitting room, helping Anya with her homework, so my plan is to bypass Aksel and Aurora and go straight to the source. If I could go to Anya without her mother there, even better.

But when I enter the room, everyone is there.

Not just Stella and Anya, but Aksel, Aurora and all their children. The adults are sitting around drinking (minus my baby mama, of course), the kids are flipping through some books and scrolling through an iPad.

And now everyone is looking at me and the cat carrier in my hand.

"Orlando," Aksel booms. It's been a few days with him now and he's still not my biggest fan. "Please tell me you don't have a cat in there."

Anya shrieks something in Danish and gets to her feet, running over to me.

"Is this Sir Mokey of Monaco?" she asks, jumping up and down so excitedly that her glasses fall off and she doesn't even bother to pick them up.

"It sure is," I tell her.

"Don't you dare let that cat out of the cage," Aksel says.

"Oh come on," Aurora chides him. "You let the girls have a pig. What's a little cat?"

"Aurora, stop being an enabler," he shoots back at her.

"I'm *allergic*," Stella says but everyone is ignoring her now because we all know she's not.

I crouch down to put the cage on the floor and hand Anya her glasses. Then I open the cage door.

Anya slips her glasses on and immediately plops down

cross-legged on the floor as Mokey pokes his head out cautiously.

She squeals and scoops him up in her arms, cooing over him. Clara and Freja abandon their books and come running over, all of them fighting to see him up close.

I leave them where they are and go over to Stella on the couch, avoiding the death glares I'm getting from Aksel, even though when I sit down next to her, Stella shoots me a Danish death glare of her own.

"Sorry," I say feebly. "I just figured that maybe Anya would like to meet Mokey."

"I can't believe you had him flown up here," Aurora comments. "That's really, really sweet."

I glance at Stella and see her glare is starting to fade, her brow becoming soft.

"I did it for Anya," I add.

"I know."

"Which also means I did it for you."

Her brow quirks up. "Oh, is that how this works?"

"Maybe?"

"You know, she's not going to let that cat leave."

I nod. "I know. That's why I thought I would give Mokey to her."

"What?"

"*What?*" Aksel repeats, sitting up straighter. Aurora elbows him.

"Orlando," Stella says in a hush. "You can't give up your cat."

"I can if it makes Anya happy. Plus, it's not like I won't see the cat. At any rate, I wanted to ask you first."

"How considerate," Aksel comments dryly.

"I'll think about it," Stella says, her attention going back to Anya and Mokey, who seem to be totally in love with each other. She sighs. "Would you look at them? Look how happy you made her."

But I'm the one who's happy here. I'm grinning ear to ear.

I hear Aksel groan. "You're going to give her the cat, aren't you Stella?"

She tries to shrug nonchalantly but she has the most sly smile on her lips. She reaches out and grabs my hand, giving me a grateful look. *Thank you,* she mouths.

Aksel groans even louder, sinking back into his chair. "This is going to be a long month."

CHAPTER 14
ORLANDO

"Well, well, well if it isn't the mysterious Prince Orlando," Francis says as he opens the door to Matilde's house. "Aren't you a sight for sore eyes?"

Matilde pops her head out from behind him and frowns at me. "You *are* looking good, brother," she says. "Or is it because I haven't seen you in forever?"

"A little from column A, a little from column B," I say, gesturing to the door. "Can I come in or are you both going to stand there like the twins from The Shining, ogling your big brother? I have to admit, it's kind of weird."

Francis rolls his eyes and opens the door. "Come in. Sit down. You have a lot of explaining to do."

I walk inside Matilde's house. Francis used to live here with her—they both moved here when they were old enough to get out of the palace—but now he has his own apartment. It's actually near mine, down by the marina, but I don't see him as often as I should.

Of course, that's one of the reasons why I called them up and asked to meet. I've been MIA for most of the month and, as Francis said, I have a lot of explaining to do. They just have no idea what I'm about to tell them.

"Here, sit, want a beer?" Matilde asks, as she pretty much shoves me down into her couch. I sink into the cushions.

"It's barely noon," I tell her.

"So? Do you want a beer?"

"Of course."

"Me too," Francis says, sitting down in an overstuffed armchair across from me. The two of them bought it from some antique shop in Nice, the only royals I know who like to go antiquing. It's not a large house but Matilde has managed to cram every single corner of it with vintage pieces and heirlooms and bric-a-brac from all around the world. There are also Turkish rugs and Danish tapestries, lanterns from Nepal and bronze statues from Malta, plus a load of pottery and woven bowls from various places in Africa. It's a cool spot and being here I always feel a little more grounded. But that's Matilde's way, too.

"Beer?" I question, looking Francis up and down. "I thought you were watching your figure?"

"Fuck that," he says. "I've turned over a new leaf. If a man can't handle me with a beer belly, he can't handle me at all." He puts his hands on his stomach and jiggles his stomach around. He has put some weight on lately, but I think it suits him and he carries it well.

"Cheers to that," Matilde says, juggling three beers as she comes out of the kitchen. She hands us both one and then sits down on the couch beside me, tucking a leg under her, her gauzy hippie skirt flowing over most of the couch.

I hold out my bottle and they reach out and clink against it.

"Cheers," Francis says. We all have a long draw from the bottles and then he clears his throat. "So, Orlando, what made you call this meeting of the Monégasque monarchy?"

I smirk at that. I love alliteration. "I haven't seen you guys in a long time."

"And why is that?" Matilde asks. "For the last month, every time I've asked where you are, you've been in Copenhagen."

"I've come back a few times," I protest feebly.

"So what is so interesting about Copenhagen?" Francis asks with a twinkle in his eye. "I've talked to mother and father about you and they keep saying you're there to learn about rally driving from King Aksel? And I don't know how they're buying it but we're not buying it."

"You've been seeing Princess Stella," Matilde says. "I thought she lived in England, though. Have you really been in Copenhagen?"

"I have. And she happens to live at the palace now, too."

"Why?"

I sigh. "It's a long story."

"Does this long story have something to do with all the explaining you owe us?"

I nod slowly, taking another gulp of my beer. Even though I've spent most of the last month living with Stella in Copenhagen, flying down here on the weekends to make sure I'm seen with Zoya or at public events, the pregnancy thing is still something I'm getting used to. Don't get me wrong, I absolutely love being there for Stella and seeing how she's progressing, I love being so involved. But Amalienborg Palace is its own little bubble and every time I step out of it, I'm met with the reality that the rest of the world has no idea what's going on.

Which is why I finally found the guts to tell my siblings the truth.

More than that, I need their advice with what to do about Zoya.

Because she needs to know the truth, too.

And this is going to *hurt*.

"Spill it," Matilde says. "We don't have all day."

"Well, I do," Francis admits. "Not all of us have Skype meetings with their charities in Zimbabwe."

"Mali," she corrects him. "Though Zimbabwe is a prospect."

"Look, the longer we talk, the less Orlando has to talk," Francis says to her and then he jerks his head at me. "You heard what your sister said, spill the beans."

"Okay," I say, taking in a shaking breath. The twins exchange a worried glance. I guess I'm not normally nervous like this, especially around them. "I have something I need to tell you, that very few people know about."

Another glance goes between them. Then they both look at me with prompting eyes, in unison. Their twin shit can be very persuasive sometimes.

"Here goes," I say, finishing the rest of my beer and putting it down on the coffee table with a clank. "I've been seeing Princess Stella."

"Not shit, Sherlock," Francis says.

"Let him finish," Matilde hushes him while delivering an elbow into his side.

"I've been seeing Princess Stella and things have grown pretty serious between us. And when I say they've grown, I mean it."

They stare at me blankly.

I go on. "Grown as in, she's growing a baby. My baby. She's pregnant with my baby."

"Noooooo," Francis exclaims after a moment, his hand at his chest.

"Oh my god," says Matilde, her dark eyes going round as saucers. "Oh my god. Orlando! Are you serious?"

"Oh, I'm serious."

"This is a big deal!"

"This is a very serious, crazy, complicated, fucked-up deal."

"I'll say," Francis says, shaking his head in awe. "Wow. I mean, wow. Okay so give us all the details."

"How far along is she?"

"Do you know the sex?"

"What does the King think?"

"Does she look pregnant?"

"Do you think the kid will learn French or Danish first?"

"Oh my god," Matilde says softly, after all of that. "Have you told Zoya?"

I wince at that. "One thing at a time."

I go on to answer all their rapid-fired questions, the ones I can anyway because, honestly, I have no idea what language the kid will speak (I'm guessing Danish) and no we don't know the sex yet.

Also no... I haven't told Zoya.

"What are you going to do?" Matilde asks. "I mean, obviously you do have to tell her and soon. I just don't know what you're going to say."

"Yeah, what are you going to say?" Francis asks.

I shake my head. "I have no clue. I figured I'd tell you and then you would give me advice."

Francis scoffs incredulously. "Listen, brother, I can give you advice on the best places to eat in Paris and Lisbon, I can tell you that you need to start incorporating a little more color into your wardrobe, and I can tell you that reality TV is the best TV. But I can't give you advice on how to break the news to your fake Russian girlfriend that your Princess mistress is carrying your baby. That is way beyond my pay grade."

I glance at Matilde, my brows raised hopefully.

"Nuh uh," she says. "This is something you have to figure out on your own. All I know is that you need to tell her.

Right away. Soon Stella will be showing, and people will wonder. And beneath it all, Zoya is your friend. She deserves to know and will be hurt when she finds out you've been keeping it from her."

"Maybe because she's my friend, she'll understand?"

They exchange another glance, this one unreadable.

"You're going to have to break up with Zoya," Francis says. "Unless you want to have this baby a secret forever, which, as we all know, isn't what you want and isn't a very Orlando thing to do. You're going to have to break it off. Get together with Stella. Hopefully marry her. At least in the end, father will be ecstatic because you finally have an heir, hopefully a boy, but I bet he could rewrite that rule, too. You know he's never really cared whether it came from Zoya or not. It was always about the fate of the country."

"And the fate of the country is in your hands," Matilde and I imitate our father in unison.

I lean back into the couch, feeling mentally exhausted. Who knew the truth would be so damn hard?

"I don't think Zoya is going to take it very well," I admit.

"You don't say," Francis comments with a wry smile. "If I were you, I'd wear some padding. Make sure to hide all her tennis rackets before you spill the truth."

I let out a dry laugh. He's right. She's going to freak the fuck out. But I'm not so much worried about that as I am about hurting her. I don't want to put her in any danger, I don't want her to think that I don't care about her, because I do. It's just my responsibilities have changed now, and I have changed with them.

Shit. This is going to fucking suck.

"Where is Zoya now?" Matilde asks.

"At home."

"With Sir Mokey of Monaco?" asks Francis.

"No, he's been relocated. He's living in Denmark now."

"Wow. The cat moved in before you did."

"Orlando." Matilde places her hand on my shoulder. "Go home. Tell her now. Get it over with."

I give her a pleading look that says, *do I have to?*

But I know I do.

I thank my sister for the beers, give both of them a hug and then I'm getting in my car (a black Ferrari, which I'm starting to think might need an upgrade if I'm going to fit a baby seat in there), and zipping across the length of our tiny little country all the way back to my penthouse. It takes about twenty minutes so I'm back home before I'm ready. Times like this, I wish the country was a lot bigger.

The lift whisks me up to the penthouse in seconds and I spend a good minute standing outside the door, gathering my courage.

I finally unlock it and step inside.

I can hear commotion from the kitchen and see Zoya standing there with a big butcher knife in her hand.

That can do *so* much more damage than a tennis racket.

"Hi," she says brightly and uses the knife to point to the table with a roast chicken on it that's been hacked away at. "I got us chicken for lunch." She puts her other hand on her hip and stares at the poultry with disappointment. "Unfortunately, they've thrown away the heart and the liver and the gizzards."

"Yes, so very unfortunate."

"Back at home we would never waste such things," she says, shaking her head at me, as if this is my doing somehow. "You don't know how to appreciate the best parts of the bird."

"I guess I need to work on that."

She frowns at me. "Are you okay?"

"I need to talk to you."

"Sure," she says uneasily.

"I need you to put the knife down and come with me," I say, jerking my chin to the door.

I swear the grip on the knife tightens for a moment. She's such a fighter.

"Okay." She reluctantly puts the knife beside the chicken carcass and follows me out of the room, to the sitting area.

"Sit down," I tell her.

"I don't want to sit down." She folds her arms across her chest and stands up straighter, almost matching my height. Oh shit, she's already acting like this is the start of a heated match.

"Okay, then I'm going to sit down," I tell her, but I actually just go stand behind the armchair and brace myself against it. I figure putting some distance between us can't hurt.

"What's going on Orlando?"

"I need to tell you something. Something that maybe I should have told you sooner, but I just wanted to make sure how things were at the time. Where I stood."

"You're in love with Princess Stella," she says matter-of-factly.

I swallow uneasily. I haven't told Stella that. I haven't even told myself that.

But I know the answer is yes.

"Yes, " I whisper. "I'm in love with her."

This is the first time I've voiced it and hearing the words aloud makes me realize how much it's true.

It's true.

"You love her." The severity of her features melts a little. "I'm happy for you," she says softly. "Really. You deserve to know what love is like Orlando."

"I loved you, you know."

She shakes her head. "No. You didn't Orlando. And I didn't love you either. Maybe it was love at the time, for the people who we were at those moments. It was love in the only way we knew. But in time, your heart grows as you grow, and you learn a new capacity for love. The love I feel for Emily surpasses all of that. It's worth everything. I know the love you feel for Stella eclipses anything your heart has felt before, including for me. And that's a beautiful thing."

"She's pregnant," I blurt out, ruining her poetry.

She stares at me for a moment, frowning. Her mouth opens and she finally says, "What? She's *pregnant?*"

I nod. "I found out a few months ago."

"*What?* And you're only telling me now?"

"I needed to figure out what to do."

"And? So? What are you going to do?" She's starting to panic, I can tell, the anger mixing in with fear. She's wiggling her jaw, something she does right before a game.

I hope the chair offers me enough protection.

"I'm going to do the right thing."

"Which is?"

"Zoya..." I say carefully. "You and me, this whole fake thing. I can't do it anymore. It's over."

It's like all the color is drained from her face.

"It's not over...." she says, voice just a wisp. She mumbles something in Russian and then says, "No. It's not over. You can't do this to me. You can't do this to me!" Tears start to well in her eyes.

My heart breaks like I knew it would.

"I have to."

"No you don't!" she yells, marching across the room to the chair, eyes blazing and on fire. "You don't have to! You made a promise to *me*, Orlando. Do you remember that promise? You said that we could pretend. You said that you would do it for me so that Emily and I can be together."

"You can still be together. Nothing will change."

"It will change! Back home, I know people already

suspect. I've seen the rumors in the press there. They already think something is going on and as long as it just stays a rumor, I'm safe. But if you do this, I'm not safe anymore. I won't be able to hide behind you; I won't be able to be with her."

"And I won't be able to be with Stella and my child!" I yell back. "I've made promises to her, too."

"But who will be hurt by the broken promise, Orlando? Me. I can lose it all. Everything. Do you know what it's like to lose everything you care about?"

"Yes! I do. I lost my mother and she was my everything. I lost her and I still feel that loss, don't tell me I don't know what it's like."

She clamps her mouth shut for a moment, breathing hard through her nose. "I know you lost your mother. But that wasn't a choice. This is a choice. You are choosing someone new over someone you have known for a long time. You say you're loyal to the bone, but I guess that loyalty ends with me." A tear spills out from her eye and she turns around, back to me. I watch as she sobs. The only time I've seen her cry is when she loses but that's out of frustration, not sadness, not fear.

She's afraid.

I'm ruining her life.

I'm taking away her love, I'm taking away her game, I'm taking away her life.

"Maybe no one will notice," I say feebly. I reach out and put my hand on her back, tentative, like she might bite.

She continues to sob and then brushes me off, head back, walks away.

"You're a fool if you think that's true," she says. "If you leave me, I'll lose her. It's too dangerous otherwise."

"Maybe that love is worth the danger," I tell her.

Maybe my love for Stella is worth the same.

But I only have the authority to play with my own heart. I can't do this to Zoya. I can't be the one with her demise on my shoulders.

"Maybe there's some way to make it work," I manage to say.

I already feel like I'm betraying myself with just those words.

She sniffs and turns around to look at me. "How?"

I shrug. "I don't know. Maybe we can just make this all work in secret."

"And then what? You're going to still marry me? We'll have legitimate heirs to your throne, and you'll be okay with keeping Stella and your child a secret?"

Everything inside me feels like it's being ripped apart at the seams. I've never felt so powerless, hopeless, helpless.

"I don't know what else to do. I don't want to break Stella's heart..."

"Have you told her you love her?"

"No."

"Has she said she loves you?"

"Well, no."

"Do you think she does?"

I think back over the last while, all our time together. The tenderness. The easiness. Love has never come up and Stella can be hard to figure out. Sometimes I think all she's really focused on is the baby, not me.

Maybe she doesn't love you, I tell myself. *Maybe you're making this into something harder than it has to be. It was your idea to make a go of it, not hers. She seemed more than fine to have this child and keep you on the side.*

"If she doesn't," Zoya continues, "then is it worth it? Maybe put your own feelings aside for once and stop being selfish."

"Selfish?"

She shrugs before wiping away another tear. "You can still be there for her and be there for me. Maybe you're not with her romantically but that's your own heart on the line, not hers and not mine."

Only my heart on the line.

And I'm choosing my heart over everything else.

Maybe that's as fucking selfish as they get.

"You have a role to play," she says to me, hands on her lips. "The role you've been playing since birth. You're going to be the ruler of this country one day and I will give you a legitimate heir. There are going to be so many more sacrifices coming your way, that you better get used to the idea of putting your own needs aside. This isn't about what you want and what you want is Stella. This is about what you've been born to do, which is to play the role that the country needs from you. I know you may hate me for it, but this is a sacrifice you're going to have to make today."

Her words have weight to them, and they sink into my brain like a fishing line with a lure.

I'm hooked and there's no escape.

Trapped by my own promises and drowning in them.

What am I going to tell Stella?

CHAPTER 15
STELLA

y phone is ringing.

I open my eyes slowly, staring up into the dark. I can't tell what time it is or how long I've been asleep.

I reach over and grab my phone, glancing at it.

It's Orlando.

And it's only eleven p.m.

I've been conking out so early these days, I'm usually fast asleep by eight o' clock.

I clear the grogginess from my throat and answer. "Hello?"

"Hey," he says, sounding tired.

I hadn't heard from him all day, which is unusual. I knew that he was going back to Monaco to tell Zoya and his siblings the truth and I also knew that he had to do it on his own time and in his own way. I wasn't going to bug him about it.

But still, I wish he'd contacted me at some point today, just so I could know he was okay. He's been back there for a few days and it seems the longer he stays, the more sporadic our contact gets.

It makes me scared, to be honest.

Each time he went back to Monaco for an appearance of some sort, I was worried that the place – and his duties there – might pull him back in to that world. Back to his family and the people he loves.

He always came back, though. With the biggest smile on his face, he'd scoop me up in his arms and twirl me around like a couple of teenagers deeply, madly in love.

And I do love him.

I always thought that when I fell in love again, it would hit me on the side of the head one day, like I'd be slapped with it and brought to my knees.

It hasn't been like that with him.

Oh, I've been brought to my knees. But the fall was gradual and slow. My feelings for him have built up and up and up over the last month until there was no place for my feelings to go. My heart had been inside a cage before, a thick-barred cage with a heavy lock that I didn't have a key for and didn't care to pick. I let it sit in that cage and paid it no attention. The only thing my heart was good for was loving Anya and it did that very well.

But ever since I found out I was pregnant, my heart began to swell against the bars. It grew and turned a beautiful shade of red. I began to notice my heart more and more every day.

It was growing for my baby.

It was growing for Orlando.

I don't know when it happened, but one day I realized I loved him. A slow, languid feeling that rushed through my veins like drugs in an IV drip. The feeling never stopped, and my heart was let free from the cage, too big now to be contained.

I love him. I truly do.

I love him truly, madly, deeply.

And the only fear I have now is that I'm not sure if he feels the same way. He's definitely sweet and tender and affectionate to me. His words are romantic, and his eyes are sincere. But Orlando is still a boy in so many ways and I feel like his past, his family, keeps him tethered, unable to grow. I'm afraid that he might not really know what love is.

I want to tell him how I truly feel but I don't know how. I just keep thinking that maybe my heart is big enough for the three of us.

"Are you there?" he asks.

I'm brought back to reality. I clear my throat again, "Yes, I'm here," I say into the phone, loving the sound of his voice. It's like an anchor. "Sorry, I just woke up."

"Long day?"

"Kind of. I didn't do much except watch that damn Disney Descendants movie three times in a row. The girls are all so obsessed and I don't know why. None of the guys are attractive."

"I wouldn't try and dissect the minds of young girls that much," he says. "Seems like a frightening place. How is Sir Mokey?"

"Fine. He sleeps a lot."

"Is he sleeping with you right now?"

"No," I say.

But that's a lie. He's curled up at the foot of the bed, completely oblivious to me talking on the phone. Sometimes I envy him.

"I guess you're right. Otherwise you'd be sneezing, right?"

Here's the thing about my cat allergy: I'm pretty sure it went away. While I sneezed a few times in Cyprus when Orlando first picked Mokey up, I haven't since. Now everyone accuses me of making the allergy thing up, making me admit that I don't like cats.

I refuse to admit it.

Especially since Mokey has grown on me an awful lot. I used to not like cats because I hated how they wouldn't give you their love, how you had to work for it and the harder you tried, the less they cared. There was no such thing as unconditional love with them and I guess in some weird way it kind of reminded me of my mother. I want the excessive love; I want to feel adored and cared for.

I want Orlando back.

"When are you coming home?" I ask, and then realize that this isn't his home. "I mean, back here."

"I was thinking tomorrow," he says.

"Good." I say. "I miss you. What is your tattoo again? *Tu me manques?*"

There's a long pause and then he says, "Yes." His voice is low and choked.

It sends a current of fear up my spine.

"Orlando, what's wrong?"

The silence hangs in the air.

Finally he says, quietly, so quietly, "I talked with Zoya."

I take in a sharp breath. "Oh? What did she, uh, say?"

"She made me realize that...that I need to make a sacrifice. That my whole role in life is to do things I don't want to do. She..."

Oh no. No. *No.*

My heart, my big beautiful red heart, is *this* close to deflating.

"What?" I whisper. "What happened?"

"I made a promise to her, Stella. And I can't break that promise."

Everything inside me cracks, right down the middle, sand rushing into the dark and hollow places. My red heart is bleeding. The pain is cold.

"You're not breaking up with her?" I manage to say, my voice breaking.

"No."

No?

Oh god.

He goes on. "I'm sorry. I'm so sorry. I made a promise and—"

"You made a promise to me too!" I cry out, the anger lashing through me, surprising me. Mokey lifts his head in shock.

"I know, I know," he says through a groan. "I know, okay? I'm just...this is fucked up, Stella. I don't know what to do."

"You keep your promise to me!"

"If I keep my promise to you and break hers, what credibility do I have?"

"You're worried about credibility?" I shriek. "Fuck you."

"Stella. Calm down. The baby."

"What the fuck? Calm down? And don't bring the baby into this, it's obvious the baby means nothing to you."

"That's not true!" he roars through the phone and sucks in his breath. "I'll come tomorrow, and we'll talk this through."

"Wait, no. What is there to talk about?"

"I need to make this right."

"How? How are you going to make it right?"

"I made a promise that I would be by your side and that's one I'll keep. I won't desert you. I'll be there for you."

"But you won't be *with* me," I say softly. The pain is so cold and so sharp that I can barely talk. It feels like I'm dying, that crack widening, spreading me apart, filling me with ice.

I'm losing him.

I've lost him.

He's choosing someone else over me and *our* baby.

How can I ever think that his word is good? How can I ever trust him to remain in our lives?

How did I ever believe I could trust him with my heart?

Now I'm more glad than ever that I've kept my love for him a secret.

It will remain in me.

And hopefully die there.

"I want to be with you," he says. There's desperation in his voice but it means nothing to me. "Don't you see? I want you. I want to be with you and the baby in the way you need, but I can't. I just can't. So I'll have to do what I can to make sure I'm still with you as much as I can be."

Now I'm angry. It's amazing how quickly sadness can turn to anger, like it's a river looking for an outlet. The ice thaws and it's raging.

I'm raging.

"No!" I yell through the phone. "You don't get to decide anymore. You made your choice and now you're done and now this is up to me, okay? It's up to me whether you get to be in our child's life or not. I don't trust you. You've broken the trust I had. You've made your choice and it was the wrong one. The right choice wasn't even me, okay? The right choice was the baby." I choke back the tears. "The right choice was the baby."

I hear a sob on the other end. "Stella. Please."

"No. This is how it's going to be. If I need you, I'll be contacting you and that's it. You can fight it if you want but you won't get anywhere. And don't for one fucking second think that I need you, because I don't. We don't. I've been a single mom for a while, and I do a damn good job at it. So you can fuck right off with your hard choices and your roles and your fake life down in Monaco. I've got a real one up here and it's going to be even better without you in it."

And with that, I hang up.

I already feel regret at my words, but the anger pushes those feelings away. He deserved it. He broke my heart, broke my trust, he chose someone else over us. Even if I know it wasn't an easy decision, even though I know deep down where he's coming from and I know he's not a bad guy, it doesn't matter.

I have to think of the baby first.

That's the only thing that matters, not my heartache, not anything else.

He has his duties.

And I have mine.

۞

"She's ready for you now."

I look up to see Maja exiting the door to my mother's room. My hands are clasped in my lap. There's another *Hello Magazine* on the table in the waiting room and there's a headline on the front that says *When Will The Royal Rogue of Monaco Marry?* But it's taken all of my strength not to open it up.

It's been a week since Orlando ended things. Or, more accurately, didn't end things with Zoya. I've been trying hard to deal with my emotions, talking to Aurora a lot, Maja too. Aksel just wants to beat the shit out of Orlando and I think Henrik has offered to smash his acoustic over his head.

But even though I've been talking it out, I'm still not over it. Not sure that I'll ever be. And I'm feeling as lost and unmoored as ever.

Maja thought maybe it was best that I pay my mother another visit.

I figure it can't hurt.

I get up and give her an appreciative smile and step inside. My mother is in her bed now and she's not looking at me. "Are you sure?" I ask Maja, looking at her over my shoulder.

"She's tired but she's listening. Somewhere, her heart is

listening," she says before she almost closes the door, leaving it ajar a few inches.

I gingerly walk over to her bedside and take a seat in the chair beside her. Maja put a poinsettia on her bedside table, since Christmas is coming up soon.

My mother stirs a little, her head lolling on the pillow toward me, but her eyes don't open. Maybe it's better that way.

"Hey Mama," I say softly, gently placing my hand over hers. I know people say that their loved ones become strangers when they get Alzheimer's but to me that's never been the case. This hand here, this is my mother's hand, the hand that fed me, the hand that used to braid my hair, the hand that wiped away tears when Anya was born. It will never stop being my mother's hand.

A wayward tear comes to my own eye and falls off onto my arm. I don't bother to wipe it away. I'm sure more will come.

"I know we haven't talked in a while and I'm sorry for that. Things have been...things in my life have changed, things you need to know about. Things I need to tell you."

I take in a deep breath. "About a week ago I had my heart broken by a prince. I know it sounds like a fairy tale, perhaps a Grimm's fairy tale, but it's true. Once upon a time I fell in love with a prince and he secretly held my heart, even though I knew he'd break it in the end. To make things more complicated, I'm pregnant." I pause, thinking if she can hear me, this is the part where she'd take interest. But so far, nothing.

"I'm pregnant with Prince Orlando's baby," I go on. "And nothing in my life will ever be the same. I just wanted to let you know because you were such a good grandmother to Anya. You really were. And I know I was hard on you when I was growing up, but all of this is making me realize that I should have appreciated you when I had you. I shouldn't have tried to change you. I should have accepted who you were and continued to love you. I always felt like...like I wasn't deserving of your love and because of that, you weren't deserving of mine. But that's not how love works. You have to have a heart with faith in it, faith that the love will be there no matter what."

Another tear rolls down my cheek and another. "I miss you, Mama. I really do. The more that time passes the more I realize how precious time is. I would do anything to roll back the clock and go through it all again with you, love you harder, love you no matter what. I have a stubborn heart. But now I can only do that from here and hope, hope, hope that you feel me."

I'm squeezing her hand and I'm crying.

I'm crying because I miss my mother and I wish I could have her back in my life, in whatever form I can get. I wish that I knew how rare and precious it was to have her love at all and that I didn't spend so much time fretting about the amount or how she showed it. I wish I had held it to my chest and hung on, even if it felt like I was just getting a morsel at a time.

And I'm crying because I know she's not really here. She can't help me with the baby. She can't heal my heart from Orlando's absence. She probably won't get to see my child, not with the eyes that I know. I'm going to have to go through it all feeling alone and while I should be used to being alone, sometimes it really fucking sucks.

Sometimes you just want someone to love.

Sometimes you just want someone to love you.

I know what I want and what makes it harder is that Orlando is still out there. The man who has my heart. He's still in Monaco, still with Zoya. He's texted me often, called too. I try not to answer him. I definitely don't pick up the phone.

But I'm torn. I don't hate him. I'm hurt by him, and I feel betrayed, but I don't hate him. I know that's a silly statement because I'm still in love with him but it's crazy how intertwined love and hate become when emotions are high. It's like a switch gets flipped and it's hard to know which way your heart will turn. Like a waxing and waning moon, it's a heart of love or a heart of hate.

It's...complicated.

So I text him when I can, just to keep him updated on how the baby is. There isn't much to report but it's the best I can do right now. I'm not sure how things are going to proceed in the future, and I anticipate things getting harder and harder, but for now, it's best if I don't have much to do with him. He has his rights to the child, whether legally or not, but I also have to protect myself while I can.

What a fucking mess.

Time usually passes slowly when you're grieving but before I know it, Maja is opening the door and coming in the room, putting her hand on my shoulder.

"It's time to go," she says softly, taking tissue paper out of her pocketbook and handing me one. "Come on. Let's get the both of you home."

I can't help but smile at that.

I put my hand on my stomach, which hasn't started showing to others yet, though I definitely notice it myself.

We go home.

❧❧❧

TWO DAYS LATER I WAKE UP IN THE MIDDLE OF THE NIGHT from an awful nightmare.

Only it's not a nightmare at all, it's just the truth hitting me over and over again.

I realize that I have to tell Anya about the baby.

I've been waiting for the right time, the right opportunity. But there never seems to be a right time to have the talk. I know I might not ever have the right answers to tell her when she asks who the father is or if he's going stay around or if he's going to end up like her own father, someone that only pops his head up on birthdays and holidays. Someone who doesn't really give a shit, someone who constantly breaks her heart.

But now I know, that this is it. There is no Orlando, not really. It's just me and her against the world, just as before, but this time with baby in tow.

The triangle is the strongest shape.

Even though it's the middle of the night, I get out of bed, throw on a robe to protect me from the drafts in this palace, and head down the hall.

Her door is open, and the night light illuminates the room. She wants Mokey to sleep with her, but I don't want her around cat dander that much, so I've forbidden it. To my relief, the cat isn't in here. Sometimes I think he's sleeping with Maja when he isn't with me. She seems to have taken a shine to him, even though she won't admit it. She sneaks herring to him every morning at breakfast.

"Mama?" Anya asks softly as I walk into the room. "What time is it?" She yawns, which makes me yawn.

"It's the middle of the night."

"Are you okay?" She sits up straighter. "Is Mokey okay?"

"Mokey is fine," I tell her, sitting on the edge of the bed. "I just had a dream and I wanted to talk to you about it."

She frowns and reaches for her glasses on the bedside table, slipping them on. "Okay. What kind of dream?"

"Well it wasn't so much a dream as it was this nagging feeling. You know the ones you get when your subconscious is trying to tell you something?"

"Like I didn't give Patches enough hugs?"

Patches is the name of her pony that stays at a nearby stable. Since she's still learning, I opted to get her the roundest, friendliest, oldest horse possible, an ex-lesson horse that needed a good home. One day, when she gets better at it and if she gets more serious, then we'll spend the big bucks but until then it's sweet, fat, ornery Patches.

"Yeah, like that," I tell her. "Anyway, sweetheart, there's something that's been happening to me and I've wanted to share it with you, but I didn't know the details. I didn't know how I felt about it and it's all so very complicated. But you're a big girl and you're old enough and so I think it's time to let you know."

"This couldn't wait until morning?" she asks dryly.

I pat her arm. "You make a good point. But now that I'm here, aren't you curious?"

"Sure. Is this something to do with your *condition?*" She says the last word dramatically.

"You remember that?"

She rolls her eyes. "Everyone in this house is always talking about your condition. I thought maybe you were hit in the head or something and didn't realize it."

I can't help but chuckle. "No, I wasn't hit in the head, though it sure feels like it sometimes." I pause. "Anya, I'm going to have a baby."

Her eyes widen and she jolts back in her bed. "Right now?"

"No," I say quickly, putting my hands on her legs to hold her down. "Not right now. Next year."

"You're pregnant?" she says. She makes a face. "Why?"

I manage a smile. "I don't know why. I guess the same reason I got pregnant with you. Just what life had in store for me."

She makes a more contorted face. "Is it Papa's baby? Is he the father?"

"No," I tell her, shaking my head. "Your father will still be around..."

"He's never around."

"But it's not him."

"Who is it then? Will he be around? Will he be a better father?"

Jeez. She's really digging in deep.

"Maybe," I say, ignoring the hollow pain in my chest. "But the most important part isn't that, it's that you get to be an older sister and we're going to have the best family ever."

"But who is it?" she repeats. Then her eyes go wide. "Your boyfriend!" she gasps. "It's Orlando!"

"He's not my boyfriend." Why am I even getting defensive with my daughter?

Grow up, Stella.

"But it's him," she says. "He's the baby daddy."

"Look, I don't really want to get into why and how you know the phrase baby daddy at your age but yes. He is the daddy."

"He's already a better dad than dad."

"First of all, he's not your dad and second of all, what makes you think that?"

"Mokey," she cries out. "He gave me my cat. That's more than you ever did."

"Anya," I warn. "You got a horse and now a cat."

"You made me move from warm, tropical England to cold and rainy Denmark."

"Okay, now I think you're the one who got hit in the head," I tell her, reaching over to put the back of my hand against her forehead. She's fine.

"So what do I have to do?" she asks.

"What do you mean?"

"I'm going to be the big sister; I have to prepare."

"Oh. Well, I don't think you need to do anything but be exactly who you are."

"I don't want to share Patches with her. Or Mokey."

"We don't know if it's a her yet."

"Oh I can tell. It's a her."

"What else can you tell?" I ask her, amused.

"That I might be the best big sister in the world. But I'm going to need to do my homework about this."

I have to admire her gusto. "Tell you what, I'll get a book for you that tells you how to be a good big sister."

"Not good. The best!"

"The best then." I laugh and kiss her on the forehead, my heart swelling for the first time in days. Just the two of us will soon be just the three of us and maybe that's all we really need. Maybe we're going to be more than okay. "Thank you for being so understanding."

She grins at me. "It's okay. It's my job."

I kiss her again and then leave the room, laughing to myself as I go. The minute I hit the sheets, I'm out like a light, falling into a deep, peaceful sleep.

CHAPTER 16
ORLANDO
ETHIOPIA

Three months later

I've never been afraid of a little hard work. My mother was actually half-American, and she wasn't born of nobility. Though her family was upper class, they also had that hardworking, make your own way persona that Americans tend to have, and they passed that down to me when I was growing up. I spent a few summers at camp in the States, in upstate New York, and it wasn't the camp you were pampered at. There it was like a working farm and we had a lot of chores to do every day, which included getting up at five a.m. to milk the cows.

When I was a teenager, after my mother died, I spent a lot of time at the military bases in France. I was too young to become a soldier, but my father insisted that the boot-camp-like mentality would toughen me up.

It did, as did the big wave surfing I did later off the coast of Portugal. Early mornings in the water, the boards smacking you in the face, the waves pummeling you into the sand, and if you were unlucky, the rocks. That was hard work too, especially if you wanted to become good at it.

But I can truly say I'd never known hard work until I came here to Gambella, Ethiopia, helping Matilde with her organization, which means setting up classrooms and education for refugees from South Sudan.

It's March but that doesn't mean much here. It's hotter than possible, the air thick with humidity. We're on the banks of the Baro River, the brown water a tributary of the Nile. Once upon a time this was a busy waterway, fulfilling the classic image of a languid tropical port in Africa. But now, because of all the civil war in South Sudan, only fifty kilometers away, there are no boats on the river and the troubles have spilled into this region.

When Matilde told me over Christmas that she was going to start moving her charity work into the area, I was against the idea. It was fine when she was working in Botswana and Mali—both those areas were considered safe. But with the fighting and the war going beyond the borders of Sudan, I wasn't so sure. I said the only way she could do it is if I went with her.

It was a crazy idea. And because it was a crazy idea, far removed from anything I would normally do or say, she didn't believe me.

But I was nursing a broken heart. I was drunk all the time. I was in the throes of depression and dealing with a holiday that has always been hard since my mother passed away. Suddenly going to Africa to put my sorrows in perspective seemed like the only thing to do.

I don't regret it. We've been here a month and while the work is physically hard, it's emotionally hard, too. I don't have a lot of time to think about Stella and the baby. I don't have that luxury. Instead all my heartache goes toward the people in the region. Seeing things I never thought I'd see; how hard life truly is for the majority of the world.

That said, it's not all been gloom and doom. There have been some close calls with attempted kidnappings, but we have military presence around us at all times, which helps. And the pupils are wonderful. We're not just helping to teach children here but adults as well, anyone who wants to learn. This particular camp gets aid from the United Nations in form of food and so our job is to take care of their minds. A different type of sustenance but equally as important.

Right now, I'm doing the laundry, which consists of washing a basket of our shirts in the river. There are a few fishermen along the water, and every now and then one of them will pull in a giant, long fish and plop it in a bucket, to be sold later at the market.

A kid runs past and points and laughs at me, saying something in one of the many different languages that they speak here.

I hear Matilde's laugh too from behind me and turn around as I'm crouched on the ground.

"What did the kid say?" I ask her as she walks over.

"That you're doing a woman's job," she says.

"I'll have him know that it's the man's job. I'm risking my life doing the laundry. There could be crocodiles in the water."

"There *are* crocodiles in the water," she says as she wipes her brow. "We're just lucky we haven't seen them yet."

"They're probably afraid of my big muscles."

She rolls her eyes. Africa suits her. She's dressed in a long-sleeved white gauzy shirt and a bright yellow skirt that reaches the ground. She's got a headdress wrapped around her head in the same color, her whole outfit a gift from one of the students.

She's tanned as hell but so am I. I'm going to go back

home a few shades darker (and covered in scars from mosquito bites. They're nasty little fuckers down here).

Speaking of home, we're supposed to be heading back in a few days. Our work here is done, and volunteers will then take over while Matilde concentrates on raising more awareness and money. I don't know how much of her own personal money she's put into it, but it's been a lot. I try to chip in from time to time but she says my actual work is what makes all the difference.

"What are you doing when you're done?" she asks, nodding at the clothes. "I decided to let everyone go home early. I need to pack and prepare for tomorrow's party."

Since tomorrow is the last day of school with us teaching, Matilde wants to have a real big party. She's got a van behind the classroom that's filled with balloons and party favors and I think she's even going to attempt to bake a cake in the kitchen of a local woman. All I know is that I'm terrible in the kitchen and should be kept far away if they want to avoid disaster. I'd normally say I'm much better at eating food than making it, but actually, since I've come here, I've dropped a ton of weight. I'm still lifting when I can, there's a makeshift gym with rusted equipment, something I made a note to replace when we return, but you can't run here for long until it gets dangerous. My weight loss is just from the heat, the stress, and the loss of appetite.

Though you can't really blame this place for that. It's part of the whole fucking broken heart thing.

I wince at the thought, the pain sneaking up on me.

Matilde sees it. She says, "I wasn't planning on making you help. I thought maybe we could go out for a beer."

There's only one suitable bar in town but we've been so busy we haven't had a chance to go there even once.

"I'd like that," I tell her.

An hour later, after the clothes are hung up and drying on

the line, Matilde and I are in a bar in the middle of town. It's dusty and run down but the beer is cold and fresh, and the bartender is happy to practice his English on us. There's a couple of old men in the corner, snacking on dried fish and playing cards and we have two soldiers stationed outside the door, just in case.

"To Gambella," I say to Matilde and everyone else in the bar joins in a cheers.

"To Gambella," she says, raising her beer for everyone. She gives me a sweet smile. "And to you, Orlando. Thank you so much for coming here, for helping me, for seeing what I do and why I do it. This really meant the world to me."

"You're welcome," I say, batting away a fly that keeps trying to land in my drink. "Just don't say anything else sappy."

"It still hurts, doesn't it?"

I don't have to ask what she means.

"Yeah," I say hoarsely.

"Have you talked to her lately?"

I palm my beer, staring down at the bubbles. "No. I mean I texted her the other day and I got a 'we're fine' and that was it."

That's all it's been.

I've tried to be as involved as possible but ever since I told Stella where I stood, where I had to stand, things have been strained.

So fucking strained. I was lucky to get her on the phone once a week over the holidays and I haven't heard her voice for a long time.

I miss her.

So, so much.

It burns.

The fear, the loss.

Like there's a void in me now that I can't quite fill, a void that was paved over during the last month here but still empty and hollow underneath.

Tu me manques.

She sighs. "You know...I didn't want to say this to you over the holidays because I knew how hard you were taking it and I didn't want to add to it. But...this is all your fault."

I'm in mid sip and I nearly spit out the mouthful of beer.

"What?" I manage to say, wiping my mouth on a tattered cocktail napkin. "My fault?"

"Yeah, dummy. You broke it off with Stella."

"I didn't break it off," I say snidely. "I just...stopped it from becoming something."

Her eyes roll to the ceiling where a fan slowly turns. "Uh huh. It was already something, Orlando. She's having your baby. She's still having your baby. That's something."

"I know. I just...look, you know what Zoya is like and I made the promise to her first."

"Sometimes you have to break a promise."

"I know. I have broken a promise. To Stella. It was one or the other. I didn't want to have to choose but I had no choice."

She twists in her seat to face me and puts her hand briefly over mine. "Listen to me, okay? As your sister. I'm going to tell you something."

She clears her throat and gives me an authoritative look. "I know Zoya, and I like Zoya. I know where she's coming from. I work with a lot of humanitarian groups; I know what it's like in Russia. I mean, Pussy Riot went to jail just for playing a concert in a church in protest to Putin's regime, a regime that punishes people for being different. They've been physically attacked for standing up for LGBTQ rights. Zoya's sexuality, whatever it may be, will not be tolerated and that's a fact. Is she going to get, like, physically harmed because of it? Maybe, but probably not. Is she going to lose the respect of her parents? Sounds like yes, but maybe in time they'll come around. Will she lose her standing in the Russian Tennis Federation? Probably but she doesn't need them. I mean, she's Zoya the Destroya, and unless she's that set on the Olympics, that won't affect her much. She plays as an individual around the world, her nationality doesn't come into play."

"And her sports line?"

"It's getting picked up by Moet Hennessy Louis Vuitton. She's *fine*. I mean, you know what a big deal that is. Technically, she doesn't have to play tennis ever again." She has a sip of her beer while I mull that over.

She goes on. "Zoya is scared and she has every right to be. But I think that if you explain to her, maybe see if you can get Emily involved because it does affect her too, if you try and make her see your point of view, she'll understand. It's scary all this change and I know she doesn't want the backlash, but we all get backlash at some point in our lives. It's inevitable. We all make choices and sometimes those choices upset other people. Sometimes those choices also make us happy. You're a noble man for doing this for Zoya, you really are, but now it's time to be noble as the father of your child. I hate to say it but *that's* the promise that you really can't break."

She's right. I know she's right. I feel it in my heart, it's the only thing that has really sat well with me. Zoya is an adult. But the baby is just a baby.

I know where I'm wanted and where I'm needed. And as much as it's going to be tough for Zoya, those are the choices she made when she wanted to be with me. It's not just on me, it's a part of her too. We both were playing roles and now it's time for us to sever those ties and become the people we're really meant to be.

Even if it's tough, even if it hurts.

We owe it to ourselves.

"I'll talk to her as soon as I get back," I tell her, feeling determined. "It's not going to be pretty."

"Well now you know what to expect."

But after we're done in the bar and we're walking back to our camp, I know that's not completely true.

I have no idea what to expect when it comes to Stella.

Will she have me back or will she keep me at arm's length?

Will she trust me again or will I be on the sidelines looking in?

Will I ever get the chance to even tell her I love her and what are the odds of her feeling the same?

I don't have the answers to any of those questions. I don't have the answers to anything. All I know is that I've made up my mind with what I'm going to do, and I can only hope and pray that Stella will let me in her life again.

She's become a missing part of me.

That night, as I'm falling asleep, I text her:

Tu me manques.

But I don't get a reply.

CHAPTER 17
STELLA

I wake up in the middle of the night with an aching back.

This isn't new for me.

I'm twenty-five weeks pregnant and during the last few weeks, as my baby grows and my belly grows with it, my back feels like it's taking the brunt of it.

But for some reason, this pain feels a little different.

More of a bruise, less like my muscles learning how to cope with my changing body.

I grab my phone to take a look at the time and I'm surprised to see a text from Orlando.

Just a few words.

Tu me manques.

Tears spring to my eyes, my throat choked, like I've suddenly been assaulted by sorrow.

By longing.

By loss.

Orlando.

Orlando.

He misses me.

But no, that's not just what he's saying.

It's that I am missing from him.

I put the phone back down and close my eyes, letting the tears spill down my cheeks in rivers, letting the pain in. I've been trying so hard to keep the agony away, ignoring the hollowness in my heart, trying to stay focused on the baby, to stay focused on Anya, to keep moving forward and being strong. I have to be stronger than I've ever been before, I have to be the best mother possible to care for my babies in the way that they deserve and need.

I can't be weak. I can't let what I feel for Orlando undermine what I need to do.

This role I need to play.

This role that feels harder and harder each and every day.

It's March now and even though I'm getting into the swing of things in some ways and the pregnancy has been fairly easy (aside from getting diagnosed with high blood pressure last month, which Aksel attributes to stress caused by Orlando, which makes him want to kill him some more), it's also gotten harder.

Or, I should say, it's not getting easier.

Emotionally.

My heart, my poor heart that is battered and bruised and confused, aching for Orlando and yet growing for the baby, still feels lost. I thought that in time, concentrating on the pregnancy would bring my heart back to the right place, that there would be no time to think about Orlando at all, let alone feel anything.

But that's not how the heart works. At least, that's not how I work.

And these three words that he just texted me, not I love you but *tu me manques*, well...

The pain won't be denied anymore.

So I lie here, and I let the tears come because deep down they've been begging for release and it actually feels good to let it out, it feels good to recognize it and acknowledge it.

I miss Orlando and I love Orlando and it gives me hope, stupid, foolish hope, to know he might feel the same.

Though we don't talk often, and honestly that's more on my part, not his, I know he's been in Africa for the last month doing charity work with Matilde. I'm happy for him, glad that he's doing something more with his life. But as proud as I am, the feeling doesn't compete with that constant pang in my chest.

I sigh and think about taking an acetaminophen for my back. I've been taking them lately for the aches and pains, with Doctor Bonakov's blessing of course. So I go into the bathroom and splash cold water on my face, fill a glass with it and take a pill. The pain really is unusual and the more I concentrate on it, the more it feels like it's spreading.

Not just my back but in my stomach.

Indigestion or baby? I think quickly to myself. *Indigestion or baby?*

It's a game I play after a heavy meal, always freaking myself out. While Anya's pregnancy was more or less smooth, there were some minor complications and I ended up having a caesarean in the end. I'm aiming for a vaginal birth with this baby, but I don't really care too much as long as the baby is healthy.

We still don't know the sex of it. I wanted it to be a surprise. I know that's kind of odd when it's a potential future heir and it's not just your family that will be kept in the dark but a whole country. I just figured it would keep something that's mine, mine. I don't want to know, and I don't think I should just because the whole country thinks it's owed to them. Let me have something private, let me have a surprise.

Anya still thinks it's a girl, of course.

And secretly, I've started calling the baby my little star.

I know that's what Orlando used to call me but I've managed to make it about the baby instead.

My little star who will show up in a few months and make their mark on this world.

I can't wait.

I smile to myself until my smile fades into a grimace.

The pain is spreading.

I take in a deep breath, trying to ignore the fear that's slowly crawling through me. I need to stop freaking out over every single thing. I've got this.

I sit on the toilet and pee.

Color catches my eye.

I glance down and see blood.

Not a lot of blood, but it's enough and it's bright red, so bright that it's shocking against the white toilet bowl.

Oh my god.

My heart starts to beat fast; my brain goes into overdrive.

The baby is coming early. Too early. I'm dying. We're going to die.

I try to take in a deep breath, but the panic is starting to grip my lungs, making me feel lightheaded.

Calm down. It's not a lot of blood and you've had contractions before, and this isn't it. Blood doesn't mean the baby is coming, it doesn't mean anything major is wrong. Just calm down. Call Dr. Bonakov.

But it might take him a while to get to me and I'm not going to chance it, not now. I'm not as young as I was when I had Anya, I have high blood pressure, I need to do this right.

I grab my robe, wrapping it loosely around my belly that's growing increasingly sore, and then I'm out the door and walking as fast as I can down to Aksel and Aurora's room.

I open their door and flick on the lights, hoping that I'm not interrupting some middle of the night antics.

"Stella?" Aksel asks through a sleepy groan, wincing at the glare of the lights.

But Aurora is already throwing back the covers and leaping out of bed, hurrying on over to me. "What is it? What's happening?"

She reaches out and puts her hand on my stomach, as if the baby will tell her.

"I'm bleeding."

Her eyes widen in horror. "No. What? Just now?"

"I'm getting the car ready," Aksel says, getting out of bed and pulling on pants. I look away before I catch him naked.

"I've been having back pain and now abdominal pain," I tell her, trying to keep the panic out of my voice. "I went to the bathroom and I saw blood. It's not a lot. I don't think. Bright red though. I don't know what that means."

"It means we're going to get you to the hospital!" she says, practically shouting. "Don't panic!"

"I'm not panicking, you're panicking."

"Ladies, come on," I hear Aksel yell from the hallway.

"Come on, come on," Aurora says, trying to steer me out of the bedroom but then she starts to flap her hands like a bird that can't quite take off. "Oh god, do I need to bring an overnight bag? Do you? Should I pack for you? You can't be having the baby already, it's too premature!"

"Aurora," I tell her. "Let's just go. We'll deal with that later. Okay? Deep breaths."

But I have to remind myself to breathe as well.

We hurry down the hall and I don't bother getting changed. I shove furry boots on my feet, grab a winter coat and go straight into the car out back with Aksel and Aurora.

Johan is driving and he's fast, probably faster than an ambulance would have been and much more discreet.

Everyone knows I'm pregnant. And by everyone, I mean the world. I couldn't stay a hermit forever, locked up in the palace as my stomach grew bigger. I had to go out. Rumors were spreading, said that I ran away with a young lover or I'd joined a cult up in Lapland. People were concerned. So I went out with my big stomach and made the news and now everyone knows I'm pregnant and won't say who the father is.

This has been the subject of a lot of debates. I've heard every royal monarch mentioned (except Prince Orlando, which, honestly, is starting to feel a little insulting) as well as a bunch of celebrities. There's a random rumor that my baby is Jack Nicholson's and I'm rather fond of that one.

But as I'm being driven to the hospital, Aurora and Aksel holding my hands the entire way, and then ushered into the emergency room, none of the rumors matter. I don't care what people think. I just want Orlando here.

The doctors do a quick pelvic examination and an ultrasound and then I get the news.

"You have a placental abruption," the doctor explains to me. He has a kind voice and dark eyes and I immediately like him. "This can be very serious, but in your case, we have hope that it might right itself."

"What does that mean?" I ask. I look up at Aurora and Aksel who have stayed by my side. Aurora holds my hand tightly.

"Yes doctor, tell us what it means," Aurora pleads. I'm not sure if she means to sound so dramatic or if it's just her accent.

"The placenta has come away from the wall of the womb. As you know, the placenta is what gives your baby life, it's the support system for giving the baby everything it needs."

My heart rate starts to increase and that's picked up by the monitors, the beeps filling the room.

The doctor puts his hand on my shoulder and gives it a light squeeze. "Yours is minor. You're bleeding but we are hoping in time that will stop. We'll need to keep you in the

KARINA HALLE

hospital for a while to monitor you. With any luck, the bleeding will stop, and we'll be able to ensure that the rest of the placenta is giving your baby all the nutrients it needs to survive."

"And if the baby doesn't get better?" Aksel asks, his voice rough and grave.

"She could be here until she gives birth. The baby will be given medicine to help the lungs grow stronger until then. Or we may have to do an emergency C-section."

I swallow hard. It feels like I have cotton balls in my throat. "Why did this happen?"

"Listen, I won't judge, but you haven't been using cocaine, have you?" the doctor asks.

"What?" I cry out.

Aurora laughs. "Did you seriously just ask the princess of your country that question?"

He gives me a sheepish smile. "I had to ask. We don't really know what causes this. Usually it's cocaine use or cigarettes. Street drugs." I give him a steady look to keep going. "But I can see on your chart you're being treated for high blood pressure, so that could be it. It could be that you're older and that you had a C-section before. But you're healthy and from the looks of it, your baby is healthy, too."

"So she's going to be fine, right?" Aurora says. "They both are?"

"I think so," he says. "But for now we need to monitor you here and see. I've called your personal physician in; he should be here soon." He faces Aksel and Aurora and straightens his posture. "I just wanted to say that it's an honor to have met you both. It's not often you're working your shift and the King and Queen of your country walk in."

I clear my throat.

He glances down at me. "And of course you too, Princess."

Of course.

Soon I'm moved into a private room, hooked up to monitors with an IV drip through my arm.

I'm sleepy, which is good, even though I can see the sun rising from my window.

"We should let you sleep," Aurora says to me. She and Aksel have been sitting with me for the last hour, going over everything that Dr. Bonakov had told us. Mainly that everything looks good, but it will be a while until we know the details of how this is going to progress and when and if I can go home.

"But we can stay if you want," Aksel says.

"No, no." I yawn. "I'm tired. This way you can go and grab my stuff."

"We can have your stuff delivered. I don't feel right leaving you alone."

"I'm not alone. There are nurses here."

"You're scared."

"I'm going to be okay," I say, giving him a pointed look, even though I don't feel okay and I'm scared shitless. I just figure if I fall asleep, I can't be scared.

He gives me one of his patented stern looks. "You need to call Orlando."

I straighten up. "I am not calling him."

"Stella," Aurora says.

"No. No, this is my choice. And he's in Africa anyway. All you would do is make him worry."

They exchange a glance. "Besides," I add. "You hate his guts, Aksel."

"I know I do," he says. "But I can put my own feelings aside to do the right thing. That's what a good king does."

I have to wonder if that's what Orlando thought, too.

I close my eyes and they take that as the hint to leave.

I'm asleep before the sun comes up.

"SO WHILE YOU'VE BEEN IN THE HOSPITAL, I'VE HAD A LOT of time to think," Anya says matter-of-factly. She's sitting on the chair beside the hospital bed, flipping through a book she's supposed to be reading for school.

I raise my brow. "I've only been here for two days, Anya."

"And that's enough time to think," she says, closing the book. She sucks in her lower lip and drums along the cover. "I've decided that I think Sir Mokey needs a friend."

Why am I not surprised? She hasn't been thinking about the baby or the fact that I'm in the hospital, but instead she's been thinking about getting another cat. Though, I guess it's proof of a child's optimism. They assume everything will be okay in the end.

So far, it looks like she might be right. I've stopped bleeding and the baby seems to be getting all the nutrients it needs from the placenta. It hasn't detached in total, so I guess what's attached is enough. The doctor still wants me here for another week just to make sure, which is annoying, but I've already made peace with it. Honestly, I'll stay here until the baby is born so as long as it means the baby is healthy.

"So, what do you think?" she asks. "Can I get a cat?"

I groan, shutting my eyes. "Why am I getting déjà vu?"

"That would be a good name for a cat. Sir Mokey and Déjà Vu."

I shake my head and give her the stink-eye.

A knock at the door saves me from having to lecture Anya about how, technically, I never got her a cat to begin with. That cat was a rogue kitty.

I look up to see a nurse stick her head in the room. "Princess Stella?" she asks. So far, none of the staff will call me Stella. In this setting it just makes me feel like I'm spoiled.

"There's someone here to see you. Are you accepting any more guests?"

I frown. I think I've seen everyone at this point. "Who is it?"

She clears her throat, looking uncomfortable. "I believe it's someone important."

I'm still confused so I just nod and look at Anya. "Sweetie, can you give me a minute? I have a guest."

"Okaaaaay," she says, grabbing her book and walking to the door. The way she narrows her eyes at me says, *this conversation isn't over.*

Just as she leaves the room and turns the corner out of sight, I hear her shout.

"Prince Orlando!"

No.

I can barely breathe and then there he is, appearing in the doorway.

Orlando.

He's here.

He's here.

And I barely recognize him.

He's tanned as hell and he's lost a lot of weight, the navy sweater he's wearing is filled out at the shoulders but seems to hang off the rest of him. His blue eyes stand out amongst his tawny skin, though there are dark circles underneath them. He looks tired, worried.

And somehow still amazing.

"Stella," he says in a choked voice and suddenly he's rushing over to me.

If we're supposed to act a certain way around each other, that doesn't matter at the moment. I know all of my feelings of resentment and hurt and loss for him are pushed to the side as he grabs my hand between his and holds on tight, staring at me in shock.

"I came as quickly as I could," he says, squeezing my hand as if he can't believe I'm real.

Honestly, I feel the same way.

How is he suddenly here?

"How did you know?" I ask. Shit, is this already in the tabloids?

"Your brother," he says, reaching over and smoothing the hair off my face. I close my eyes, surrendering to his touch. "Aksel called me. I dropped everything and came right away."

"Weren't you in Africa?" I ask, opening my eyes and taking him in again. The fact that he was there is obvious on his face. It's not just that he's gotten so dark being under that sun, it's that there is strength in his features where there wasn't before. His eyes have aged, they've grown, acquired wisdom. This is a new Orlando.

"I was. In Ethiopia," he says. "I caught the first plane out. Let me tell you, that was a doozy. Some of the roads were blocked due to rioting so we couldn't take a convoy. We had to fly on a tiny four-seater plane that could barely get off the ground. We almost hit powerlines. And all I could think about was Ernest Hemingway."

"Why Ernest Hemingway?"

"Because he flew in the same plane in Africa and it crashed; he barely survived."

"It wouldn't be the same plane if it crashed...like, sixty years ago."

"I just couldn't help but think that would be my fate. The irony. You know? Go to Africa, fly home to see my baby, die in a plane crash."

"Well, your baby is fine."

"I know. I was talking to the doctors. But what about you?" he asks, trailing his fingers over my cheekbones. "I came back to see you."

"I'm fine," I manage to say, my voice coming out soft.

I'm better now that you're here.

I want to say that to him, too. I should. But I'm still mad, still hurt. I don't know what it means with him being here, I don't know how to act, how to be. I know if I wasn't pregnant, I'd make him grovel for weeks. I'd push him away and keep him out of my life. I'd be stubborn because it's okay to be stubborn with your own heart.

But it's not okay to be stubborn with your child's heart. I know I should do all of those things and make him pay and suffer like I did, but when your child is involved, there is no time for that pettiness. I need Orlando back in my life, not just for my own sake but because of the baby.

Shit. It's so fucking complicated.

Then again, it's always been so complicated between us. It's never been easy.

But it's been worth it.

He gives me a sad smile, his eyes searching mine like he's looking for something. Maybe the truth. That I haven't been fine until he got here.

"I don't know where to start, Stella," he whispers. "I don't know what to say. I don't know how to repair the damage that I've done to you. I don't know how to regain your trust. All I know is that I will do everything in my power to make it up to you and the baby. I want to be a part of your lives; I want to be with you."

"How?" I ask. "How can you do that? How can we make this work? It all seems impossible."

"We have a saying in Monaco, that anything is possible. Even the word impossible itself says *I'm possible.*"

I manage to laugh. "That's not a saying in Monaco. That's a quote from Audrey Hepburn."

"And so it's my saying now and it's a good one." He chews on his lips for a moment, those lips I've missed so much. "Look, we're going to make this work."

"I don't want to keep you a secret," I tell him. "It's not right. I'll do it if I have to but..."

"I don't want to be a secret either," he says. "I won't be. I told you I want to be with you and that's what that means. It means it's going to be you and I together, as a team."

"Just a team?" My heart starts to lurch inside my chest.

What if we announce the baby to the world and stay friends?

What if that's how it's going to be? There will be no secrets, but I also won't have him in the way that I need him. I don't just need him as the father of my child, I need him as a lover, too.

"Stella," he says gruffly, his voice now thick with emotion. "I love you."

Oh my god.

"I love you," he goes on as my heart and mind struggle to keep up, to soak those words in, "I love you so fucking much. I wish I had a chance to tell you earlier, but I wasn't sure how I felt. I wasn't sure if my feelings were for you or for the baby. Or because of the baby. I was so confused and it's so complicated. But then I realized that love can seem complicated at times, but really, it's pretty simple. It's a yes or a no. And I love you, Stella. It's a yes. It's a very big fucking yes."

He kisses me on the lips, soft, full of yearning and passion and...love. "I just needed you to know," he says as he pulls away. "And I understand if you don't feel the same way and I get it if you don't trust me. I don't blame you. What I did... I'm ashamed I made the wrong choice there. I should have always chosen you and the baby. It's just that I loved you so, I thought maybe I was being selfish by doing so. Choosing that love for myself." He pauses. "Honestly, it was the first real choice I've made for myself, not for the person I'm supposed to be, but for me. *You're* that choice."

Tears are prickling behind my eyes and my nose feels hot.

I'm struggling to keep it together. "What about Zoya?" I ask. I don't want to ask but I have to ask.

"I'm going to tell her my choice. She won't like it, but it doesn't matter this time. It's the right choice to make. I'm choosing love, I'm choosing my life, I'm choosing you and the baby. I won't be made to feel bad or guilty for making any of those choices. Zoya is an adult, so is Emily. They have the means to figure shit out. But our baby is our baby. I won't have her grow up without a father, without having me in the picture every step of the way."

My eyes flutter. "Her?"

A slow, sheepish grin spreads across his face. "Shit."

"Anya told you she thinks it's a girl, right?" I ask him, searching his eyes. "Right?"

He rubs his lips together for a moment. "No," he admits, sounding wary. "The nurse told me."

"*What!?*" I cry out. "The nurse told you! When, why?"

"I asked. I'm the father after all."

"It was supposed to be a surprise!"

"Well," he says, putting his arms out. "Surprise!"

I shake my head. "A girl?" And then it dawns on me.

We're having a little girl!

I put my hands on my stomach and think about my little star.

He puts his hand on top of mine.

"I love you," he says. "The both of you. Very much."

"And I love you," I tell him.

Oh god, it feels good to finally admit it.

The most breathtaking smile spreads across his face, radiating so much joy that I feel it in my bones. "You do? You love me?"

"I love you, Orlando," I say, giving his hand a squeeze. "So much more than I can say right now without crying."

"I don't mind if you cry."

I shake my head, pressing my lips together and taking in a deep breath. "No," I say when I've calmed down. "Once I start, I won't stop. Everything...the baby, you, being here in the hospital. It's been too much."

"And I'm so sorry that I did that to you."

"I know you are. I trust you. Don't think I can't feel it from you, see it in your face. I know you Orlando, just as you know me." I manage a small smile and we lapse into silence for a few minutes. Just holding hands on top of my stomach, hoping she can feel us, feel the love and the hope and everything else that's good and pure and beautiful.

After a while I say, "So I've been thinking about names for the baby."

"You have?"

I nod. "But only one name came to mind, a girl's name. So maybe, deep down, I knew."

"Or maybe Anya is that persuasive."

"Maybe. Probably, actually."

"So what's the name?"

"It's French," I tell him. "In honor of you."

"Technically it should be in Monégasque then."

I raise my brow.

"I mean, I'm flattered," he says quickly. "Go on, go on."

"It's Estelle."

"Estelle," he repeats, looking awestruck. "Of course. It's perfect. A star."

"Our little star," I say.

"Our little star."

CHAPTER 18
ORLANDO

O ne of the scariest things I ever had to do was get in that plane with Matilde in Gambella and fly all the way to Addis Ababa.

When I got the phone call from Aksel, well, that was scary, too. But he didn't tell me much, just that Stella was in the hospital and that she needed to see me. That's all I needed to know anyway. She could have fallen down and scraped her knee and I would be rushing to her side. So I immediately started making plans to leave, with Matilde in tow. I wasn't going to leave her behind.

The plane was small, and the pilot seemed under a lot of stress, maybe because there was fighting breaking out, maybe because I was stressed, maybe because it was hard to find a pilot at the last minute and he had been drinking in the bar.

Regardless, the plane barely took off and we just managed to skirt over the powerlines at the end of the runway. All I could think about was (other than Ernest Hemmingway, who happened to cheat death many times, by the way, until he welcomed it with a shotgun. But that was on his terms, so I guess there's that), what would happen if I died? Who would

I leave behind? I would leave behind a child I never got to meet and a woman I never got to tell the truth to, that I loved her. I would leave behind a life that I never got to sink my teeth into and really live, for myself.

Somehow, though, we made it and then onto a big jet in Ethiopia's capital. It flew to Paris and from there, I went to Copenhagen and Matilde went to Nice. She offered to come with me, but I said I had to do this on my own.

When I went into the hospital, ushered in secretly through the back door, I didn't know what to expect. Once I talked to the doctors and found out the baby was going to be okay (and once a nurse spilled the beans about the sex), then the rest of the fear kicked in. That same fear I had on the plane.

What if I go in that room and see Stella and she rejects me?

What if that life that I want gets left behind anyway?

Aksel was at the hospital too, which didn't help. I guess he wanted to meet me in person, to see how legitimate and serious I was about her. I only got a few words in before he seemed to dismiss me (in a very king-like fashion, I must add). I guess he saw the truth in me. Either that or he figured he would deal with me later.

Then I saw Anya, who seemed genuinely happy to see me.

And then I saw Stella, who, thank the lord, looked like she was happy to see me, too.

And just like that, everything was okay. Even before I said a word, even before she said a word, I knew that we were going to work it out, that this was the right choice to make and the only choice to make.

I'll never choose anything but her again.

And Estelle, of course. Our shining little star. I couldn't be happier about the name Stella chose, couldn't be happier to learn that she's a girl.

I just can't be happier. Period.

But even with all the happiness that seems to be bursting through me like a meteor shower, I know that this isn't over yet. I have to make things right by talking with Zoya and ending it for good.

I also have to talk to my father and tell him the truth.

I've been in the hospital on and off for the last forty-eight hours. I sleep next to Stella in the chair, though sometimes, when Aksel or Aurora or Maja or Anya come to visit, I steal away to the palace and get some shut eye and a shower. I even get a chance to say hello to Mokey.

This morning I'm taking the opportunity to place a call.

But when I call home asking for my father, I get Penelope instead.

"He isn't here," she says. "He's in the council meeting." She pauses. "Where are you, Orlando? I talked to Matilde and she's being rather secretive about it. Are you okay?"

"I am now," I tell her. Well, I wasn't about to let it all loose to Penelope. I would have rather she heard it from my father. But I guess it's going to be the other way around.

"I have to tell you something," I add. "I was going to tell the both of you but..."

"What is it?"

I take in a deep shaking breath. I have had this damn talk with every single person I know at this point and it never gets easier. I mean, I know where I stand but I can't predict how others will feel and my father and Penelope are total wild cards.

"I'm in love with Princess Stella," I say bluntly.

Long silence. "From Denmark?"

"And she's pregnant with my baby."

An even longer silence. "What?"

"Yup."

"Orlando...are you serious? This isn't a joke?"

"Very serious."

"How pregnant is she?"

I laugh. "She's very pregnant. Almost six months."

"I can't believe this." She sounds shocked. Very shocked. "Wait until I tell your father."

I can't tell if that's a good thing or a bad thing.

"I mean...he's going to be so happy," she goes on, her voice growing excited. "Maybe I should film his reaction. Those videos are always a hit on YouTube."

"Happy?"

"Yes. My god. We'll finally have an heir! You know that's all we ever wanted."

"Well, I also figured you would probably want my happiness, too."

"But we do! You said you're in love with her. That's wonderful."

"Aren't you wondering about Zoya?"

"I guess," she says slowly. "I assume she knows."

"She does."

"I haven't seen your break-up in the news, though. You've done an excellent job at being discreet. That's a hard thing to learn."

"We haven't broken up yet," I admit.

A pause. "But...you said she knows."

"Yes but you see..." Part of me hesitates. Maybe Zoya doesn't want them to know the truth. But then again, it's my truth, too. "Zoya is in love with someone else. A woman."

"Oh...*oh*. Wait. Since when?"

"Since maybe a year or two after we started dating. I agreed to stay with her as a front. She was afraid of coming out."

"I don't blame her," she says.

"I tried to break it off with her before but...it's just so complicated."

"Yes, well life is like that sometimes. But Orlando, you have to break it off with her. You're in love and you have a baby on the way and I'm sorry but there's nothing more important than that."

"I'm just surprised. I thought you liked Zoya. You guys were pressuring us to get married from the start and have kids."

"Of course. That's what parents do. And we thought you were in love, though in hindsight now, I can see the signs. We just wanted to give you a little boost."

"You said that Zoya was getting too old," I point out.

"There's nothing wrong with a little pressure. And anyway, it's all worked out."

"For everyone but Zoya," I say under my breath.

"You don't understand, Orlando. Choosing your child is the most important thing you can do. In the end, Zoya will come to respect your decision and respect the mother of your child. You know," her voice goes low, "there's a reason why I always wear black in public. It's out of respect for your mother."

"My mother?" This is news.

"Selene was beloved and even though I loved your father, I knew that I would never be her. So I never tried to be. I stayed out of her role and fulfilled my own and I wanted you and everyone else to know that I respect her and her influence on your life. The black is a sign of mourning. I've never actually told anyone that, but it's the truth Orlando. I thought by wearing black, it showed that I would never forget who came before me. Your mother."

Shit. I mean...*damn*. I know I've been a mess of emotions lately but this confession from my stepmother is hitting me deep inside.

"I love you, Orlando," she says, and I think she's said it before but this time I really feel it. I really let it in.

I swallow back a choked word before I manage to say, "I love you, too."

She sniffs loudly. Then she says, "You're ruining my makeup."

"I'm sorry."

She laughs. "Listen, why don't you call again after dinner. I'm sure your father will be waiting to talk to you."

"You'll break the news to him?"

"I'll film it." She pauses. "Is it a boy or a girl?"

I was waiting for this, the potential disappointment. "It's a girl."

"Perfect. Do you have a name?"

"Estelle."

"Even more perfect."

"You're not, like, upset? Doesn't it have to be a boy to be an heir? That's all Matilde complained about while growing up, how she'd never be the ruler."

"It's the rule for now. But I'm sure your father can rewrite that law if he wants. And if you don't have any more children with Stella, I know that's what he'll do. We aren't losing our country to the French."

"That's going to piss off Matilde."

"I think she's over the whole royal thing by now," she comments.

After I hang up the phone with my stepmother, it takes me a while for everything to sink in. Penelope is happy, which means my father will be too, something I didn't expect. It's amazing how we let ourselves get carried away imagining other people's feelings. If we could just ask about them outright, we'd probably save ourselves a lot of grief in life.

I get back to the hospital, an extra spring in my step, excited to tell Stella the good news, when I'm met with a huge surprise.

Zoya is sitting in the chair beside Stella, laughing to her about something.

I stop dead in my tracks as they both look to me.

Zoya quickly gets to her feet and gestures to the chair. "Here, sit down."

She's smiling. She genuinely seems happy.

What's going on?

"Uh," I say as I slowly walk toward them. "I don't mean to sound rude, Zoya, but why are you here?"

"Matilde called me and told me everything," she says.

What is up with siblings making all these phone calls behind our backs?

But I can't complain. Without Aksel's call, I wouldn't be here.

"So you came all the way over here?" I ask, not getting it at all. "To see Stella?"

"To see the both of you," she says. She walks over to me and grabs my hand and leads me over to Stella, placing her hands on my shoulders and pushing me down until I'm sitting on the chair.

I glance over at Stella, my brows raised in confusion, but she just gives me a small smile that I can't read much into.

Zoya stands in front of us. "Matilde called me and told me what happened. I went over to her house. She made me some tea. Then she really told me what was going on." She looks between us. "I just have to say...I am so sorry for the way I acted. I know now that I was acting irrationally, out of fear. I panicked, you know? I thought I would lose everything."

I want to tell her that she absolutely had every reason to panic since there was a chance she really could lose everything but she goes on, "But after I talked to Matilde and the way she explained it, I realized I had to talk to Emily about it, too. That I was making decisions for her without taking in how she was feeling. All this time, she was the mistress, she was the one who was the secret. Emily didn't want that. She felt hidden and ashamed and jealous of you, Orlando. Jealous that you got to be with me, and she didn't. Emily wanted us out in the open. She doesn't care if we lose everything because in the end, all we really need is each other. And you know what? She's right. That's all that matters. I don't want who I love to be a secret, I don't want to live in fear, and I don't want to feel ashamed. Love is love is love, as they say. And as long as I have love, as long as I have her, they can try and take it all, but I won't lose everything."

I hear a sniff from beside me. Stella is crying.

Now Zoya is crying.

Shit.

I hold it together.

"So what are you saying?" I ask her.

Zoya smiles at me. "You guys are in love and you have a baby together. I'm letting you go, Orlando. I'm making that choice, so you don't have to. I'm choosing Emily. You're choosing Stella. And who knows, maybe one day Emily and I will be as blessed as you are."

Blessed.

I look over at Stella and grab her hand, kissing the top of it, feeling every single emotion burning away inside me. Happiness, relief, joy.

Gratitude.

Because Zoya is right.

We are blessed.

***

STELLA WAS ONLY IN THE HOSPITAL FOR A WEEK IN TOTAL, but it felt like forever. Even after all the tests were done and it was shown that the bleeding had stopped, they wanted to keep her under observation. I have a feeling that because she's royalty, they were being extra cautious and I guess there's no harm in that. But it felt like heaven when they finally allowed her to be discharged.

We could go back to normal, at least our new normal.

Me, Stella, and Estelle.

Little does Stella know that her life is going to change yet again. And for the better.

At least, I'm crossing my fingers that it does.

News had traveled fast that Stella was in the hospital, though no one in the press could quite figure out who the baby daddy was. At first, anyway. Then I think one of the hospital staff must have said something and sold us out.

It didn't matter, though. We knew that we would announce it soon. We were waiting for the right time. And so while news of us together spread like wildfire, the two of us decided to have a little press conference in front of the palace.

This isn't something new. Aksel and Aurora held a similar conference when they announced to the world that they were together. I guess we're just following in their footsteps.

"This is it," I tell Stella, holding onto her hand and giving it a squeeze. We're both bundled in winter coats, though I tried to take the advice of Francis and pop some color into my life, so my coat is olive green. Probably not what he meant, but it compliments Stella's grey trench that does nothing to disguise her pregnant belly.

"I'm ready if you are?" she says, flashing me her sweet smile.

I kiss her on the cheek and hand in hand, we exit the palace doors and step out in front of the crowd of reporters and onlookers.

There are a lot of people here, which makes me feel more nervous than ever, to the point where Stella basically has to rip her hand out of my grip. But she doesn't get why I'm nervous.

She will soon.

Stella smiles at the crowd and waves like a princess and then she launches into her speech. It's in Danish but she told it to me earlier and it's all diplomatic bullshit along the lines of "I wanted to protect the identity of the father because we wanted to love on our daughter in privacy, etc, etc, but I have a duty to my people to keep you informed, etc, etc." That sort of thing.

In fact, I think it's more than that because Stella talks for a really long time (I'll have to tell her this later, but she's more of a royal than she thinks) and she fields a lot of questions. I have no idea what everyone is saying, but they all seem to be really happy.

"I have a question for Prince Orlando," a woman with a British accent says to me once Stella has finished talking and we've posed for a few photos.

"Yes?" I tell her, thinking it's going to be about Zoya.

"Your Serene Highness," she says, adjusting her scarf around her neck. A light snow has started to pick up, though we're under some cover. "What does your father think about the fact that you're having a girl? Don't you need a male heir to the throne or Monaco will revert back to being part of France, as per the treaty?"

I was ready for this one. "My father is delighted that we are having a girl. If one day we need to change that rule, we will. My daughter may very well be the first female ruler of Monaco. I know the Monégasque people would rather that happen than let the French take over."

She nods. "And how does your father feel about the fact that you're having a child out of wedlock? Doesn't that count against the child's eligibility?"

Perfect fucking segue.

"Funny you should ask that question," I say to her, flashing my smile at the crowd. "Because there is a solution to that."

Stella is staring at me, curious and confused as to what I'm about to say.

I turn to her, take both her hands in mine.

Look deep into her beautiful eyes.

Smile.

She smiles back, that smile that reaches right into my heart.

"Princess Stella of House Eriksen," I say to her and only to her. In seconds, it's like the crowd completely disappears. All I see is her eyes, the rest of the world falls away. "The day I first met you, I knew we knew each other. Deep down inside, my heart saw something in yours. I think what it saw, was the ability to be a better person. The ability to love. The ability to find myself and the happiness that was always in me, that had always escaped me. I saw that in you, and I wanted to be a part of it."

My breath is starting to shake, and I grip her hands tighter. "But you were like a shooting star. So quick and so bright across the sky, almost impossible to capture. Being with you, I can imagine what it must have been like to be as the first humans were, staring up at the night sky and wondering how something so beautiful and mysterious could exist. Wondering if they would ever see such magic again."

Her lower lip is quivering.

I drop to one knee and hold her hand.

Everyone in the crowd gasps, including Aksel, Aurora, Maja and all the children who have been standing off to the side of us. I pull out a ring from my pocket, a giant yellow diamond surrounded by three smaller ones.

Everyone gasps again.

"Stella, my star in the sky," I say as I stare up at her. "I managed to pull off the impossible and capture your magic in my hands. And I want that magic to last forever between us. I want the light to shine brighter with the birth of our little star; I want to keep it going until our days grow dark. Stella, will you marry me?"

She swallows. Eyes fluttering. Mouth falls open.

"Yes," she manages to say. "Yes, I will marry you Orlando. I love you."

"I love you, too." My words come out hushed because I'm smiling so damn hard.

With shaking hands I slip the ring on her finger.

The diamond in the middle is her. The star.

The three other diamonds are me, Anya and Estelle.

Forever together, burning bright, as a family.

I get to my feet and we kiss.

The crowd is swooning, the cameras are flashing.

The tears flow.

I place a hand on her stomach.

The stars are mine.

EPILOGUE

ORLANDO

Three months later

"Welcome home, little star," my fiancée whispers to Estelle, holding her close to her chest as we step inside the palace. As the doors close behind us, the shouts of the photographers and the press fade away. I didn't necessarily want to have them here on the day we returned home from the hospital and told Stella as much. But she said she felt like she'd kept our daughter a secret for so long, that she wanted to show her off, much like I did with my proposal. She thought her people deserved to see her.

Her people.

I liked the way she was thinking—I don't think I'd ever heard her refer to the Danes as her people before, even though it's true. It's like with Estelle being born, she's finally feeling like a princess, and almost like a queen.

I know in the future she'll be living with me in Monaco but that won't be for some time and even then, they will always be her people. And one day, so will the Monégasque. Honestly, I've never seen the people so happy and excited as they have been over Estelle's birth. I heard that the entire country had a holiday in honor of her (at least that's what Francis says—he's probably pulling my leg).

Stella glances up at me as I guide her through the palace, my hand protectively at her back.

"We made it," I tell her.

"And not a moment too soon," her aunt Maja says to us. She's standing in the middle of the foyer beside Aksel and Aurora. To the side of them are Clara, Freja, and Anya. And behind them are the rest of the staff, also looking equally as eager. All of them are staring at us with the biggest smiles on their faces, almost twitching for us to get closer. Henrik has a guitar, which doesn't bode well for any of us.

Before I can ask where my own family is since I heard they were supposed to be here, I hear Penelope's shriek of excitement ring throughout the halls.

"They're here!" she yells and suddenly the small crowd gathered in front of us becomes a bigger crowd when Penelope, my father, and my siblings join them.

Chaos ensues.

All of us are swept up in kisses and hugs and cooing and I don't think I've ever had so much attention before. Okay, I know the attention is all for Estelle, but still, I had a minor part in her creation.

"She looks just like you Orlando," Penelope says, as she gazes at her adoringly.

"She looks just like Stella," counters Aurora.

"No offense but she looks like a ball of mush to me," Francis comments and when everyone gives him a look, he says, "but a beautiful ball of mush. Don't get me wrong."

"You must be exhausted," Maja says to Stella.

"But you don't look it," Matilde adds.

"Is it just me or does the girl look like her grandfather?" my father asks, peering closely at her face. He's very wrong.

Somewhere in the background, Henrik is playing "Twinkle, Twinkle, Little Star" until it starts to morph into "Wonderwall."

"I said maybe," Henrik sings in his deep booming voice. "She's gonna be the *star* that saves me."

Stella looks up at me and rolls her eyes but I just shrug.

I don't hate it.

"I think it's time we had a proper toast," Aksel says, sidling up to me. He touches my elbow and then jerks his head to the hall. "Don't worry about the girls, we can come back in an hour and everyone will still be *right here*."

I follow him down the hall and away from the crowd, feeling a little uncertain where this is going. Aksel and I occasionally butted heads over the last few months of my living here and while I think he's come to accept me always being around, he has a way about him that's hard to read. I think I've seen him smile a handful of times and they've all been for Aurora or the kids.

We walk into his study and he grabs a bottle of Scotch from behind the elegant bar he has set-up. The man has bars all over the palace, but I feel like it's this one that's the most personal. This is the room he comes to when he wants to be alone (no kids allowed).

Actually, I'm honored to be in here, especially when he hands me a glass of Scotch and a cigar.

"You're a father now, Orlando," he says. "This is the day that everything changes. For better or for worse, you're a man now."

I don't know why it feels like Aksel is giving me the talk that my father never did with me, but I'm not going to complain.

"To being a man," I say, raising my glass.

"To being a father," he says. "The best role you'll ever have."

We clink our glasses together and have a sip. The Scotch is as smooth as silk.

His face grows grim for a second. "But if you ever fuck over Stella or my niece in any way, I will seriously behead you and feed you to the pig."

I let out a nervous laugh, but he doesn't laugh back.

Finally he pulls out his lighter and flicks on the flame. "Shall we?" he says.

He walks toward the French doors and opens them, stepping out into the fresh spring air, lighting his cigar.

I follow the king and hope for the best.

***

It took a few days for Stella to recover enough from giving birth. She was in labor for a long time and everyone was being extra cautious because of her previous complications.

But when she was finally feeling better, we decided to take Estelle to meet her grandmother.

I'd come with Stella to see her mother a few times before and it's always been tough. But today, Stella was full of hope. Even though she was trying not to expect much, I know she thought it was important that Estelle meet her mother, even if it wasn't really the other way around.

While Stella goes to talk with the nurse in her mother's ward, I hold Estelle.

It's indescribable the love that I feel for her, so I know I shouldn't even try.

But it's like there's a trapdoor somewhere in your soul and it's been there your whole life and you never even knew it existed until someone showed you the way.

Estelle showed me the way. She showed me that trapdoor and she opened it and let me see all the treasures that were hidden inside.

Love. The purest, deepest love imaginable.

That's what I feel for Estelle. She's shown me the love that the human heart is capable of, she's given me my purpose in life.

To love her.

To love her mother.

To protect them both until my dying day.

"Okay," Stella says to me. "She's ready."

With my other hand I reach out and put it at the small of her back, just to let her know we're here, and we go inside the room.

Her mother is sitting in a chair, staring out the window.

We walk halfway across the room and stop, waiting for a sign of some sort to approach her further.

Her mother turns her head to look at us, curious for a moment, but then it fades and there's no hint of recognition at all. It's like we're not even here.

Stella is starting to shake a bit. I know what she wanted to happen and it's not happening. I can tell she's about to cry.

I grab Stella's hand and give it a squeeze, then I go straight over to her mother and sit down across from her.

"Liva," I say to her gently, showing her the baby. "I wanted you to meet someone very important and very special. This is Princess Estelle."

Liva's eyes go to mine, blank as snow, then they slowly move down my face until they rest on my daughter's tiny form.

She stares at Estelle for a good minute. No confusion, no reaction at all.

And then...

A tear appears at the corner of her eye.

I swallow hard and look over my shoulder at Stella, knowing her mother has never given any kind of emotional reaction in this state.

But Stella is beaming, her hands covering her mouth in shock, gasping with joy.

I look back at her mother.

The tear is rolling down Liva's face.

She's smiling at Estelle.

Stella
Monaco
One Year Later

THE CHAMPAGNE CORK WHIZZES THROUGH THE AIR IN A perfect arc, reminding me of a shooting star, reminding me of my beautiful little Estelle.

Then it nearly takes out Viktor, the Prince of Sweden, causing him to duck at the last minute before it bounces off a palm tree and then lands in someone's soup.

Everyone laughs. The champagne is poured into my glass, into Orlando's glass and then Prince Pierre, my father-in-law as of now, raises his glass in a toast from his table.

"Here's to my dear son Orlando and his beautiful bride, Stella," he says warmly, alternating between looking at us and looking at the huge crowd like a moderator. That's the thing about royal weddings, they aren't small intimate affairs and since this is the first big wedding they've seen since Pierre and Penelope got married, it seems like every single royal, politician, celebrity, diplomat and aristocrat had been invited. And in a small but prosperous country such as Monaco, it feels like every citizen happens to be one of those important people listed above.

"Here, here," the wedding guests cheer, while someone lets out an overly loud wolf whistle. Oh, that was just Prince Magnus of Norway, who seems to be really into the festivities. He's one of Aksel's friends and he's a real piece of work (in the best way). He's here with his wife, Princess Ella, and their children. Beside him is Prince Viktor and his wife Princess Maggie (that's what the press calls her, anyway. Her mother-in-law, the Queen of Sweden, insists that it's Princess Margaret but at no time has Maggie ever tried to correct the press. So Maggie it is).

They have children too, as well as Maggie's younger siblings, who all joined the family when she married.

They're at the children's table at the back of the reception, along with Clara, Freja and of course, Anya. Agnes is there too, the only adult supervising, and keeping a close watch on Estelle who (thankfully) seems to be sleeping through everything. Other than Estelle, though, they're a rowdy bunch, perhaps even rowdier than Magnus and Viktor, all hopped up on sugar and boredom. Weddings are boring to me, too, and this wedding in particular was *looooong*. I should be used to that, my first wedding was the same and Aksel's was no different, but even though it was my own wedding, I couldn't wait to get all of this over with and get to the "I do" part.

That's really the only part that matters.

That's the only part that really feels real.

That I'm now officially Orlando's wife and he's my husband, my prince, and nothing else in the world matters. Not this wedding, not the semantics, just that we're together.

But most of this wedding is for the parents—or maybe all weddings are? And my new in-laws are having a grand time showing off. I'm pretty sure this wedding will go down in history as either the country's biggest or the most expensive. But if I've learned anything in the last year of Estelle being born it's that this is one country that truly spares no expense.

Of course, now that Orlando is getting more serious about fulfilling his role as leader one day, he's beginning to notice some things about the country he'd like to change. Already Monaco has a lot of investments into clean energy, but he says that isn't enough. He also wants to follow in Matilde's footsteps and start doing more charity work. His first project was something simple yet meaningful to him— opening up a neuter and spay program in Cyprus. All the stray cats and dogs there are given medication and food and the organization has done a lot so far as to controlling the population and providing proper homes. Sir Mokey's Program (that's actually the official name and the mascot is a cartoon tabby with a crown) may seem like a small change to make and in another country entirely, but it's just a stepping-stone for him.

Orlando has often said that he didn't feel any purpose in his life until he learned I was pregnant with Estelle and that purpose has only grown for him over time. Now, with me at his side, he says he wants to do all he can to change the world in all the ways he's able to.

Love changed him.

It sure changed me.

"Speech!" Magnus yells from the crowd.

"Watch yourself," Aksel says to him disapprovingly.

"Hey, who invited the Viking?" Orlando says with a laugh.

Aksel and Aurora are seated at the head table with us, right beside me. On the other side of Orlando is Francis and Matilde.

Francis actually has a date here.

So does Matilde.

They're seated together somewhere near the back and it's

hard to see them buried among all the royals and famous people. Matilde's date is a shy guy from her charity organization. He seems like a nice person, but they haven't been dating that long.

Francis, however, has been seeing this dude, a photographer, for the last six months and I think it might be something serious. Francis seems to think so anyway. He only came out about two months ago but to everyone's surprise, the press hasn't been that bad or intrusive. I guess all the rumors that had been spread about him were more or less true anyway, and people took it at face value. He's happy though and that's all that matters. Even his parents were understanding. I think it helped that Orlando and I already had Estelle, so the pressure for Francis to marry and have kids, AKA future heirs, was off anyway.

I do know that the reason Francis found the courage to come out publicly is because a few months earlier, Zoya had done the same.

Zoya and Emily are now married. They had a secret ceremony that we attended in Copenhagen of all places. The city is known for being a popular destination for same-sex marriages because of how liberal we are and Zoya thought it was fitting.

Shortly after that, she announced her marriage to the world.

There was backlash.

A lot of it.

But Zoya knew it was coming and had time to prepare. She withdrew from the Russian Tennis Federation before they even had a chance to kick her out (and because they ended up publicly distancing themselves from her, it's obvious she wouldn't have lasted long). She worked on getting a new coach, pushed aside any Olympic dreams and instead focused on winning her Grand Slams. She may have lost every single one of her Russian sponsors, but her sportswear line has only grown in value. People from all over the world buy it to support her, much in the same way Nike has attracted consumers with liberal values.

She's doing good. She said she still talks with her parents too, and though she said their relationship is strained now, the love she shares with Emily was worth the sacrifice.

As sometimes love is.

Actually, as love always is.

"You look beautiful," Orlando says, as he whispers in my ear. "Did I tell you that tonight?"

I laugh into my champagne, the bubbles tickling my nose. "You have told me that. Many times. But you know I never tire of your compliments."

"That's funny," he says with a wry expression, "because I very clearly remember a time where my compliments seemed to annoy you."

"That's because they were crude," I remind him. "You were trying to get a rise out of me. As usual."

"As crude as they were, they were still complimentary." He leans in closer, his breath tickling my neck, his lips on my ear. "Like if I told you I can't wait to rip this dress off you later and taste your sweet, wet cunt, you'd take that as a compliment, right?"

My cheeks immediately go red. The whole entire wedding is staring at us right now, or at least staring at Pierre as he's now going on and on about the country or the wedding or who knows what, and yet they have no idea the things Orlando is saying to me.

"Go on," I tell him, my voice getting throaty. And yes, I am already wet. The man—my husband—he just does it for me. Every time.

"I'm not sure what else there is to say," he murmurs,

kissing behind my ear. "It's more that I need to *show* you. Right here, under the table."

I tense up and pull back to give him a warning look. "Don't you dare," I whisper. Sexual innuendo is one thing but I'm not going to have him fingerbang me under the table in front of every single guest and every single camera.

"Are you sure?" he asks playfully, his hand going down under the table and resting on my knee. "Because I think you're just being demure for the fun of it."

"Orlando, if you try anything, I will..."

"Speech!" Now it's Aurora yelling it, right in my ear. I think she knows what was about to go down. "Speeeech. *Stell-llllllllaaaaaaaaaaa.*"

Oh boy.

The Queen of Denmark might be drunk. This is that *Seinfeld* episode all over again.

I smack Orlando's hand under the table and then I get up, smoothing down my dress. I give Aurora a complacent smile and look out to the crowd.

"In a night of speeches, I don't want to bore you."

"Too late!" Magnus yells. I think half the crowd laughs, the other half looks horrified.

I go on, making a mental note to keep the mic away from him. "But I do want to say one thing and that thing is thank you. Thank you for accepting me into your hearts and into your countries. Thank you for being so open and supportive, not only with me but with the people I love. Thank you for showing us compassion and respect. Thank you for coming here and sitting through boring speeches."

Everyone laughs, because it's true.

I look to Orlando, at his beautiful face, those clear blue eyes that are brimming with so much love for me, I know my heart is spilling over.

"And thank you to my husband, to my prince. Thank you

for coming into my life at the right time, the time I needed you the most. Thank you for the most wonderful gift of Estelle. And thank you for making me realize that I, too, am deserving of happiness and a happy ending. That used to be all I ever wished for."

I once wished it upon a star.

THE END

THANK YOU ALL SO MUCH FOR READING THE ROYAL Rogue! I hope you loved it!

As an author, we depend on reviews from readers such as yourself. You really make our world go around!

From now until October 31st, if you leave a review of The Royal Rogue on Amazon.com, you will receive an invitation in the mail to Stella and Orlando's baby shower! You will also be entered to win one of ten signed limited edition paperbacks.

—> All you need to do is click here and enter your info. This is open internationally and this offer expires on October 31st. Please allow 4-6 weeks for delivery of your special swag.

If you're wanting to check out any of my other romances,

I have too many to list, but here are some of my favourites (and all are available on Kindle Unlimited):

Start here, with my Nordic Royals series (all standalone!)

- THE SWEDISH PRINCE

(The Prince of Sweden falls for an American girl - spin on Roman Holiday)

- THE WILD HEIR

(The bad boy Prince of Norway has to marry a good girl princess in a marriage of convenience)

- A NORDIC KING

(The widowed King of Denmark falls for his much younger nanny)

AND IF YOU LIKE AGE GAPS AND FORBIDDEN ROMANCE, TRY:

- BEFORE I EVER MET YOU (young single mom falls for her father's best friend)

- LOVE IN ENGLISH (the ultimate forbidden romance with the sexiest Spanish soccer star ever)

LIKE BEST FRIENDS TO LOVERS?

- BAD AT LOVE (a quirky friends-to-lovers romance)

- THE PACT (two best friends agree to marry each other by the time they're thirty)

HOT SEXY CANADIANS? START WITH WILD CARD...

- THE NORTH RIDGE SERIES (A trilogy about three rugged mountain men from Canada with very dangerous and thrilling jobs and the women who love them)

-> If you want to connect with me, you can always find me on Instagram (where I post travel photos, fashion, teasers, etc, IG IS MY LIFE and the easiest place to find me online)

-> or in my Facebook Group (we're a fun bunch and would love to have you join)

-> Otherwise, feel free to signup for my mailing list (it comes once a month) and Bookbub alerts!

THANK YOU SO MUCH!!!

ABOUT THE AUTHOR

Karina Halle, a former travel writer and music journalist, is the *New York Times*, *Wall Street Journal*, and *USA Today* bestselling author of *The Pact*, *A Nordic King*, and *Sins & Needles*, as well as fifty other wild and romantic reads. She, her husband, and their adopted pit bull live in a rain forest on an island off British Columbia, where they operate a B&B that's perfect for writers' retreats. In the winter, you can often find them in California or on their beloved island of Kauai, soaking up as much sun (and getting as much inspiration) as possible. For more information, visit www.authorkarinahalle.com/books.

ALSO BY KARINA HALLE

My Life in Shambles

Discretion

Disarm

Disavow

The Royal Rogue

Ashes to Ashes (EIT #8)

Dust to Dust (EIT #9)

The Devil's Duology

Donners of the Dead

Veiled

CPSIA information can be obtained
at www.ICGtesting.com
Printed in the USA
LVHW041225020623
748690LV00003B/409